FOUR DOCTORS, FOUR WIVES

The pleasant river town of Bayard is the scene of this story about four doctors and their wives. The couples had been almost inseparable until one September afternoon the four young women decided they had become too dependent on each other. Now they would trust their own judgment, live their own lives, unhampered by criticism and advice.

In the weeks that followed, minor incidents seemed to grow into problems. Crises arose over an unwanted child; an impressionable medical student; a fear that threatened a marriage. The doctors, at first bewildered, found themselves helpless to stem the rush of events their wives had set in motion.

The action takes place in hospital rooms, in the doctors' offices and in their homes. Told with insight and humour, this delightful novel explores the emotional undercurrents of closely entwined lives as well as revealing the strengths and tensions of married love.

by the same author

Substitute Doctor
The Doctor's Husband
The New Doctor
Love Calls the Doctor
Home-Town Doctor
Doctor on Trial
When Doctors Marry
The Doctor's Bride
The Doctor Makes a Choice
Dr. Jeremy's Wife
Ordeal of Three Doctors
Doctor with a Mission
Bachelor Doctor
For Love of a Doctor
The Doctors on Eden Place
The Doctor's Promise
The Doctors were Brothers
Doctor Tuck
Rebel Doctor
Two Doctors and a Girl
Two Doctors, Two Loves

Four Doctors,
Four Wives

ELIZABETH SEIFERT

COLLINS
8 Grafton Street, London

William Collins Sons & Co Ltd
London · Glasgow · Sydney · Auckland
Toronto · Johannesburg

First published in Great Britain 1976
This reprint 1984
© Elizabeth Seifert 1975
ISBN 0 00 222245-0

Made and printed in Great Britain by
William Collins Sons & Co Ltd, Glasgow

FOUR DOCTORS, FOUR WIVES

Chapter One

"I love September," said Nan Shelton contentedly.

The heads of her three friends and co-workers lifted for a surprised second.

"Why September?" asked Ginny Ruble, deftly quartering, then slicing, still another apple.

"We are going to make jelly out of the peelings," Hazel Windsor reminded her. "Try not to get seeds into that pan."

"We'll strain it."

"Yes, but apple seeds are poison."

Gene Cornel snorted, not elegantly.

"Ask your husband," said Hazel loftily. Her husband was a doctor. All their husbands were doctors.

"She's right," said Ginny. "I read it in a mystery one time." Carefully she removed a brown, glossy apple seed from the pan of green and scarlet peel. "Why do you like September, Nan?" she asked.

Nan's brown eyes looked at her blankly for a moment. "Oh!" She recovered herself. "I did say that. Why, I like it for the cosmos that blooms, and the chrysanthemums, and the faint drift of cobwebs over things in the early morning—the voices of children going to school . . ."

"Thank the Lord!" said Gene Cornel fervently.

Again the heads lifted, and the lips smiled. "Why should you . . . ?" Ginny asked.

Gene grinned sheepishly. "I'm grateful that I did get them through grade and high school," she admitted. "But Susan left for college only on Friday, and I still haven't swamped out her room."

"Anything else you like about September, Nan?" Ginny asked.

"Oh, yes. The smell of cinnamon in this kitchen when we make our apple pies for the winter."

"Nutmeg, too," said Hazel, a bit of belligerence in her voice.

"Be sure to mark her pies," Gene cautioned the others. "She makes only three."

"That's three too many for our house if they have nutmeg in them," said Gene firmly.

"If you'd taste it . . ." suggested Hazel.

"I would taste it, but Alison," said Alison's wife, "is an entirely different matter."

"Badly trained," sniffed Hazel, and the others laughed softly.

Each year in the late summer the four wives of the four clinic doctors met to make pies to freeze for the coming winter. They liked the summer apples in their pies. Now Nan and Ginny got up and took the balls of pie dough out of the refrigerator and prepared to shape it into thin shells for the apples and sugar and cinnamon —and nutmeg. There was discussion about which balls of pastry had been made by Ruby, the Sheltons' cook, and which by Mag, here in the Ruble kitchen.

"We should make our own crust," said Hazel virtuously.

"Gene's always falls apart."

"Too flaky," Gene agreed smugly.

Nan and Ginny continued to roll, to cut, and fit the dough into the waiting thin aluminum pans. They had that discussion each year, too. "Why I like September," said Nan softly into Ginny's ear.

"Hazel knows she doesn't make good pastry dough," Ginny agreed.

"But she really slices her apples thin."

"Yes, she does."

Out on the porch, the two remaining apple peelers were discussing the clothes which Susan Cornel had taken to college. If she'd had her way, declared her mother, jeans and knitted shrinks would have been the whole wardrobe. A flight bag would have contained the whole bit.

"But you sent . . ."

"Oh, sure. The first new boy she meets, she'll want to dress up." Gene rested her knife on the edge of the table. "Maybe I just wish she were back in grade school," she said. "How many more apples will we need, Ginny?"

"Hold up a little, until we get these shells filled. Why can't we use the peels in our apple butter?"

There was some discussion about that. There was discussion about Kitty Sims's hair, and what her daughter, Cornelia, was doing that year. They told and laughed about Ike Kibbler's adventure at the V.F.W. stag party.

"Wasn't it the American Legion?" asked Ginny.

"What difference does it make? Spanish American War Veterans, for all I know. What was Ike doing there?"

"What the rest of the men were doing. Waiting for, and watching, the girlie show."

"When I heard that story, it was the first I knew we had such parties in Bayard," said Hazel.

The others hooted at her. But she insisted that Dewey never went to such affairs.

"I don't think Bob goes either," agreed Ginny Ruble, "but he knows what goes on. And usually I do, too."

"I didn't," insisted Hazel.

"All right," said Ginny. "Put your halo on straight and come add your nutmeg to your pies. Those three sitting on the stove."

Hazel obeyed, tall, slim in her orange slacks and white blouse. "Dewey never told me exactly what happened at the barbecue either," she said.

"We could tell you, but you may want to stay innocent," Gene teased her.

"I can promise you that Dewey could enlighten her," said Ginny. "We'll need about ten more apples, ladies."

"We can do them while you cut strips," decided Nan. "Tell Hazel, Ginny. I think it makes a funnier story than it does a dirty one."

"Naughty, not dirty. And quite a few faces are red that don't usually get red." Frowning down at her pie dough, talking to herself, she began to roll it out flat, stretch it, then, using a wheel, to cut it into fluted strips.

The others peeled apples and listened while Gene told the funny story.

Ike Kibbler was a friend, a respectable and respected farmer in the neighborhood. He was a deacon in his church, and generally well thought of. He and his wife joined in almost any civic and social activity; they were very popular.

And about a month ago . . . "Ike went to the barbecue on Labor Day," Gene said. "I know that Alison stopped in because he brought home ribs, which were delicious. But he didn't stay for the stag party which always winds these things up. Or down, in this case."

The parties, the picnic-barbecues, were held every year in a parklike area on the bluff overlooking the town. There was an immense screened building with a dance floor. This was rented for all sorts of affairs—wedding parties, church picnics, district meetings, church revivals . . . And for this particular barbecue and stag party.

"This fellow," Gene said, "his name is Pat Adams, and he has a TV business in some town south of here."

Ginny supplied the name of the town.

"That's right," Gene agreed. "He came for the barbecue and the stag party. I suppose he was a Spanish War Veteran himself, because he sued Ike, not the picnic givers."

The other women nodded. She had things straight.

"When the girls come in," said Gene, "they dance and sing on the stage at the end of hall. Chairs are set in rows. Folding chairs, most of them, but that night they had brought in some of the lawn chairs from outside. Ike sat in one of those."

"Front row?" asked Hazel.

"Pretty near front at least," Gene agreed. "Anyway, he's tall, as you know . . ."

They did know. Ike was several inches over six feet, thin and rangy.

"And," Gene continued, "this Adams character, who was sitting behind him, began to fuss because he couldn't see. Finally he came and sat on the wide arm of Ike's chair. That way, they both had front seats to watch the

5

girls who were singing and dancing, and coming down into the audience to sing to individual men, and to sit on the laps of some of them—the way they do."

"I've seen it on TV," said Hazel, and her friends laughed merrily.

"I guess Ike had seen it, too," agreed Gene. "And because he was afraid one of the girls—they don't wear much in the way of clothes, and he didn't want one of them sitting on his lap. So he jumped up to prevent it and the chair tipped; Adams fell off of the arm of it and broke his arm."

"Oh, dear," said Hazel.

"Yep," Gene agreed. "Because now Adams says he will sue Ike for damages."

"But . . ."

"Sure he's crazy. Alison told him so when he was setting his arm. Now the lawyers want him to settle out of court, and he would maybe, but Ike's mad and won't pay a penny. That's why the story has got around town. Why even you have heard it, Hazel."

"Maybe they won't have any more barbecues," she suggested.

"Oh, of course they will. Men have to have their parties."

"Stag parties, you mean."

"Yes," Ginny agreed. "I do mean that. They need to get together, just men, every so often."

"They bring girls in."

"They do, but not wives or family."

"And why expect them to be consistent?" asked Nan. "There! That's the last apple, if ten will be enough. I wouldn't want men to be different, would you, Hazel?"

Hazel stared at her in astonishment.

"She's been working on Dewey for years!" laughed Gene.

"I'll bet he always was a darling," said Nan. "He has been ever since I've known him."

"Well, Dewey's all right," Hazel conceded. "But, Nan, you know that men—I'll bet Garde does things, and you surely are teaching Butch . . ."

"Trying," said Butch's mother, speaking lightly. "Just trying, Hazel. That's the best I can do for Garde, too, and all his bad habits."

"Somebody's going to say *he* doesn't have any," Hazel warned the others. "But of course he does. And I don't want you to tell what they are, Nan. I'm not going to talk about Dewey's either. Because I do think the trouble with this bunch is that we talk too much, that we talk things to death."

Her companions stared at her.

"Yes, we do," Hazel insisted. "An hour ago you all talked for thirty minutes about whether I could or should wear brown."

"You said your say."

"I know I did. That's my point. We all four of us talk things to death."

Hands stilled, faces were turned her way, their eyes inquiring, Ginny's blue eyes, Gene's hazel ones, Nan's soft and brown and a little troubled. Ginny set her sugar cup down, Nan looked down at the sliced apples under the water in her pan and shook the pieces about a little. Gene scratched her elbow and shifted her feet.

"I think it would be better," Hazel continued, "that we'd be better off, if we didn't do this way."

Ginny gulped. "How would we be better off?" she asked. She looked around her big kitchen, and the wide porch which opened from it. Afternoon sunlight came in through the leaves of a vine and made patterns on the shoulder of Nan's blue and white blouse, touched Gene's light red hair with gold. Ginny loved having her friends about her; that was why she and Bob had bought this big old farmhouse and had remodeled it. To have places for her family, and these dear friends, to gather and talk.

Hazel was answering her. "Why should you all be concerned whether I can wear brown or not?" she asked.

"Because we have to *look* at you when you do wear it," said Nan.

"And listen to you moan if you put out big money for a brown cashmere coat and find out for yourself that you look awful in it," said Gene.

"But it still isn't any of your business," Hazel insisted. "And that's what I mean. That we should stick to our own business, to our own people, and the interests of our own families."

"Oh, Hazel," Ginny protested.

"We should," Hazel declared.

"You mean the four families shouldn't bother about Kitty Sims's hair, or Ike Kibbler's law suit."

"No, I don't mean that. I mean we should stop thinking and acting as a group, but be, each family, a unit. We should tend to our own affairs, and—"

"Not keep you from making a big mistake when you buy your winter coat."

"Well, yes, that, to some extent."

"Perhaps you'd better limit those extents," said Gene coldly. "Give us some examples of what we've been doing wrong so we can change our terrible ways."

"Gene, don't make me quarrel with you."

"I won't if you won't. So—go ahead. Cite some examples."

"Well, let's see. Surely we don't need a four-family conference over whether Butch Shelton should be corrected when he sings 'My Country Tivoli.' "

Ginny giggled.

"He sings 'There's a wildness in God's mercy,' too," said Butch's mother. "At the top of his lungs."

"Father Linders loves it," said Gene.

"But my point is," said Hazel, clinging to her argument. "Nan and Garde are the only ones who should decide whether he should be taught different. We don't need a conference on that any more than we need one on the length of Susan Cornel's skirts."

"There isn't length enough," said Gene dryly, "to confer about. I'll grant you that point, Hazel."

"And we don't need a conference when we make pies. Whether mince pies should have whole top crusts, or lattice, whether . . ."

"But it's fun to be together," said Ginny wistfully.

"Yes, it is," Hazel agreed. "But isn't it rather ridiculous to argue as seriously as we do about the use of cinnamon or nutmeg for seasoning, and the merits of tapioca, cornstarch or arrowroot for thickening?"

"They all work," said Nan softly.

"Of course they do. So why don't we all make our own pies our own way, then serve them to each other as we happen to be guests in one house or another?"

"You mean, make our own pies?"

"Yes, Gene, I mean just that. For instance, Nan's cook, Ruby, makes better pies than Nan does . . ."

Nan shrugged and began to clean the table where the

apples had been peeled. The others stood up and also began to clear things away, to wrap their own pies to take home for freezing.

"My point is," Hazel persisted, "we—we *units*—should live in our own homes, live our own lives. We are individuals and should live as such."

"But can't we be *friends?*" Ginny asked. "We have been for such a long time."

"Certainly we can be friends. We are friends! Just as we are with the Kibblers, and the Copelands—but we don't think we have to discuss every single thing with *them!*"

But the doctors' wives did discuss this idea of Hazel's. They cleaned up the kitchen, they carried the carefully wrapped and labeled pies out to their cars, they stood about on the driveway, and they talked. Nan and Ginny wanted no part of Hazel's latest idea. If she wanted to buy her brown coat, she could! But she'd know what the others would advise. Why shouldn't they make pies and popcorn balls together? And worry about their kids, and—

Gene thought the idea was a good one. She, for one, would like a little independence. "And we'd have more time to ourselves," she announced. "There would be much less calling everyone on the telephone—finding out what each one thought before putting turnips in the stew."

"Oh, Gene!" Nan protested, laughing.

"Well, we do that way."

"I know we do, and I've loved it."

"So have I," said Ginny mournfully. "I'll feel left out in the cold . . ."

"Don't be silly," Hazel admonished her. "If you like, we could categorize the things we could consult about."

"Nothing doing!" cried Gene. "You and your big words! We don't need rules and stuff. It's enough to say that we won't consult about every damn thing that comes up! We never made rules for the close intimacy we've built up. Why should we make rules now? I say, let's try independence, and see if we can live with it."

"Don't you think it will work?" Hazel demanded.

Gene shrugged and got into her car. "I know what the men will say."

"What?"

"That we won't stay with it," said Gene, driving away.

And two or three days later, at the hospital, the four husbands said precisely that. It had taken them that long to discover what was going on, though Hazel told Dewey at once about the new procedure.

"What did you work that up for?" he had asked.

"I think we all need a little privacy."

"What for? What are we going to do with it?"

Dr. Alison Cornel and their daughter Carol noticed that Gene was more often around the house now, and hardly ever used the telephone. Carol told her father that she was that way all day, too. "Do you suppose she's sick?"

Alison inquired. Gene said she was fine. And what was wrong with *him?* She could recall his beefing because she didn't stay in the house all day, and because their telephone was always busy when he tried to call home.

Alison unfolded his newspaper with such vigor that the sports section sailed across the room. He swore and got up to retrieve it. "You may not be sick," he grumbled, "but something sure as hell is wrong with you."

Gene did not answer him.

But when the men gathered in the doctors' lounge at the hospital that early morning and compared notes, they pieced together what their wives had said and done.

"Nan cried," said Garde. "She had got a fine book on Michelangelo, and she wanted to show it to the other wives, but she told me that they had agreed not to see so much of each other—and she cried."

"Ginny's washed every blanket and curtain in the house," Bob Ruble said. "She says she doesn't have anything else to do since the girls stopped coming in."

The men stared at each other. "Who started this crazy thing?" asked Dr. Cornel.

"Hazel," said Dewey, his voice muffled. He was bent over, tying his white shoes.

"Did she say so?"

"Didn't have to. She's the spawning place for any and all crazy ideas." He stood up. "Diets," he grumbled, turning to his locker. "Home improvements. Social reform. My reform."

The men laughed. "Failure doesn't stop her, does it?" asked Garde.

"It's my resistance against hers," said Dewey cheerfully. "And I resist pretty good."

"Well, I hope the girls do, too."

"Oh, this will blow over by the end of the week."

"I hope."

"It will," said Bob. "The girls can't possibly hold out. As many things as our four families get into— Hazel's going to see Jan on the street with her hair curled. She'll just have to come around and ask Ginny what's going on. And then there is the new idea Ginny has of seeding her flower beds in the fall . . . Naw. This idea won't possibly work. It's doomed." Bob slammed his locker door.

"Maybe not," said Garde Shelton quietly.

Bob turned sharply. "Maybe not what?" he asked.

"Maybe it's not doomed. Maybe it will work, to some extent."

"I don't understand," said Dewey, advancing toward the pediatrician.

"Well, like this: maybe our dear wives won't get into so many things, or get tangled up into such big things— maybe the big things won't happen if circumstances and little happenings can be allowed to languish and die."

Dewey turned away. Alison Cornel stood shaking his head. "That isn't going to happen," he said. "Ever."

"Why not?"

"Because the women themselves won't let it happen. They won't like this new procedure. They enjoy getting involved. They like building a half pint of green paint into enough to cover a sun porch."

The men all laughed and prepared to start on the day's work. "We'd miss their conferences as much as they would," Garde declared.

"I think they plan to try the thing," said Alison.

"Oh, yes, they do," Dewey agreed.

"And perhaps we should decide to let them," said Garde Shelton. "At least, not interfere. Perhaps we should wait and see what happens."

"Plenty always does," said Bob, going into the hall.

By the end of the month, the weather had turned cold and rainy, the leaves began to fall, and the flowers looked rusty. Then the sun came out again, the river sparkled, and the Windsors' fat cocker spaniel, Bitsy, turned up missing.

Bitsy was an iniportant resident of the street where Dewey and Hazel lived. He was an integral part of their pretty white home. He was the owner of a large, fenced back yard, with his own entrance into the house, his own bed there, and the large, comfortable chair which was his. His diet and regime of exercise were as closely considered as the habits of the human members of the family.

Until on that sunny afternoon when Hazel decided to take Bitsy for a walk. She began talking about it as she tied a scarf around her shining gray hair, and took the leash from its hook. "We'll walk toward the woods," she said, "but we won't go into them, and you're not to insist that we do." She glanced at the chair, and then at the rug in the kitchen where Bitsy sometimes lay if he became hot. Bitsy was getting old. He had put on weight, and he puffed, but the Windsors loved him. Ten years ago they had got the puppy, announcing to all concerned that he would not be a spoiled, fat dog. Within a year, he was both—a fact admitted, but never discussed, by Hazel or Dewey.

That afternoon, the dog evidently was not in the house, so he must be in the yard. Hazel pulled on a wool jacket and went out through the back door to the patio; she called Bitsy's name and rattled the leash. For all his weight, the cocker loved to walk.

He did not respond, he did not appear. "He's sick," decided Hazel. "He's lying under the bushes, sick."

She explored. She called. She went inside again, calling, hunting. She looked under the beds, behind the couch . . .

By then she was getting panicky. The meter reader, or some neighborhood child, had left the gate open. She went the length of the block, calling, searching.

"What's wrong?" The neighbors all asked that. Two or three children said they would help hunt.

Hazel even called the police. No blond cocker had been picked up. No, not even a dead one.

"He has our name on his collar," said Hazel, her voice breaking.

"Yes, ma'am. We'll call you if he turns up anywhere."

Hazel sat, exhausted by fear and grief, and stared at the telephone. She knew that she must not phone Dewey. A doctor's wife knew that she did not call her husband during office hours unless somebody had died, or the house burned down, or—or their dog was missing. Hazel picked up the telephone.

Dewey's secretary said, sure, Mrs. Windsor could talk to the doctor. "Hold on, please."

Hazel held on. And after what she claimed was "hours," Dewey's hearty voice came over the wire. "Hello, Hazel, what's up?"

He sounded so—so cheerful. Hazel began to cry, which she never did well. She always gulped, and found it hard to speak.

Dewey, no longer cheerful, tried to calm her. What had happened? Who died? Well, what *is* wrong?

Finally she told him and he was upset, too. But, no, he could not come home at that minute. His office was full. Yes, he'd be as early as he possibly could be. By the time he got there, Bitsy would probably be home . . .

But he was not. And Hazel was as close to hysterics as Dewey had ever seen her. He was himself disturbed. Together they retraced every step she had taken earlier. Dewey whistled for the dog.

"He loves you most," Hazel told Dewey. "He'll come if you whistle. He always does."

But that night he did not. Sadly, Dewey and Hazel went inside. They would eat supper and think about what to do.

"The Rubles have so many animals, they'd know what to do," said Hazel.

"We know whatever they'd know," argued Dewey.

"Maybe not."

Dewey lifted her hand from the telephone. "Don't call them," he said.

"But—why not?"

"Remember? For the past two weeks, we doctor families have been a unit? And this is the Windsor unit's problem."

Hazel's face flushed. "You're teasing me!" she cried. "At a time like this!"

Dewey put his arm around her. "I'm not teasing you," he said. "Believe me, I'm not."

But Hazel was certainly in a fine state. Their dog was lost—probably killed. If there was anyone who could help find Bitsy . . . She faced Dewey accusingly.

"It's still our problem," he insisted. "The dog's got out of the yard some way, and he probably has followed some bitch . . ."

"Dewey Windsor!"

He looked inquiringly at his wife.

"You said . . ."

"Dogs do that sort of thing, Hazel," he said mildly.

"Not Bitsy!"

He laughed, then had to apologize and comfort her. But he still was firm. Even stern. She was not to appeal to the other families. Yes, he would do something . . .

Hazel consented to prepare some sort of meal; Dewey changed his clothes, and he called the police.

While they ate the warmed-over stew and the ice cream, he drafted an ad for the newspaper.

"Make it a notice," said Hazel, showing the size she had in mind. "With a border. And offer a reward."

They didn't eat much supper, and after the dishes were in the washer, they put on jackets, took flashlights, and went out in the neighborhood streets again, calling the dog's name, looking into yards, under hedges. Hazel wanted to go up to each house and inquire . . . Starting with the Gaines house across the street.

"We barely speak to those people, Hazel," Dewey protested.

"Well, we *know* them. And they have a little boy. He may have seen Bitsy."

Dewey walked on down the street. Past the brick bungalow, and the big, two-story white house with its deep porch and green shutters, past the little Cape Cod, and the Tudor brick and stucco set back on its sloping lawn. Acorns crunched under their feet, and Hazel stumbled over a broken place in the sidewalk. Dewey caught her arm and told her to watch where she stepped.

"I'm watching for Bitsy," she said, as crossly as he had spoken. But he was tired. He wanted his chair and his newspaper.

"Let's go on to the Rubles'," said Hazel.

"I don't think so, Hazel. I think we should go back and be there to welcome the prodigal."

"He's so familiar with their house," Hazel pointed out, not wanting to turn back. "And with Nan's and Gene's as well—he might go to one of them. I mean, if he did wander off, and got tired, and . . ."

"And those families are well acquainted with him," said Dewey. "If he'd show up at their door, they would return him or at least phone us. Provided we were at home to take the call. Besides, I forgot to tell the hospital where I'd be . . ."

So Hazel, though reluctantly, consented to return home. Once there, she went into the yard again and called.

"We're the only ones," she said mournfully, when she finally came inside and pulled the scarf from her head, "who think he's much of a dog. He's fat, and he's getting old. And he snuffles." She sniffed herself, and would not be comforted, though Dewey tried.

"I'm upset, too," he assured her.

Together, they put in a very bad night. At each sound, Hazel was up and going to the door, Dewey usually following her.

The next morning, he was fifteen minutes later than usual getting to the hospital. The other doctors, including the Public Health man and part-time staff member, Rufus McGilfray, were in the lounge changing, checking schedules for the day, and talking. The coffee urn bubbled and hissed fragrantly. The morning was cool.

The men glanced at Dewey when he came in; he said "Good morning," and went to his locker, setting his medical bag on the table. "Anything happen last night?" he asked Garde Shelton.

"Elmer Attaway died," Garde told him. "That's what we were laughing about."

Dewey nodded, then turned and looked sharply at Dr. Shelton, and beyond him to Alison Cornel.

"*Laughing?*" he asked.

"Yes. Oh, not that the old gentleman died . . ."

"Old buzzard," said Alison, coming up behind them. "You know him, Windsor. Last year you had me do some surgery on him."

"Yes," said Dewey, not too interested in Elmer Attaway, who *was* a buzzard. He took off his suit coat and his necktie.

"Remember how I insisted that the old man make a will?"

"Yes . . ."

Bob Ruble brought him a cup of coffee. Dewey said "Thanks," and added that he'd not had any breakfast.

"Why not?" asked Bob, but Alison was talking about the arguments he'd had with Attaway, and how good he'd felt when the old man finally capitulated and sent for a lawyer.

"You always feel good when you bully a patient into making a will," said Dr. McGilfray.

Alison took that up quickly, ready to give all his arguments over again.

"You said Attaway died last night?" Dewey asked Dr. Shelton.

"Yes, he did. Rather quickly, at the end."

"But he'd made a will," drawled Dewey.

The men began to laugh again. "He most certainly did," said Dr. Cornel; he and McGilfray were dressing in scrub suits. "His wife called me at six-thirty this morning, and laid me out about it."

Dewey turned to look at him. "Why?"

"Oh, he'd left her the third she would have got anyway. The geezer has a sizable estate, it seems."

"He owns property all over town."

"Yes, I know that. Well, he left his wife a third. And then he left the rest in trust to three other women."

Dewey stared at him. "What other three women?"

"You wouldn't know their names," McGilfray told him. "Hazel would not stand for your knowing . . ."

Dewey's face flushed up. "Leave Hazel out of this, will you?" he cried angrily.

McGilfray stepped back. "I'm sorry . . ."

Dewey shook himself. "No need. I— Tell me who these shady women are."

Mac listed them, and they were shady indeed. Dewey said he thought Attaway, at one time, had kept one of the women, had furnished an apartment and given her a car.

He had. And now she and her "sisters" were the beneficiaries of a trust fund.

"Sizable?"

It was.

"Well, maybe Mrs. Attaway can manage to survive them. They aren't young either."

"Won't do her any good," said Dr. Cornel. "If any money is left, after the juicy lawsuits there will be, I mean—if any money is left in the trusts, it is to go to Billy Graham."

Dewey stared at him. "Billy . . . ?" he asked in disbelief.

"That's right. Attaway had never seen or heard him, but he thought he must be a good man."

Dr. Windsor laughed shortly. "I suppose he is," he

20

agreed. "And I have learned my lesson," Alison told him.

"What lesson is that?"

"To keep my mouth shut."

Dewey nodded and sat down to change his shoes.

"Dewey?" asked Bob Ruble. "Is something wrong with you?"

"You said you'd had no breakfast," Garde reminded him.

"I didn't. Things were—well—upset at our house."

"What happened?"

Dewey told them about Bitsy. "I wouldn't let Hazel draw the wives into this, but maybe you fellows have some ideas to pass on to me," he concluded. "I hope so. She's gone to pieces like an old bird's nest. And I'm not in too-good shape myself. A fellow gets fond of his dog."

His friends all agreed. They could sympathize, and they knew that Hazel would be in a state. They asked questions; they offered suggestions.

Dewey told about his idea that Bitsy had followed some dog in heat.

"I'll bet Hazel took to that," said Alison Cornel, glancing at the clock. The surgeon and Dr. McGilfray had surgery scheduled for eight.

"About the way Mrs. Attaway is taking to Elmer's girl friends," Dewey agreed.

"Do you suppose," McGilfray asked, bringing Dewey the plate of toast he had ordered from the kitchen, "that someone stole the dog?"

"Who'd want him?" Dewey asked. "Thanks, Mac."

"I don't want you fainting on rounds. But— *Couldn't* someone have stolen the dog? You don't lock the gate, do you?"

"No, but who would *want* him? Besides us, I mean."

"Mac means that someone may be keeping him for the reward we know you've offered."

"Yes, we are. That's why I was late. I went past the newspaper to put in an ad. But that would mean . . . *kidnaping?*" Dewey asked loudly.

Dr. McGilfray shrugged.

"It's a thought," agreed Garde Shelton.

The two surgeons left. The other men watched Dewey eat his toast and drink a second cup of coffee. "I don't know how Hazel will take the idea of kidnaping," he said gloomily.

"I'll bet she is upset."

"We both are, Bob. We couldn't sleep last night."

"Why didn't you tell us then?"

"Hazel wanted to. But, remember the pact the women made? That we would live our own lives, solve our own problems?"

Garde Shelton made a soft sound of protest.

Dewey nodded. "This was—is—important to us. But to the rest of you, a wheezy old dog . . ."

"*Agggh!*" cried Bob. "We might be able to help. The kids could, surely. We all know how much Bitsy means to you. They could fan out . . ."

"We don't have so many kids in our group any more, Bob," Dewey reminded him. "With your Bobby and Susan Cornel at college, and Mary gone too from your house . . ."

"Married, not *gone*. Well, yes, she is not here, of course. But Carol Cornel is at home, recuperating from that cyst surgery she had . . ."

Dewey nodded. "Is she all right?"

"Oh, yes, but Gene and Alison and I have persuaded

22

her to take some time to get over it. She'll be at home until Christmas, we hope. Then—Jan's still among us."

"Yes, and she probably will have ideas. The ad will be on the air as well as in the newspaper."

"Sarah will hear it," said Bob Ruble. "That transistor of hers has grown fast to her ear."

"I'm afraid Butch and Fiddle are too small," said Dr. Shelton.

"Yes, they are, but—"

"We'll keep alert, all of us. Of course Bitsy had a tag."

The men moved out into the corridor. "Yes," said Dewey, "with our name and address."

"He'll be found. And if a reward is mentioned . . . How much did you offer?"

"I wouldn't specify. But if the finder reaches Hazel first, it will be a whopper."

"Well," laughed Bob, "whatever it is, and whatever the women have decided, you can count on the kids involving themselves in your problem."

The men parted, each to read the night's charts and to make the necessary rounds.

Only an hour later, Ginny Ruble was in the church. She was on altar duty that month, and she had decided to do the wood waxing and the brass polishing before her always busy Saturday descended upon her. She let herself in through the side door and went up the steps to the hall, and the sacristy, liking the quiet of the church building, the mixed perfume of candle wax, cedar furniture polish, wine, and faded flowers, the warm security of the shadowy place. She gathered her supplies and put on the smock which Nan had persuaded the women to wear.

Polishing the carved front of the pulpit, pushing her soft cloth into the crevices of grapevine and wheat, Ginny thought about Ferrell Linders, who had been their rector for the past six months. For several years, their church had been beset by sorrow and tragedy; they had known a succession of priests who had not lasted, any of them, for more than two or three years.

Last Christmas, when Mary Ruble and Storm Linders were married, Storm's father had officiated, because— well, everyone wanted him to, but also because the Bayard church was without a rector. Mr. Linders was doing town and country field work for the church . . .

He liked Bayard, liked the old houses, the river, the people. After the wedding, he and his wife had stayed on with the Rubles for a few days, and Bob had asked him . . .

It was his wife who first jumped at the suggestion that he stop traveling, accept a church, and give them a chance to "get acquainted." Ferrell Linders' eyes had smiled at her. "Have you missed me?" he asked quietly.

The Sunday after the wedding, he preached, conducting the service beautifully, and the vestry decided to ask him. . . .

He had to have the Bishop's approval. There were many details—the farm in the Ozarks, an invalid aunt— Mr. Linders' father, still practicing medicine . . . Could all that be entrusted to the new bride?

All of it need not be. The aunt could be moved to Bayard. Mary and Storm could care for Grandpa. And he could care for them. Uncle Ike Toy and Storm's brother Harold, both farmers, could and would take care of the ancestral acres. Ferrell and Gertrude Linders, with Aunt Sophie, moved into the rectory before Easter.

"Mary should not have her mother-in-law living in the same house," said Gertrude contentedly.

Anyone could have got along with Gertrude Linders, Ginny thought, but the new family arrangements seemed to be working out happily for everyone. Ginny, as she worked that morning, hummed a little tune of contentment, thinking about how glad everyone seemed to be to have Ferrell Linders at the head of things. There was peace in the church family, they enjoyed the fine sermons preached from this pulpit, and the dignified services he gave. She gave the pulpit an affectionate pat and moved on to the altar rail, a small, intent person with her brass polish, her furniture wax, and her thoughts. The church, she decided, and not for the first time, was as it had been when she and Bob had first come to Bayard, the children little, Sarah not yet born, and Nan's father the rector—an old man then, glad to serve out his years in the parish.

Ferrell Linders created the same atmosphere of loving service. Not making rules, not demanding too much of anything—just establishing a good center of worship, which was as a church should be established. The people of the town had accepted him as warmly as had the church's congregation. And his handsome wife as well. Nearly everyone spoke of the tall woman as a good wife. Which she most certainly was. A good wife, a good mother. She looked like Storm and was like him. Ginny sank down on the red carpet of the footpace and looked at the jewel-like glass of the big window at the back of the church. She remembered the day when Mary and Storm had been married . . .

Did she *ever* remember that day!

The excitement, the crowds of people in her home, the

talk and laughter—and tears—they'd never get anything
—everything—done on time!

But of course Hazel and Gene and Nan all had helped.
It was the first wedding the group had ever had, and each
was convinced the affair could not have been happily
accomplished alone. As it was accomplished. That day,
the blessed peace of this church had enfolded all of them.
With his father and his oldest brother Chauncy, Storm
had waited, his eyes fairly glowing!

Sarah did not falter—or run!—as she came up the aisle,
her slippers peeping in and out from under the bottom
of her long red velvet skirt. Jan's knot of flowers and net
did not slide down, or sideways, on her head; she had
looked solemn, and really pretty—later she said she *felt*
pretty!—in her dark green velvet, with the cascade of red
carnations and holly steady in her hands. And the bride!
Bob, so handsome and proud of Mary, his first-born—the
loving way she smiled at her father when he put her
hand into Storm's . . .

Beyond the big window the sun had come out across
the snow, and everything—just everything!—was
beautiful. The sun made stained-glass patterns on the
white aisle runner, and across the shoulders of their
friends, the bride's lace-veiled white satin and her golden
hair.

Ginny sighed, and rubbed brass, and remembered.

"A penny wouldn't begin to pay for them this morning, would it?"

Ginny jumped and looked around. "It's a wonder I
wasn't thinking aloud," she said. "I do at home. Good
morning, Mr. Linders."

"Good morning, Ginny. How are things at your
house?"

"Fine, I think. Kids in school, Bob at the hospital—no babies last night."

"And you're ahead with your altar duties."

She smiled and tossed her dark hair back from her face. "That doesn't happen often, does it?" she asked. "I'm usually the girl at the end of the parade, her tongue hanging out."

He chuckled. "You get a lot of things done that way," he assured her.

He's a lot like Storm, too, Ginny told herself. Not in looks, but the quiet way he has of knowing what he wants, and doing it. Storm *looked* like his mother—dark red hair, rich brown eyes—while Mr. Linders . . . Ferrell was a tall man, but his hair was gray, and thinning. Receding. He wore glasses behind which his eyes were steady and quiet.

"I have something I wish you would do for me, Ginny," he was saying.

Ginny's eyes flew to his face. "Oh, dear," she said apprehensively.

The Rector smiled and sat down in the front pew. "You fear the worst," he confirmed.

"Well, Mr. Linders, I get gun-shy."

"I expect so. Ginny, could we talk a little, again, about my name?"

"No," she said firmly, sweetly. She spoke so to Jan or to Sarah when a point had been argued and settled. "I know you're a member of our family. I know Bob calls you by your first name, and many of the women do. But since you're the rector of my church, it just has to be Mister. For me."

He nodded. "I'll not mention it again. And certainly not when I am asking favors."

Ginny spread the cerecloth again upon the marble top of the altar. "Let's hear the worst," she said.

"I want you to agree to serve as den mother for the next year for a pack of the church's cub scouts."

He saw her shoulders rise and fall. He heard her deep sigh.

"I understand you are experienced," he said.

She turned. "You want me to be a den mother," she said. "Again? Or still?"

His eyes twinkled. "As experienced as that?" he asked.

"Yes. I am afraid so. And I just can't, Mr. Linders. I just can't. I gave that up last year."

"You're not having a baby, too, are you?" he asked.

Ginny's head snapped up; she dropped her dustcloth and stooped to retrieve it. "I certainly hope not!" she cried emphatically.

"Then I beg you to do this thing for me, Ginny. Your replacement *is* having one. The boys need you—if you've had experience—"

Ginny sighed again and dusted the office candlesticks, and then the missal stand. "You back me into a corner," she told the clergyman. "And I suppose I'll have to say yes." She moved toward Ferrell Linders. "I remember the way Gene Cornel took over for me when Sarah was on the way."

"You women are very close, aren't you? You clinic doctors' wives."

"Well, yes, we have been. We came here to Bayard together, you know. Young wives. The clinic was new; the town was strange. Nan lived here, of course, and she wasn't yet married to Garde, but she joined the group as soon as she was—and we got into the habit of doing things together, deciding things together. When you came in this morning, I was remembering how the girls helped me when Mary and Storm were married. Coming at Christmas, there was so much to do! But Nan took charge of the church and the decorations. Gene and Hazel arranged the reception—and we four talked over every detail! Mary's slippers, the punch, the— Oh, just everything! We'd get together every day and call each other a dozen times a day. It drove the men crazy."

"They enjoyed it, I suspect."

"Well, I don't know. Lately—" Her dark-lashed blue eyes darkened. "Lately, when we decided that we did do things too closely, that no one of us ever made a separate decision—that we should perhaps decide things, and do things, on our own, the men agreed. And they are letting us do just that."

"But you're not happy about it."

"I don't know. Perhaps I should wait and see if it works out. Just now, I know I liked the other way better."

He stood up. "You'll make an adjustment," he said confidently. "Be sure you stay friends."

"Oh, we are that. It's largely a matter of not being such *close* friends."

"And you will be den mother."

She smiled at him wryly and reached for the brass polish.

"Thank you, Ginny," he said warmly. "Thank you very much!"

She nodded, said good-by, and sighed again. She gathered up her cleaning supplies, put them away, and started for home. She had hoped her new car would not need to be another station wagon.

* * *

Her impulse was, of course, to stop at Hazel's and talk about the pickle she was in. And, once home, to call Gene, and Nan, and moan a little.

But, as things were, she went straight home; she paused for a few minutes to admire her beds of chrysanthemums. Then she went into the house where Mag had the vacuum cleaner going upstairs. Ginny put her cleaning cloths into the laundry hamper, found a large tablet and two ballpoint pens, and went out again to a chair on the sun-warmed patio.

". . . have to make the best of this weather," she said half aloud. Willie, the dachshund, tucked himself into the chair with her, happy to have her at home.

"We have to make lists," Ginny told him. "We're a den mother again."

He would like having the boys around—and so would Ginny, if she were honest. Though some of the kids— What would she find to do with and for the group? Advancements and stuff took up some of the meeting time. She must look up her book, and get some supplies, check with the store downtown about badges and uniforms and—and stuff. She supposed her pregnant predecessor would have a list of names and addresses, telephone numbers—but Ginny must make plans for the months ahead. A lot of plans. There would be field trips, and—

"I will not give up my weekends!" she said firmly. "We'll meet after school. And—well, maybe one Saturday a month." But the regular meetings would definitely be after school. Jan would have to agree to keep an eye on Sarah. She would . . .

Let's see. There would be Hallowe'en, and Thanksgiving—and Christmas. Ginny groaned softly. What would they make for Christmas gifts? Those had to be started in November—supplies ordered. Paperweights? Picture frames of extruded aluminum—shadow boxes with dried flowers—*that* would have to be started right now! She must call the present den mother—she must ask Bob if the gang could visit the hospital? He'd say no, then change his mind. Rufus McGilfray would be glad—or say he was—to have the boys distribute public health literature. That could be a service project . . .

Ginny's pen flew.

She was surprised when Mag brought her a tray with a sandwich, a glass of milk, and a peach. "Lunchtime?" she asked.

"Yes, ma'am. And I'm fixin' to leave."

Ginny thanked her and gathered her papers into a heap. "I've agreed to be a Scout den mother again," she said. "It makes me weary just to think about all the work."

"Yes, ma'am."

Ginny drank her milk and watched Mag make her substantial way down the driveway. She was one of the few maids left who didn't need to be driven home or have a taxi pick her up. Mag was a jewel. But even Mag went along with the other "girls." First, they had stopped coming on Sundays. Now they no longer stayed all day or came back to prepare the evening meal. But Mag was honest, she was faithful, she was kind. And in time of trouble, she would do anything asked of her. On six days a week, she cleaned, she washed and ironed, she prepared things for dinner.

But with a cub pack, thought Ginny, it would be easier if Mag were getting dinner, the way she had used to do. Now— "I'm in despair," she said aloud, feeding the last bite of sandwich to Willie.

Well, maybe she could find help. Her friends had talents; she could get them to take over some of the projects. She could ask Ruth and Ike Kibbler to give the boys a morning on the farm. Gene, a former nurse, could teach first aid. Nan knew about painting, and Hazel had all sorts of things going. Ceramics, wood finishing—Ginny could count on them. She could go inside soon and phone to each of them in turn; they would sympathize with her despair. Maybe she'd ask them all to come over and help her lay out her whole program. If Carol had to be home until Christmas, she might want to help. She was very good with children. Yes, she would call Gene, present her problem . . .

She was in the house, with her hand on the telephone, when she remembered. She sat back in the chair and regarded the instrument. She felt exactly as she had done the time she and the children—Mary was about ten at the time—had gone exploring in the fields and woods behind their house. Ginny had run along a path and, suddenly, without warning, she had come upon a steep, sharp drop before her very feet. The path had ended; below her lay rocks, and farther down, a small lake or pool of water.

She had caught herself just in time, and could warn the children. But she sometimes remembered and lived again through the shocked fright of that moment. And today, eagerly ready to call her friends and summon them, she remembered their—their resolution. The others had formed it and accepted it. They would not want to hear about Ginny's despair. They would not be interested in knowing about the fix she was in, or be ready to help her extricate herself.

Oh, dear, oh, dear! What was she going to do?

She had not yet decided when Sarah came home from school, having been delivered by bus to the nearest corner. She had not decided when Jan blew in, running, from *her* bus—her dark hair bouncing, her short skirts whirling.

And she was full of Bitsy's disappearance. Had Mrs. Windsor called her mother? But why hadn't she? Had Ginny heard it on the radio? Mrs. Windsor had called the school and asked the students to help her find the dog. "*Bitsy,* Mom! He's *disappeared!*"

Ginny was properly upset to hear this. She believed she was even more upset that Hazel had not told her.

She immediately called Hazel and told her that she had just learned . . .

"Didn't you hear it on the radio?"

"I'm afraid not, dear. What happened?"

"Well, nothing really has happened," said Hazel in a dispirited tone of voice. "He just disappeared yesterday afternoon."

"And you don't know . . ."

Hazel did not want to prolong the conversation; she didn't want the phone tied up. So Ginny hung up, feeling worse than ever. If they had known last night . . . They could have offered sympathy, at least.

She asked Jan if she would want to go to the Windsors and offer to help.

"Have you and Mrs. Windsor had a fight?" Jan asked in her forthright way.

"No, dear. Of course not. We just get busy . . ."

She felt awful about Bitsy. The Rubles were crazy about their pets, too. She felt even more "awful" that twenty-four hours had gone by, and Hazel had not asked

Ginny and her family for help.

By the time Bob came home, she was in a real state. When he asked her what they were going to have for dinner, she stared at him in shocked dismay. "I haven't given it a thought!" she cried. She put both hands to her temples and shook her head. "This has been such a terrible day!" she told him.

"Where's your week's menu list?" He knew she made one up on Thursday nights, and shopped on Friday, and—

"Today's Thursday," she said solemnly.

He laughed. "Yes. That began eighteen hours ago."

But she was not amused. She went to the kitchen, opened the cabinet door where she always hung the menus. And there the list was. The last dinner planned ...

Split pea soup, Crax. Ro beef. Potatoes. Head lettuce. Cookies.

All right. She smiled wanly at Bob. "We'll have dinner," she told him. "I made the soup yesterday. And I can put the potatoes in the oven right now. If Mag made the cookies . . ."

She had. The big ginger "shin plasters" the kids and Bob loved.

Ginny scrubbed potatoes and talked to Bob about Bitsy and Hazel. "I felt so lost myself when I realized she hadn't called us," she said woefully. She turned to face him where he sat at the table. "It's terrible to lose all your friends at once."

"Have you lost them?"

"Well— Of course this was all Hazel's idea to begin with. But Bitsy's disappearance is a real tragedy in their house . . ."

"Yes, it is. Dewey was shook—and that takes doing."

"But they didn't tell us."

"We couldn't have done much of anything."

"We could have gone down there and *talked.*"

"Yes. And tonight I could take them some of your good pea soup."

She nodded. "I suppose that would be all right. I really don't know the rules of this game."

He made no comment, and she glanced at him. He had taken off his jacket and loosened the knot of his tie.

"Do you think it's a good idea?" she asked, putting the potatoes into the oven. "Not talking things over with each other?"

"I don't know, Ginny. You girls thought you'd try the thing. And you really haven't given it a full try."

"I never wanted it. Nan didn't. But since we're part of the group . . ."

She fetched the large jar of soup from the refrigerator and poured half of it into a pan, the rest into a smaller jar. "That's to take to the Windsors," she said. "Let Sarah go with you, but don't take Willie. Hazel won't be interested in our dog."

He smiled at her. "I'll go down there as soon as you tell me about the rest of your terrible day."

She stared at him. Then she remembered. "Oh!" she said. "Oh, yes. Well . . ."

And she told him about the cub scouts. "I just don't want to do it, Bob. I just don't!"

He comforted her, he laughed at her. He assured her that she did want to do it. And she was to think of all she would do for this batch of cubs. "They'll remember you all their lives, sweetheart. You're such a *good* den mother!" He picked up the jar of cold soup.

"That," said Ginny bitterly, "is where I made my first big mistake!"

He patted her shoulder and started for the door.

"We're going to eat in the kitchen," she called after him.

He waved his hand at her, to say that he had heard, and strode down the driveway. Ginny called Willie and kept him firmly on the porch. She told *him* they would eat in the kitchen. "Bob hates that," she reminded the little dog. "He believes in dinner. In the dining room. With flowers."

And as soon as Bob and Sarah were safely on their way, she cut enough pink mums for the blue glass vase and spread the cloth in the dining room. "Can't let my whole life fly to pieces," she said aloud.

Chapter Two

Up and down one green hill, and up on the top of another one, there stood the Cornel home, serene and lovely. Alison liked to get home early enough to do some work around the place, to give him an excuse to gaze out across the river below them, to enjoy, as on this afternoon, the way the oak leaves were turning. They had to be raked, and oak leaves were heavy, but he preferred them to the nasty little curls of elm leaves or sweet gum. Carol came out to watch him and offer to help, knowing full well that he wouldn't let her rake. She contented herself with scuffling through the pile of leaves which he had raked, and laughing at the antics of their new cat chasing a leaf across the grass.

She—Carol—was a tall girl, with smooth, "dishwater blond" hair. She was thin, and too pale still from the surgery she had had a month ago. It was because of that surgery that she was at home, under the pale blue sky, smelling the fragrance of the smoke from the leaf burner, instead of working her shift at the big, busy hospital in the city.

"I was to do Children's this quarter," she said discontentedly to her father.

"It will be there when you get back."

She sighed and sat down on a stump of the tree which had had to be cut down in the spring, a real tragedy in their family.

"I didn't know you were all that crazy about your nurses' training," said her father.

"It's all right. I like it," said Carol. "But mainly because I am busy doing things away from home. Mother can't fuss at me all the time."

"Maybe these weeks of rest here at home would be a good opportunity for you to learn to get along with your mother."

"She doesn't like me, Doc."

"Oh, of course she does, Carol. You and she—you don't see things alike. Not many things."

"It's not all my fault. I agreed to study nursing, as she wanted me to do."

Her father grinned. "But now you don't want her to tell you how things should be done."

"She forgets that things have changed in the years she's been out. We hardly ever have to sterilize syringes now; medications are different."

"I know that. But why not let her give her little lectures, if giving them pleases her?"

"That's your method, isn't it?"

"Not always. I quarrel with her, too. It never gets me anywhere."

"And you don't think it will get me anywhere."

"I think you'd enjoy your rest here more if you would relax. I am sure there are points where you should make your own decisions. But on little things—just ride along, dear. Then, at the end of this time, you can go back to the nursing program, completely well and strong."

"I get bored."

"Oh, there's no real need for that, Carol. Find yourself a hobby. Take walks, beginning slowly, of course. Use your imagination. I have a plan for our Christmas that you can look forward to. I thought I'd take all three of my girls to Florida, or maybe Bermuda, for Christmas. Wouldn't you like that?"

Carol sat thoughtful. "I'd like it," she agreed. "But I can think of three people who would be sure to object to the suggestion."

"What three people?" asked Alison.

"Nan, Ginny, and Hazel. "It's Mother's year—our year—to have the Christmas dinner, I think."

Alison Cornel raked a long strip of lawn. "Are they going to have a four-family dinner for Christmas this year?" he asked when he came back.

"Ask Mother. She's coming out."

Alison turned and put his question to Gene. Was the group of clinic wives going to have their joint-project Christmas dinner that year?

Gene looked at him in surprise. "Why not? It's going to be at Nan's. I have the Thanksgiving one."

"I thought you'd all seceded from each other." He watched her closely.

"Don't be silly. Of course we'll have the dinners, as we always do. Carol and I will work out our part of the Thanksgiving menu, and the decorations. I thought maybe we'd play games."

Alison stood shaking his head. "I don't see how you

can do it," he said soberly. "If you ladies can't go into consultation over whether to have radish roses or turnip lilies . . ."

Carol laughed aloud.

Gene smiled at her. "Let's go away from this creature," she suggested. "Men never understand the finer points of life. I'm going to the market. Wouldn't you like to come along?"

"I think I'll go on helping Doc rake leaves," she said.

"Well, don't work too hard . . ." Gene went back toward the house and her car. Alison and Carol waved to her as she drove around the circle of the drive.

"Why does she wait until five in the evening to do her marketing?" Alison asked his daughter.

"She meets a lot of people at that hour," Carol told him.

Which may or may not have been Gene's reason. But when she reached the large and glittering supermarket, almost the first person she did meet was Hazel Windsor.

"You look terrible," Gene greeted her friend.

"Well, thanks a lot." Hazel ran her fingers through her short white hair. "I feel terrible," she admitted.

"Bitsy is still gone?"

"Yes, he is. I can't understand how he could disappear so completely. Unless someone picked him up and carried him clear out of town."

Gene thought this unlikely. She could not imagine anybody stealing an old dog like the Windsors' cocker.

"Dewey made me come here," Hazel was saying. "He found that I didn't have milk or bread in the house."

"And he wanted you to get out, too."

"Yes, he did. He knew I wouldn't leave unless he was there to answer the phone."

Gene selected a head of lettuce. "I haven't the least idea what I'll have for dinner," she said. "I'm not as organized as Ginny is with her week's menus, and all."

"Why don't you let Carol organize your menus?" Hazel suggested. "How is she doing?"

"Oh, she mopes about. Says she has nothing to do. And she doesn't, of course. I asked her to come here with me, but she wouldn't. I can't get her interested in anything. She's unhappy and restless. She doesn't want to stay at home, and I can't much blame her. There isn't anyone of her own age. Her friends are at college, or married and having babies. She thinks Alison and I should let her go on with her training."

"That's pretty strenuous, isn't it?"

"She thinks the school would adjust things."

"Does she like it? Her school?"

"It's hard to tell about Carol. She doesn't bubble the way Susan does. I do know she wishes she were back in the dormitory with the other girls."

"Maybe there's some man back there, too. Maybe she's in love."

Gene whirled. "*Carol?*" she asked, and more loudly than she had expected. She saw heads turn.

"Why not Carol?" asked Hazel. "She's at the right age."

"The right age is all she is. She has no looks, no charm, and absolutely no idea about how to dress."

Hazel sniffed. "Good grief, Gene," she said loftily. "Where have you been? Look around you. Girls don't *dress* or try to be pretty any more. Their jeans, their posture . . . And not only here. Look at the pictures of them in the magazines, even the pictures of the week's brides in the newspapers. Think about the girls you know, right here in town. They either wear barefoot sandals, horrible canvas sneakers, or clunky shoes. They let their hair hang like seaweed, and they wear hideous eyeglasses. Great round circles or those nasty little granny things on the ends of their noses. And their clothes . . . What appeal can any of them have to men? If they wear long dresses, they don't know how to walk . . ."

"You don't admire the younger generation," said Gene. "That's evident."

"I'd like to admire them."

"I've been told they need understanding," drawled Gene.

"Well, that certainly must be what I lack."

"They must have some appeal to the opposite sex," Gene pointed out, trying to decide between pork chops and hamburger. "These girls are always getting pregnant."

"Perhaps it's their brains that attract. They are supposed to be smart."

"I don't think that's Carol's strength, either," said Carol's mother.

Hazel laughed shortly. "I wish you'd give that girl a chance."

"I give her every chance she'll take. But brains—that isn't Carol, and you know it."

"I know she hated studying—book reports and term papers. But she did well in some things."

"Okay. Okay. She's pleasant, and she's clean. She says she's doing all right in nurses' training, which takes some intelligence. But maybe you should be the one to ask her if she's in love. It would help me to know, I guess."

She looked expectantly at Hazel. "I don't think I should interfere," her friend said primly. "Remember, we are going to attend to our own affairs, live our own lives . . ."

Gene gazed at her thoughtfully. "Which leaves me in a fine spot, doesn't it?"

"No worse than the one I was in last night when we couldn't find Bitsy." Hazel looked at the milk and bread in her cart, turned abruptly, and went along the aisle toward the checkout counters.

Gene shook her head. It would be easy, she supposed, to resent Hazel's implied—and spoken—criticism. But the woman was terribly upset about her dog. Gene wondered if Bitsy might not have got out of the yard, perhaps have been injured, or caught somewhere and not able to get home . . .

If all you had to worry about was a dog, you—well, you would worry!

She said this to Carol when she got home and asked her daughter to help her get some sort of dinner on the table.

"Sure," said Carol. "What are we having?"

"Oh—strip steaks. A vegetable. There are several boxes in the freezer. Egg salad, and the cake we had earlier this week. If it seems dry, we can put sauce or ice cream on it."

"Sounds good, but Doc will call it fattening."

"Yes, and eat every crumb. He's a big man; a surgeon uses up a lot of energy."

"Mmmhmmmmnh. He raked a lot of leaves this evening, too."

"What's he doing now?"

"Checking the hospital, and reading."

Gene nodded and filled the tea kettle.

"Did you see anybody besides Hazel?" Carol asked. "At the store?"

"I saw dozens of somebodies. The place was crowded. The ammonia plant pays on Thursdays."

"And people swarm to spend their pay checks."

"Well, of course they do. Wait until you begin to draw one."

"I am waiting," said Carol.

Gene glanced at her. "It gets dull, doesn't it?" she said. "You don't feel bad enough to want to do all this resting."

"I suppose Doc knows what he's doing."

"He certainly does. And maybe, after a month, he'll let you go down to the hospital and do things there. They always need help."

"Be quite a bit different from working at the Center."

"Yes. Sure it would. Fifty beds isn't much like a thousand. But it's a fair cross section."

Carol touched her arm. "I wasn't criticizing. I'm proud of our hospital and clinic."

"I'd hope so. Did you get the vegetable?"

"Yes. Cauliflower. Could we have cheese sauce?"

"In case we don't have enough calories already on the table? Sure, we can have cheese sauce."

Gene moved alertly, capably about the kitchen. Like her daughter, she was more plain than pretty. Her light red hair had a shine, her eyes were good, and her bones. She wore flat shoes where some heel would have called attention to her pretty legs and ankles. She didn't "bother" to change from the denim skirt and gingham blouse which she had put on that morning. She, too was clean and . . . pleasant.

"Some interesting things happen down at the hospital," she assured her daughter. "In about the same proportion as they do at the Center. Funny things, too, sometimes. Your father was telling about a woman they had to deal with. Her husband had had a stroke or something, and been transferred to the Veterans Hospital, where he died. The widow needed the compensation due her, and our hospital was trying to help her all it could. Of course they provided his records, and so on. And tried to help her make out the application. To do this, she had to provide her marriage certificate. That was needed as proof she was married to this particular veteran, you see."

Gene looked at her steaks in the broiler.

"Go on," said Carol.

"Well—I can just *see* her! She didn't come back for three days, and when she did, she said she'd had to go up into the attic to find the old papers. While up there, she'd cleaned the attic, and threw out enough stuff for a rummage sale. But she'd also found what she thought she needed. And what do you suppose she brought to Father?"

"How would I know?"

"Well, what she brought was an old, yellowed wedding invitation." Gene laughed and looked at Carol, who didn't even smile.

"I don't suppose that worked," she said after a lengthy pause.

Gene sighed and came to her daughter. "Carol," she asked, "is there something wrong?"

Carol stepped back and shook her head. But her face threatened to collapse.

"Are you worried about yourself?" Gene asked, frightened herself. "Is there some pain or trouble you haven't told us about?"

"Oh, no, Mother! I'm fine. Scar healed, insides functioning . . ."

"But there *is* something . . ."

"Don't let the steaks burn."

"I won't. But I wish . . ." Gene turned her steaks. "Five minutes," she said. "Could you begin to tell me?" she urged.

"Well, there isn't much to tell. I'm bored here, and I wish I could be working. But I realize I wouldn't have any fun there either. Susan's letters come, and in each one she's found some new boy, and she tells about dates and stuff. When she comes home on vacation, she writes letters, and gets letters, phone calls from boys . . . Me, there's nothing. I just don't have any skill with boys or men. The other trainees and nurses have fun. Dates . . ."

"Don't you ever . . . ?"

"Well, yes. A few. One or two . . . But I'm not around there any more. Where all the men are, interns and hospital workers. I'm here in Bayard. And there's not a soul here. You know there's not!"

"Well, at least not many," Gene agreed. "But you could write to your friends, maybe invite some of them to come up here for a weekend."

"I have written some letters. I've thanked the ones who sent me cards and stuff when I was in the hospital. I do all right with the girls. I think I do. But the boys— I freeze right up. I cannot seem to write a letter that would hold any man's interest or make him want to answer, let alone come up here for a visit with me."

Gene began to serve the cauliflower on the warm plates, and carefully add the cheese sauce. "What do you say?" she asked. "In your letters."

"What can I say? When I don't *do* anything, how can I write a newsy letter?"

Gene laughed. "I'll think that over while we feed Father," she promised.

She evidently did think about it. After dinner, clearing away, then later when she followed Carol upstairs at bedtime, she tried to suggest a man or two in Bayard. Jan Ruble had told about a teacher in the high school who was—according to Jan—both fabulous and single. And there was a fellow who came to church—he was a conservationist, or an engineer, or something . . .

Carol nodded. "I've seen him. But I can't really say he saw me."

"Now, Carol . . . But before dinner you were talking about letter writing. You surely don't write to your men friends and *say* there is nothing to write about, and then stop on that note?"

Carol looked at her in dismay. "What else can I say?" she demanded. "Not that it makes any difference. They don't care if I write or not."

"How do you know?"

"Well—"

Gene leaned forward. "Carol Cornel!" she said sharply. "You don't complain to *him* that *he* doesn't write often enough. Do you?"

"Well, if he doesn't write . . ."

"All right. He's not a prompt letter writer. He's busy, and you're not. But you must not hound a man, my dear. You simply must not *press!*"

"Oh, I know. Or I guess I do. But—"

"You can protest. But keep the light touch."

"About what?"

Oh, dear. Gene sat in the bent wood rocker and watched her daughter go into the bathroom. She looked at the pretty bedroom with its frieze of ballet dancers stenciled around the pale blue walls, its good prints of Degas and Renoir.

She rocked back and forth and thought. She was impatient with that girl splashing around in the shower. But Alison had urged her to try to help Carol. "Try to enjoy her in the way you do Susan."

"Susan responds."

"Yes, she's an extrovert, so you have only the problem that she makes a fool of herself every third month in the year. Carol—you have to hunt for ways to reach her. But do be patient with her. In time you'll get results."

Well, maybe . . . At any rate, Gene would control her inclination to fuss at Carol. To throw up her hands and resign herself to an old maid in the family. Forty years old, and still moping around the house . . .

Carol came out, finally, and sat down before the dressing table to comb her hair. Gene wished she would roll it up, but she wouldn't. Though, tonight, she was drawing it back into two dog ears, away from her face.

"What did you do today?" she asked her daughter.

"Here at home, you mean?" Carol's tone was dry.

"You went somewhere this afternoon. You asked me if you could drive . . ."

"And you said to be careful and not go far."

"The abdominal muscles . . ."

"Mother, I know all about the abdominal muscles."

Be patient. Gene told herself. *Be patient.*

She waited, rocking.

"I just went to the club," Carol said grudgingly. "And down to the beach."

"It was lovely and warm. Sunny."

"Yes, it was. But hardly anyone was there. Except some little kids making sand castles."

"But you need not say it that way when you write about it in a letter."

"I know," said Carol, sighing. "I should keep the light touch, be gay and whimsical."

Gene laughed. "Well, yes, you should. Besides, if you'd look at it that way, I think you would find yourself enjoying the hour you spent on our nice beach. Were there any boats out?"

"Yes. Even a sailboat."

"That would be pretty. We have such a wide basin on our part of the river."

"Ye-es. And I do think we have a nice beach, Mother. And the river is really wide here— But my trouble—in writing gay, whimsical letters—is that I don't know *how* to write them, what to say."

Gene said nothing. She watched Carol put some sort of cream on her face, then turn off the dressing table light and go to the bed. She got up and helped fold back the quilted, blue-flowered spread. Carol slipped in between the sheets and turned on the bedlamp.

"Do you have things to read?" Gene asked her.

Carol pointed to the magazines and a book on the table. Gene bent over to kiss her daughter. "I'll turn off the light and open the window," she said.

"All right."

Then—"Mother?" she said when Gene was at the door, ready to go downstairs.

"Yes?"

"Don't talk to Doc about this?"

Gene came back to the foot of the bed. "About what?" she asked.

"Oh, about what a poor letter writer I am."

"We both thought you did all right in the letters you sent home this past year. They were short, but—"

"Writing *home* isn't any problem."

Gene chuckled. "No, it's just—'Thank you for the Care package. I shared the apples, but hid the cookies.' "

Carol laughed, too. "And thanks, Doc, for the check."

"I see what you mean. Your material is different."

"It sure is. But, Mother—maybe— Would you help me write the kind of letter . . . ?"

"Oh, I certainly would!" said Gene. "It would be fun."

"All right."

"Tomorrow. Now you should go to sleep."

"I will. And remember. Don't tell Doc."

"I won't. Good night, Carol."

She went downstairs. She surely would not tell Alison that she was going to help Carol write letters to her boy friends. He would have a jumping fit!

The next day, Gene and Plumy, her cleaning woman, worked together until noon. The Cornels did not have anything like the cook-maid which Ginny and Nan had, nor the good, trustworthy girl-three-mornings-a-week who came to Hazel's house. Gene always found some woman—usually crippled, sometimes just mentally impaired—whom she felt she helped by giving her work. Gene had to work right along with these people. One woman had let the garage door down on Gene's head and shoulders. Once the woman had decided to take over Alison's liquor cabinet while Gene was busy on the telephone. Sometimes this kind of "help" worked out quite well. And nearly always Gene felt better for her charitable deeds. She paid the women well, she transported them to and from work. "She'd do more work and get better results," Alison said, "if she'd just pitch in and clean the cupboards herself."

"But she won't."

"No, she won't. And Gene's *won't* is a fearsome thing."

That Friday morning, Carol said she would go down and ask Hazel if she could help find Bitsy.

"Just let her talk to you about it," Gene advised. "She really is upset."

But at noon, mother and daughter came together for a bowl of tomato bisque, crisp crackers warmed in the oven, and a dish of apple sauce. And Carol reminded Gene of the promise to help her write a letter. "About that dumb afternoon on the beach," she said bitterly.

"She's only being shy," Gene assured herself. "Sure, I'll help right away," she said aloud. "Let's put these dishes into the washer . . ."

That was quickly accomplished. They sat on the porch, with the louvered glass open to the breeze which, Gene said, "smelled like rain."

"Begin it that way," she advised. "You—*I*—am writing this on the big porch here at home. It is going to rain, though I wish it wouldn't. Yesterday I had a fine, sunny afternoon down on the beach. We have a really good one, you know. It's kept clean, and our river widens out into almost a lake here. The sailboats . . ."

"Boat," Carol corrected, her pencil flying.

"Some days we have a dozen. I think you could say boats."

"Okay. What about 'em?"

"Well, let's see. Oh, yes. The sailboats were pretty, because there was a good breeze. When I get stronger, I hope the weather stays nice enough for me to get out on the river. We—everyone has some sort of boat here. Yesterday—let's see. I set up barriers so I would be left alone. To do this, one tilts the beach umbrella, piles up the box of gear and the thermos jug of lemonade—and pretends to be asleep. And do you know? I did go to sleep, all cozy and warm."

"Mother!"

Gene gazed blandly at her daughter.

Carol shrugged. "Okay. Okay. If that's what gets 'em."

"It's what gets them," said Gene, thinking that it was just as well her friends were not in on this project. Both Nan and Ginny would have been startled into protest or hilarity. As for Hazel . . . She laughed aloud and continued.

"For real excitement, I watched a crawdad," she dictated. "And when he went away, I helped some little kids build sand castles. In short, I really *relaxed*. It was wonderful. Did you ever try it? It's great."

She glanced up at Carol.

"Say 'neat,' " Carol suggested. "We use that word more."

"You can change the wording. I was only making suggestions."

"I know," said Carol. "And—thanks."

An hour later, Gene watched the girl go down the drive, a white envelope in her hand. She had asked if she might walk as far as the post office.

"I think so. If you get tired, sit down on somebody's

steps and rest. Or call me. I'll fetch you."

So Carol departed, and her mother watched her go. The girl was tall, slender—thin, really. She was inclined to slump a little, and Gene was inclined to fuss about this too much. It made Carol self-conscious. She had better taste in clothes, really, than did Susan. Susan was inclined to put on everything at once. Carol wore straight skirts, or slacks, and looked pretty well in them. This afternoon her slacks were brown plaid, and her blouse was tan. She had pulled on a sleeveless sweater that had ribbings of red and gray. Her hair was tied back, safe from the breeze, with a length of red yarn. Compared to a dozen girls Gene could have called by name, Carol looked attractive.

She thought about the letter which was probably in that square white envelope. The afternoon on the beach sounded like fun. It only showed what the right choice of words could do. Gene believed she would call Nan and tell her about the incident. Nan read a lot, and she might have suggestions for further letters. If this one was a success . . .

But Gene went back to the kitchen, shaking her head. She couldn't call Nan about this sort of thing. The hospital wives were leading their own lives—which, Gene suspected, made things rather less interesting for them. She was glad she had Carol to talk to. Otherwise she'd be up the wall.

At the hospital, the doctors had made way for the staff meeting they tried so hard to hold at least once a week. At these meetings, all sorts of things were handled—a personnel dispute, a decision on some repair or purchase for the hospital and clinic buildings, and they made their tissue and surgical reports—sometimes brief, sometimes extended because of the nature of a particular case.

On this day, Dr. Windsor said he thought there should be a law against people riding with their elbows stuck out an open window of a car. "These funny bone things could hurt the doctor quite as much as the patient."

"Did your patient tell you that?" drawled Dr. McGilfray.

Dewey laughed and shook his head. "He was—is—my patient, and I got called first. Rode in the ambulance with him . . ."

"And it was excruciating."

"Sure was. Okay, Cornel. Make your report."

Alison nodded and hung X-rays in the viewer, then dimmed the lights. "I can say 'funny bone,' too," he agreed. "If it's going to make anyone happier."

Dewey waved his hand in dismissal of the point. "This isn't my week to be happy," he said. "Call the thing an olecranon fracture—I think everyone will understand that."

Dr. Cornel described the case and his treatment, making a nice little speech of gratitude to the steel industry for providing medicine with aids such as this stainless contour medullary screw used in reducing the fracture. He showed the length of finely tempered steel, switched on the lights, and asked Dewey if they still had heard nothing about the dog Bitsy.

Dewey shook his head. "I can't understand it. You just don't lose thirty pounds of dog! Everybody knows Bitsy; everybody knows me!"

The men began gathering up their papers. Garde Shelton, sitting next to Dr. Ruble, said he thought his wife,

Nan, was pregnant. And then he laughed. "To see the ears prick up," he explained.

"We're all interested," said Bob. "And we like to hear that kind of good news. How old is Fiddle?"

"She's three."

"Then Nan should be in fine condition. Butch is five . . . Have Nan come around to see me."

"Of course."

The men began to move out into the hall. Tall, dark-haired Dr. McGilfray, going swiftly down the corridor. Serving as public health doctor for the district, he was always urgently in a hurry. Dr. Windsor, who these last couple of days had let his usual good-humored smile fade, went to the chart desk, sat down and turned on the light. This silvered his white hair and, from the papers on the desk, reflected a glow upon the planes and hollows of his strongly featured face, sparkled from his very blue eyes. He studied the charts with complete absorption, oblivious of what went on or was being said around him.

Dr. Cornel went directly to the side door, out through it, and over to his office in the clinic building. He shivered a little and told himself that he must begin to pick up a coat or use the covered passageway. "Though that thing's drafty," he said. He'd better post a memo to have blankets ready for any patients transported between the two buildings. "They might have as bald a head as mine," he said, rubbing his shiny pate when he came into his office suite.

"It isn't really cold, Doctor," his office nurse assured him.

"I don't know about 'it,' but I got cold coming across the lot."

"Use the corridor."

"It's drafty, too."

"A little, yes. Doors are left open, and even a window sometimes."

"Do we have heat there?"

She smiled at him. He knew that they had both heat and air conditioning in the corridor.

He said "Humph!" and went into his own office, a large room walled with bookcases and cabinets. There was an X-ray view box, a small TV set, framed certificates and diplomas, his Army Medical Corps discharge, a picture of his family taken when Susan was five and Carol seven.

"Wonder how Gene's making out," he asked himself, sitting down and pulling forward the memo pad on which Mrs. Graham would have listed his appointments and affixed any messages. He read this and pushed the intercom button. "Let's get to work," he said gruffly.

Dr. Ruble and Dr. Shelton lingered longer in the conference room. Garde's announcement had given them things to talk about.

"Is Nan happy about a third baby?" Bob asked.

Garde nodded. "I think so. We wanted another one."

"Of course you did. Fine, healthy children, with a good ancestry. I perhaps should warn you that two children get along fine, while a third makes for cat fights."

"And perhaps I won't say that our children will be different."

"If you did, I wouldn't argue with you. Nan has a serene way, and you have firm convictions."

"Well, thank you, Bob. I'll quote you to Nan." His

black eyes showed his pleasure. "There's one hitch in this matter," he said.

Bob looked at him in alarm. "Really?"

"Nothing for an OB man to handle. But I do think Nan would be happier . . . I am sure she misses being able to talk over this blessed event with the other wives."

Bob laughed. "Not to mention what they are missing. Gene telling her not to buy one new thing for the new baby, to use what's left over from Butch and Fiddle. And Ginny would have her knitting needles out. While Hazel . . ."

"There must be new books out on childbirth and child care," said Garde.

"There are. And normally she'd be right there with everything from diet to natural childbirth. Oh, they are missing a *lot* of fun!"

"I suspect they know that. I've been expecting them to give the thing up. But they seem to be taking the decision more seriously than I realized at first."

"Too seriously, I believe. Or," Bob added, "they seem to be in danger of doing just that. Ginny was visibly upset when she realized that Hazel had not told her about Bitsy's disappearance."

"I don't like this development myself. Those girls need each other. Each one is a capable individual, and I suppose one could say that each of us doctors could carry on his medical practice alone, as an individual . . ."

Bob considered that. "I hope I never have to."

"Me, too. But my point is, we work better as a group, and the girls do, too. Oh, *work* isn't the word. *Function* is better. Those four women have a particular, a peculiar place in this town. In the society of the town. They are the wives of the hospital doctors; they are as conscious of that fact as we men are. Their tongues and their opinions can't be as free in public as is the case with other women. They must always be on guard. Okay. That means that they need to express themselves freely and frequently to each other. They've recognized that, and have enjoyed it. They depend on the freely expressed opinions of each other, or they *did*. They seemed to know that their little group was their best and only chance for free communication."

"To let their hair down," Bob agreed.

Garde put his hand on the door latch, but his thick black eyebrows were drawn together in his continuing concern. "I think we men are to blame, Ruble," he said. "I believe—just maybe—that we men have made too much fun of the girls and their huddles. They've worn paths between the homes, and the telephones automatically dial those numbers . . . And we have made fun of them. A time or two one of us has become angry . . ."

"Well, exasperated."

"At least that. And if we are to blame for this clampdown, I for one am sorry."

"Me, too. Now, if I were you, I'd urge Nan to talk about this new baby of hers, to tell the other wives. She's going to need them."

"Of course she is. And I shall tell her."

"And get an appointment to see me."

Bob went down the hall one way, Garde went the other. Both tall, strong men. Bob was the older, and perhaps the more handsome. He was, except for McGilfray, the most handsome of the hospital staff doctors. He had kept his slender, lithe grace of movement. His thick, dark hair was frosted at the temples, but he carried his head erectly. There was warmth in his fine eyes, and in his voice. He liked the work he did.

With the pill, and population growth a matter of consideration, there had been some talk of reducing the number of beds in the maternity ward. Bob had asked to be allowed to make adjustments. There were fewer babies. He knew that better than anyone. But his Gyn work kept up, and often seemed to expand. He would keep the beds, fill one side of the hall with ob's, use the other for his Gyn patients, and have his work somewhat localized.

Now it was good to go into his own territory, to look through the door window to see if he had any patients in the suspect room. Here, if possible, entering women were kept until they had been bathed and put into sterile gowns, their bodily health observed and checked for enough time to avoid their bringing infection into the ward.

Today there was one patient; she would have surgery in the morning. Bob would see her before he left the hospital that afternoon. In the hall there was a young woman, come to nurse her baby, not yet discharged. The tiny thing had weighed but three pounds, though he was doing fine now. Bob heard the floor nurse sternly ask the mother if she was scrubbed, then say, "Well, you know good and well you must be."

There was a murmur—of assent, or dissent, he could not be sure.

Then—"Of course your friend cannot go into the nursery. No, not even if she scrubs, too."

Smiling, the doctor sat down at the chart desk, glancing at his watch as he did so. *Friends.* Sometimes wonderful, sometimes . . . He thought about what Garde and he had discussed. Everybody needed friends. He reached for the phone and told his secretary to leave some time open for him to see Mrs. Shelton. There would be an appointment made.

"Sure, she's all right. Just one of her regular visits." He smiled at his feeble joke.

Chapter Three

A week slid by; a day or two of drizzly rain brought the calendar into October. The sun was setting earlier, and there were long autumn evenings with a chill on them, though not yet a biting cold. The hunter's moon rose only an hour after sunset, and back in the hills the coon dogs were running. At the Rubles' house, and the Cornels', their barking could be heard. Dewey Windsor and Hazel, still hoping to find their dog, went out for a walk to feel and see and hear the autumn evening mists about them, missing the leash around a wrist. The afterglow was still on the maples. Along the walk the grass was still soft, though here and there one could feel a crispness underfoot.

The afterglow faded, and they spoke of the stars—the Dippers, big and small, Cassiopeia, the polestar. A flight of geese gabbled across the moon, stopping them dead in delight. A barred owl hooted . . .

"Looks like fall is here," said Dewey.

Hazel sighed. Dewey hugged her arm close and turned their steps homeward. He wished he knew of some way to comfort her. But he himself was not ready to give up hope, to stop missing the furry rush of welcome when he came home, the idiotic yapping at nothing—the wheeze of the old dog in the small hours of the night.

They returned home, and Dewey checked the hospital. Then they settled into their usual chairs, Hazel with a book, Dewey with a stack of medical magazines, a pad and pencil at his hand.

He had half filled the top sheet with notes when something—a faint scraping of feet on the brick stoop?—raised his head. Then there was a knock, faint, tentative —and was it? Could it be? A bark? He and Hazel were out of their chairs. They nearly collided at the end of the room—and Dewey threw the front door open.

Hazel snapped on the outdoor light and cried out. "Oh, Bitsy, Bitsy, *Bitsy!*"

She went down on her knees; the dog sprang into her arms, nearly tipping her backward. Then he was leaping, and yelping, licking Hazel's face, leaping at Dewey, whimpering, barking, and crying.

"I don't know who made the biggest fool of himself," Dewey would tell afterward. "There we were, with the door left wide open, Hazel sitting on the floor—and Bitsy running in circles around us, out into the kitchen, into the bedroom—back, jumping and barking. I shouted and Hazel talked and laughed and cried. Just pure Hell broke loose, that's all. And that poor kid . . ."

"What poor kid?"

Well, there had been a boy. A skinny boy—red-headed —hair cut shagged—probably did it himself with a fish knife. Oh, about twelve. At the most. Freckles. Wide eyes. He watched the grown people and their crazy goings-on over that dog. Kissing and hugging each other, kissing and hugging that dog.

Somehow, he told, a week ago—a good week ago—the boy, Jay, had found the dog nosing around the packing case where he lived, down in Fishtown. Must have followed somebody all that way. First, the boy told, he'd tried to run the dog off. But he was tired, and wouldn't go very far, just sat and shivered. So Jay had offered him some food—he didn't remember what. Probably fish; that mainly was what he lived on.

"Fish!" cried Hazel shrilly. "With bones?"

"Well, yes'm. Fish have bones. Don't hurt none. They're soft."

"He's never had anything but beef bones," said the lady. By then she was sitting on the floor, rubbing and cuddling the dog, who seemed to like it.

Jay talked to the man. He said he had let Bitsy sleep in his packing box.

"What were you doing in a packing box? Where was this?"

"Down on the levee. I live in that box. It's a real stout one. I dragged it down there from behind the telephone company. Don't see those big wooden ones much any more. I caulked the seams . . ."

"Swiped the caulking?" asked Dewey.

"Sure. There's always some lying around. Fishing boats, or up where the swells keep their boats."

"How old are you?"

"Eleven, maybe twelve. I lose track."

"Didn't Bitsy have his collar?"

Dewey knew that he did. It was still around his neck, hidden under the dirty, matted fur. "Why didn't you . . . ?"

"He showed up pretty late, Mister, and he was tired. I let him sleep that night. The next day I had a sort of job at the tavern—I carry out stuff, and swab the floor. Sometimes they pay me money. Usually just leftover sandwiches and stuff. And I thought I'd make it up into town, but I didn't that day. And the next one I found the newspaper saying you'd offer a reward . . ."

The boy could read.

"But that was a week ago!" Dewey sounded angry. The lady was feeding her dog crackers made like little bones. She said he was thin.

"I'm thin, too," the boy pointed out.

Yes, he was. And his teeth needed attention.

"Why didn't you bring the dog back before this?" the man persisted. "Or turn him loose? He might have found his way home, or someone would have brought him in . . ."

"Heck, no!" said Jay. "I needed that reward. Worst way! It's going to be winter any day now!"

"You'll get your reward," Dewey assured him.

"I would have given him ten bucks," he told, "but Hazel—she brought out twenty-five. And maybe she would have given him more. She was so hysterical to have that dog back. About as pleased as Bitsy was. He looked a mess. His fur all matted and dirty. His breath would have knocked down a telephone pole."

Hazel could not wait to bathe Bitsy. The boy watched, then helped fill the tub out in the garage. One car was moved out to make room. These were really rich folks! As he had guessed they would be. And the fuss they made! The water must be warm, not hot. They had pieces of soap in a net bag. They scrubbed that dog, and talked to him. The man washed his eyes special. And when the bath was done, they used four towels—four!—to dry him. Four towels for a *dog!* Good towels, not one of 'em tore!

The man—he was a doctor—he talked to Jay, kept asking questions. All about where Jay lived. Didn't he have a family? They'd moved out after his ma died. His pa and his grandpa. Jay didn't know where they were by now. That was a time ago. First, he'd lived anywhere he could. In an abandoned boat, under a porch—then the packing box. He'd scrounged food. Stolen some. Stolen things he needed, or found things at the dump.

Did he know Dr. McGilfray?

Mac? Oh, sure, he knowed him. Kept wanting a kid to go to school.

"Haven't you been to school?"

Yes, sometimes he still went. Schools were warm, and they fed a kid. But he couldn't take being shut up that way. And they kept wanting him to show up a family.

He was not an unattractive boy. Freckles, red hair—Dewey could picture him playing baseball, or skinny dipping off a pier into the river.

Hazel asked what they could do for Jay. Besides the reward money, she meant. By then, Bitsy was snoozing in his favorite chair. Clean, warm, and fed.

Jay said he guessed he'd be going.

"But wait a minute!" cried Hazel. "We'll drive you home."

"Oh, no, ma'am."

"But we'd like to help." Did he need a warm jacket? What about food? She had a lot of canned things . . .

"Lobster, anchovies, artichoke hearts," Dewey said dryly, and she protested. "We owe this boy so much!"

"We owe him thanks, and the reward. Remember, he

kept us on the anxious seat for a week."

Yes, he had. But still—

Jay himself solved the impasse. He didn't need a thing, he said. He fished and worked at odd jobs. He was doing fine. Then Hazel again asked him how old he was, and he shrugged.

By ten o'clock, Dewey had called the other doctors— and the police—to tell that Bitsy had been found and brought home. He repeated about the same account in each case. With the police, he said only that a Fishtown boy had found the dog and had brought him home. Later he said he guessed gratitude had made him want to protect Jay.

Dr. Cornel took the call to his house, and told the news to Gene and Carol. "Maybe we can get Windsor settled down to work now," he grumbled.

Gene smiled at him. "I believe we all have been watching and looking for Bitsy," she said. "Even you."

"Sure. Wanted to get some work out of Windsor."

Then Gene smiled at Carol, who was holding a hank of green yarn while Gene wound it into a ball, her hands and forearms moving gracefully, skillfully.

"Is that hard to do?" Alison asked curiously.

"Not really."

"You use excellent coordination."

Gene nodded. "I'd better. A poorly wound ball collapses and makes an ungodly mess."

"Who's going to get a green sweater for Christmas?" her husband asked.

"You were, but now I think I'll make a coat for Bitsy."

"Mother!" Carol protested.

Alison went back to his chair and his football game.

"Let her alone, Carol," he said. "I'd rather she would be smart-alecky than cranky."

Garde and Nan were in their small, cozy library when Dewey called them. Dr. Shelton set the phone down and smiled at his wife. He could always smile at the picture she made in the lamplight, some sewing in her hands. Tonight it was needlepoint. Her brown hair caught every light and shadow, her pretty mouth showed her concentration. Now she looked up.

"News?" she asked. "You kept saying 'Good!'"

Garde laughed, sat down again in his deep chair, and picked up the book which he had been reading aloud to Nan.

"It was good news," he said. "Bitsy has been found and returned."

Nan dropped her sewing. "What else could you say?" she asked. "It *is* good news! I expect Hazel is lyrical."

"Windsor was. Some kid in Fishtown found the dog and brought him home."

"Was he all right?"

"Dewey said he badly needed a bath."

"Which no doubt he already has had."

"I suppose . . . He didn't talk long."

"No." Nan selected a length of red yarn and threaded her needle. "I'm afraid I prayed for his return," she said.

"Why shouldn't you? Bitsy's one of God's creatures, and the only child the Windsors have."

"And that's too bad, isn't it?"

"Hazel accepts it. I don't believe Dewey ever has. He talked, for a while, of adopting a child. But not lately."

"Perhaps Hazel didn't want to."

"Hasn't she talked about it?"

"I don't remember. I think she's been too busy telling the rest of us how to raise *our* children."

Garde laughed. "She tells me, too," said the pediatrician.

When Dewey called the Rubles' house, Ginny answered the phone. Bob, she said, had gone to bed. "He had three deliveries between three and four this morning. He crawled home about five, but of course he didn't get more than a nap."

Dewey said he could imagine, and then told her about Bitsy. Ginny was delighted. She turned to relay the news to Jan. "Sarah's in bed, too," she explained. "Now! Tell me all about it."

"Well, this boy . . ." And he told about Jay, the packing box and the reward.

"Smart kid," said Ginny. "Hazel gave him a big reward, I'll bet."

"Too big. I myself was rather provoked that he'd kept the dog for a whole week."

"Yes. Dewey, do you suppose . . . ?"

"That he stole Bitsy on purpose? The thought has crossed my mind. But anyone could have opened the gate. So I've decided to accept his story."

"Dewey?"

"Yes?"

"Do you suppose Rufus McGilfray is behind his returning the dog?"

"I don't know, Ginny. There are a lot of things I seem not to know as I think about this matter. Jay—the boy —said he knew Mac. Mainly because Mac has a nasty way of sending him to school."

"Well, thank you for telling me. I know Hazel is happy."

"Dithering."

Ginny set the phone down and talked to Jan about Bitsy and the boy from Fishtown. Jan had a dozen questions which Ginny could not answer. Ginny could think of another dozen herself.

Tomorrow . . . A month ago, the wives surely would have gathered on one pretext or another, but primarily to talk about Bitsy's return and the Fishtown boy and what had really happened, what could be done for the lad now . . .

Ginny sighed. No gathering would happen. In the vacuum they themselves had created, nothing ever happened. Not in the old, warm way. She didn't know if Hazel had bought that brown coat, she wouldn't know about the night Bitsy came home, she wouldn't know a *thing!* The four women had made their usual apple butter together, but they had been so blamed polite! So careful to stay off personal matters. Why, Nan had asked the others if they knew where she could buy wool socks for Garde; he could not take the man-made fibers, not even just heel and toe—and then she had apologized for "bothering" them. That same evening, Ginny had deliberately called her and told her about Pendleton socks. Bobby, her son, couldn't tolerate nylon or Orlon either.

But the doctors were under no such restrictions. They had the same dozens of questions and commentaries to make, and they made them. Consulting over a case, during lunch in the staff dining room, Cornel and Dr. Windsor in the office suite they shared in the clinic building

—and especially when they came together at the end of the day to shower and change out of the hospital clothes, to adjust their minds and interests to their homes and other lay preoccupations.

Dewey told of Jay's astonishment about the bath they had given Bitsy. "I guess he saw no reason for such measures. But if you could have smelled that dog!" He stood shaking his head. "And the *boy!* Except in the summer when he probably swims in the river, I don't think he uses much bath water."

"How does a kid like that survive?" asked Bob Ruble.

"Plenty of them do in the city ghettos," Garde Shelton reminded him.

"Yes, but Bayard has tried to clean up Fishtown."

"And succeeded to a comparative degree. Mac knows about this kid. He evidently can't keep him in school. But that packing box! In winter?"

"I gather he's proud of his independence."

"Cocky," said Dewey. "I expect he has his times of being scared. And something should be done for him, but last night I couldn't figure what. I can't now."

"He should be made to go to school."

"He goes. But for the hot lunch, not learning. He can read. He read the reward offer strong and clear."

"What if he should become ill? Or get hurt?"

Dewey nodded. "That could happen. The police must patrol the neighborhood."

"They didn't find Bitsy. Do they know the kid lives in a packing case?"

"Perhaps it looks better than some of the shacks. I mean to look at it myself."

"Be careful," cautioned Dr. Cornel.

"Of what?" Dewey demanded, turning to stare at him.

"Well, the kid can be a nuisance, if nothing worse."

"Aggh!" Dewey protested. "Anyway, now that I know about him, I expect he'll be on my conscience. A kid that age needs raising, Cornel!"

"Yes, he does. But . . ."

"You know?" said Dewey. "He's a hard-boiled rascal. Hard-nosed. But I do think he possesses a core of honesty. And I admire the guts he must have to survive as he has done."

"Well, at least talk to McGilfray."

"I mean to."

Nan was happy about being pregnant, and she agreed with Bob Ruble that she should tell her friends, the wives of the other three doctors. He felt that Nan would enjoy their participation, and she was inclined to agree with him. "It might bring us together in the old way," she told Garde one morning when she kissed him good-by as he left for the hospital.

"Why not call them together? They could listen to Fiddle sing. What on earth *is* she singing?"

"Mary has a little lamb."

"Oh, yes. And his . . . his *what?*"

"His wheat," said Nan serenely, trying not to laugh. *"His wheat is white as so."*

Garde groaned. "Did she learn that from Butch?"

"No, in nursery school."

Garde turned back from the doorstep. "You mean we have *two* kids that butcher the English language?"

Nan giggled. "They *love* the English language. Not just the way we love it, but . . ."

"And then there will be three?" asked her husband.

"I'm afraid so, darling."

He hugged her slender shoulders. "Okay," he agreed. "In some way we must be to blame."

Nan spent the morning busy at other things, but trying to formulate, as well, a plan for seeing her friends and spreading the news. She told Ruby what she was thinking about, and the big, capable woman who had helped raise "Miss Nan" cut the problem down to size.

" 'Tain't no use figuring, honey," she said. "Jes take a walk like Dr. Ruble say you should . . ."

"He hasn't told me to do that."

"He will; he will."

"Yes," Nan agreed. "And I could stop at Mrs. Windsor's today and tell her how glad I am that Bitsy is home again."

Ruby looked over her shoulder. "He come back by hisself?" she asked.

"No. A boy had found him, and brought him back for the reward."

Ruby crashed her rolling pin down on the noodle dough. "I figgered that would happen," she said.

"Did you? You didn't mention it."

"What good would that do? We all had to wait until the fella whut had him brought him back."

"Yes, we did. Well, I'll take my walk. I'll be back by the time Fiddle gets home."

Ruby made a sound of assent. She knew as well as Nan did that the Sheltons' curly-haired little girl would always be called Fiddle. That was what Butch—Garde, Junior—had called her from the first he'd been told her pretty name. Felicia.

The big woman told Miss Nan to tie up her head. "They's a right smart wind."

"I shall," said Nan, and she did. Ruby saw her go down the street; she was wearing her denim jacket, and had tied a red bandanna around her own dark hair.

"Don't look no older than Fiddle," said the woman, who loved her family.

Nan stopped at Hazel's house first with her news, because that house was the one nearest her own. She found Hazel out in the front yard clipping the yews.

"Do you want to come inside?" she asked.

Nan laughed and sat down on the step. "Not if you don't want me to."

"Well, I'd stop this if you do want . . ."

"Oh, go back to your snipping and clipping. We can talk out here. How's Bitsy?"

"He's sleeping. I took him to the vet and had some tangles plucked out of his coat. He was in an awful mess, Nan."

"I can imagine. He isn't used to doing for himself. It would be like turning Butch out on his own for a week."

Hazel made no comment to that. A car went down the street, and the driver honked a greeting. Hazel said something about the way she looked. "But I can't work in the yard in my good clothes."

She was not attempting anything of that sort. She had a plastic rainhood tied firmly about her head. She wore an old zippered jacket of Dewey's, three times too big for her, and a pair of old plaid slacks, the cuffs tucked into the tops of rainboots. She cut the yews, put the litter into a garden cart, wheeled it back to the compost pile, Nan following her.

And Nan told her news. She was going to have a baby in the spring.

"I don't think you should," Hazel answered the announcement.

"Well, if I'd known you felt that way . . ." said Nan, laughing.

"I'm serious."

"Oh, dear. Are you, really?" Nan wondered what difference it should make to Hazel.

"Yes," said Hazel, bending over from the waist to retrieve some leaves from under the hedge. She did look terrible! "Two children in a family are enough," she explained a bit breathlessly.

"We don't happen to think so," said Nan. "We love the children we have, and we know we shall enjoy them as they grow up."

"I suppose you've heard and read that the world is overpopulated."

"Oh, yes. But not the Shelton home. We can afford three children; we feel that we can do much for them."

"It's intelligent people like you and Garde who should limit their families and create social space."

Nan laughed and shook her head.

That trip, she let Hazel go alone to the compost pit. Nan was not entirely sure that yew trimmings made good compost. Hazel should have asked Ginny. Not that it mattered. Dewey would fish them out if they were wrong. He didn't quarrel with Hazel, or often dispute her, but he managed to have the important things done his way.

"I'm memorizing poetry for this baby," she told Hazel when she returned.

"What sort of poetry? Modern?"

"Some of it. I know an e. e. cummings thing, but I put capitals and commas into it."

Hazel laughed. "Will that make any difference to the baby?" she asked.

"I feel the poetry does. Some. Anyway, it helps me to be serene, and that surely helps the baby. As for the rest of it, you probably are right. Before Butch was born, I read theology and religious books. I hoped he would one day go into the church, and be like my father. But of course Butch is so crazy about *his* father that we both are sure he'll become a doctor."

"Won't that be all right?"

"Well, of course it will be, Hazel. With me. I'm crazy about his father, too."

Hazel said nothing, which, with her, meant little.

"With Fiddle," Nan continued, "I concentrated on music. I listened to it, played it—and now about the only tune that child knows is 'Jangle Bells.'"

Hazel turned her head, ready to correct Nan. Then she laughed. "That's as good a name as the right one," she conceded.

Nan started down the walk. "I must get home. The poetry I'm memorizing now is something by Sir Walter Raleigh. Did you know he wrote poetry? He wrote this one. I rather like it. It goes:

> Give me my scallop-shell of quiet,
>   My staff of faith to walk upon,
> My scrip of joy, immortal diet,
>   My bottle of salvation,
> My gown of glory, hope's true gage,
>   And thus I'll make my pilgrimage.

She smiled at Hazel. "Bye," she said. "Ruby's making noodles. Would you like some?"

Hazel shook her head. "I don't think so, Nan. I know they are delicious, but Dewey and I are cutting down on wheat."

Nan said good-by again and walked along the sidewalk, wondering if Dewey knew about this, and what he thought of it. "I could slip him some soup," she told herself.

But the visit had upset her enough that she only called Ginny and Gene on the phone to tell them her news. Yes, she said, she and Garde were happy. "I wanted you to know." She did not mention Hazel's reaction, as she would have done in what they all were calling "the old days."

But that evening, Hazel quoted herself to Dewey when he came home. He asked if the vet had examined Bitsy. Yes, he had. And had advised extra feeding for a week. "But I don't want him fat again."

"Look, my good woman, you do what the doctor tells you to do!"

"Oh, I'm feeding him, Dewey."

"You see that you do. He seems happy to be home."

"Yes, he is. But I'm almost afraid to let him out in the yard alone."

"Then you'll have to walk him four times a day."

She would, she said. Dewey knew that she would, for a time.

"He likes the yard," he pointed out, settling down with the evening paper. "What's for dinner?"

"I have some chops."

"Good."

"Nan came by this morning," said Hazel from the kitchen.

"Oh? That's nice."

"Yes. She told me she is going to have another child."

"Mhmmmn."

"You knew?"

"Yes."

"I told her I thought two children were enough in any family."

"You did, did you?"

"I firmly believe the world would be better . . ."

"Yeah, but Nan and Garde probably figure that the Windsor quota is wide open, and available."

She came flying in from the kitchen, her eyes popping. "Mad as hops," he told the other doctors the next morning. They had laughed at his quoted logic.

"Why should she be mad?" asked Garde.

"Well, now maybe you could get her to tell you, Doctor," said Dewey silkily. "She had a lot to say, but nothing to answer your question. My general impression was that the Windsors were to do their part for the world, and other families had the same obligation."

The men laughed, and then Bob Ruble and Alison Cornel became a little heated in their comments.

"Ordinarily," Dr. Windsor reminded the men, "we could count on the girls to set Hazel right. Or at least to quiet her down a little."

"You don't mean . . ."

"Jumping Jehoshaphat, no! It'd be as much as your life was worth, or mine, to argue with her! Just let things ride. Please!"

Had the wives pooled their reaction to Hazel's stand and declarations about the baby, "We'd be having a tornado," said Bob and Alison. Individually, each woman was shocked. Ginny said that Hazel was being silly. "But then she always is when faced with any sort of human crisis. I remember how she acted when she thought Dewey might be interested in another woman."

"What other woman?" asked Bob mildly.

Ginny flapped her hand at him. "You know as well as I do what other woman, Bob Ruble. She still works as anaesthetist at your hospital."

"Oh," said Bob. "And she is safely, completely married besides."

"I know she is, but Hazel did get into a flap."

"Mhmmmn."

"And she became dreadfully silly. I think she gets frightened."

"Why should Nan's baby frighten her?"

"The *baby* doesn't. But the realization that Nan can have babies whenever she wants one . . ."

"And Hazel cannot. Yes. That would be a scary thought."

"It is."

Gene Cornel told her husband and Carol that she hoped Nan did not hear some of the wild things that Hazel was saying. "It's a good thing," she concluded, "that we wives are not talking such matters over just now. At least three of us would blow our stacks."

Carol laughed. "Nan, too?" she asked.

"Oh, she can. She can."

"She's always so sweet and ladylike."

"Yes, she is. I envy her. But when the right time comes, she can speak her piece."

*　　　*　　　*

The right time must have come, because Nan Shelton paid another call on Hazel. This time she phoned and asked if she might come.

"You sound very formal," said Hazel.

"I know. I wanted to be sure you had time to talk a little."

Hazel said of course Nan was to come—anytime. Well, would early afternoon do?

"Yes. Thank you, Hazel."

Hazel put the phone down and frowned at it. "Perhaps I should have offered to go there," she said. She had seen Nan at church service only the day before . . . She seemed strong and healthy. Pretty as usual in her blue hound's-tooth suit and her blue beret. Nan would be the very last one in the congregation to stop wearing a hat.

"She'll probably come calling in a hat and gloves both," Hazel said aloud, glancing around her immaculate living room. She herself should put on a dress. Well, at least a fresh blouse and good slacks.

She also saw to it that she could serve Nan a proper cup of tea and some oatmeal cookies if that seemed called for . . .

And she greeted her friend cordially when she came up the walk to her front door. "Your button mums are darling," said Nan.

"We had a good year. All that rain. Come in! Did you walk?"

"It isn't far."

"I know."

Nan came into the house, spoke to Bitsy, who flapped a friendly though indolent tail. She looked around to see if Hazel had acquired anything new, or had changed anything.

She had not. So Nan went to sit in a low "lady's chair" which she knew would let her feet rest on the carpet. She was wearing a shirtwaist dress of brightly printed Quiana—no hat, no gloves, but her shoes had "sensible" heels. She said she admired Hazel's slim blue slacks and the white jersey shirt she wore with them.

"I don't look well in slacks," said Nan. "I'm too short, I think. Though I do wear them sometimes on the boat."

"Ginny is as short as you are."

"But she doesn't wear slacks often, either."

No, she didn't, Hazel agreed. "I hadn't noticed."

They were sparring. Like two cats, come together on a fencetop. And that was not the way Nan wanted this call to go.

"Hazel," she said firmly, "I came over here to tell you that I think, and others think, you are being silly about the baby which I am expecting." She spoke gently, she spoke sweetly, and firmly.

Hazel's mouth fell open.

"You were talking about it after church yesterday," said Nan. "Gertrude Linders was pretty upset. She was shocked that you should even think such things. I told her you didn't really mean them. That you were just being silly, and quoting a lot of stuff you had read."

Hazel's face flushed. "How do you know what I mean and don't mean?" she demanded.

"Well, I don't, really. But I understand you pretty well. We've been friends for a long time."

"Yes, we have," said Hazel. "And I suppose you think I should be all a-twitter about the new baby."

Nan laughed. "That wouldn't be like you," she agreed.

"But the things you said to Gertrude and to some of the others . . ."

"They were not silly things!" cried Hazel, her eyes popping. "I was just expressing the results of my thinking largely, and my conviction that you and Garde should not have an extra child."

"Oh, dear," said Nan, "I don't want you to call my baby an 'extra child.' "

Hazel leaned forward, her forearms resting on her knees. "But you do understand what I mean," she cried. "We must stop this proliferation. Intelligent people like you and Garde should not do one thing to increase the population of the world!"

"You mean that we should step back, limit our family, in favor of the—of the nonintelligent, the poor, the illiterate and the retarded?" Now Nan's cheeks were pink. "And be rewarded, twenty or thirty years from now, by a much lower average of people. Not fewer, just less intelligent, less enlightened. Because they don't know about population proliferation, and they care much less!"

"I know that is the position often taken," said Hazel stiffly. She never reacted well to argument.

"Yes, it is. So instead of congratulating us on our happiness . . ."

"Why should you be congratulated?" asked Hazel. "On your morality and unselfishness in adding still another child to the already overpopulated world?"

Nan laughed softly. "Oh, Hazel, *dear!*"

But Hazel was not to be deflected. "Adding an extra child to a world already reeling under its population load can't be called unselfish, Nan!"

"You don't understand, Hazel . . ."

"Because I don't and can't produce a child? Am I supposed to admire you for your fertility? Why, Nan, clams and chickens—and—and—"

"Hamsters," said Nan softly.

"Yes! Hamsters! They can beat you at *fertility.*"

"But they don't produce Butches and Fiddles."

"I'll grant you that your small children are attractive, but I'm not ready to congratulate you on your fine family. Not yet, I'm not. A fine family sets a fine example. and who knows what your children will grow up to do? Your examples may be the ones to kill off the human race in a few generations."

That was what she had been saying! "I still think it is silly to talk so," said Nan.

"Well, I don't happen to agree. As for Gertrude Linders—she probably thinks she should be praised for producing four sons . . ."

"They are fine men, Hazel."

"I like Storm. The others seem all right."

"A lawyer, a good farmer, a priest of our church, and Storm, a surgeon. I think that is a real contribution to the world. Don't you like Mr. Linders, their father?"

Hazel got up and walked around the room, plainly exasperated. "Oh, yes, I *like* him. That isn't my point, Nan."

Nan folded her hands in the lap of her bright, silky dress. "All right," she said. "Explain your point to me. The Linders should not have had four sons, I should not have three children."

"They had their children before we knew enough to be concerned about the population of the world."

"Yes, and they educated them, raised them . . ."

"Well, they are not to be congratulated, either, that they could afford to have four children. Because they didn't pay for them, just as you and Garde won't pay for yours."

Nan watched her gravely. "Go on," she said.

"I mean to. Of course you will provide food and clothing and shelter for your children. But the rest of the world will pay for their roads, schools, hospitals, air and water . . . I suppose you and Garde think you are being patriotic citizens, but you are not. This tremendous proliferation of people in our country is absorbing fifty percent of the world's resources."

"I'd not feel that my three would absorb more than they would contribute, Hazel. Where do you get all your information?"

"I read. I listen to discussions of these things . . ."

"And do you have some solutions?"

"There are some, Nan. If you want more children in your home, why don't you adopt one or two? As I said before, I am thinking largely on this subject. And I definitely feel that you should not be pregnant."

Nan smiled and shook her head. "You're a little late, because I *am* pregnant."

"Then," said Hazel, "I think you should have an abortion."

Nan jumped out of the low chair. "Hazel Windsor!" she cried. "Have you said any of this stuff to Dewey?"

"I'm saying it to you. You're the one involved. You're the one . . ."

Nan laughed. "I'm the one who thinks having another baby will be a lovely thing."

"Oh," cried Hazel, "you're being sentimental."

"Of course I am," said Nan. "And you would agree

with me if you were the one having the baby. You would think it was wonderful, too."

"I'd think it would be a miracle," said Hazel dryly. "Here I am, forty-two years old, married twenty years . . . ."

Nan went to her and kissed her cheek. "I'm sorry, Hazel," she said softly. She moved toward the door.

"I know I've shocked you," said Hazel, following her.

"Yes, you have. I won't act on your advice, of course. But I'm afraid I shall think about it. A lot."

As she went down the few shallow steps from Hazel's front door, she knew that she was trembling. That was not good. She should have brought her car. If she had her car, she could quickly go home and think about all the terrible things Hazel had said.

Or—if she had her car, she could go on to Ginny's, or Gene's, and tell them about the past half hour. Oh, she desperately *wanted* to talk to them! They knew Hazel, as they knew Nan, and they would help her get things back into perspective. She knew that she was going to worry about Hazel. The woman could not be well! Gene and Ginny could talk that over with her, too, and the three women could lovingly and sympathetically watch Hazel, perhaps talk to her, all of them together . . .

But she shook her head from side to side and turned her footsteps down the hill toward home. She would just have to think this out alone; Garde would never understand the situation. He—any of the men—would get angry and call Hazel a fool. Perhaps one or two of them might say the exactly wrong thing to her!

Nan did not consider that Hazel, galloping off on this latest idea of hers, had already spoken her thoughts to those same men. But she had, and Nan was right. Garde Shelton and Bob Ruble, at least, were angry.

That same night, those two doctors were kept late at the hospital. Bob had a difficult delivery, and he feared the child might need immediate attention from the pediatrician. So when the mother came in, experiencing first labor pains, both doctors decided that they would stand by.

They did all the necessary things. Changed to whites, Bob examined the mother, talked to the father and to the grandmother. Garde had his measurements, heartbeat— and the blood that would be needed, he felt sure. This was an RH baby, and there had been no prenatal treatment. He had asked for a technician to be available for the probable interchange.

He and Bob spent much of the time in the doctors' lounge. Garde did some reading, Bob had paper work. And they talked. At midnight they drank coffee, ate sandwiches, and talked about Hazel and the damfool things she was saying about the Sheltons' expected baby.

"I'd like to put a muzzle on her," said Garde grimly.

"She won't sell Nan on any of her silly ideas."

"She can upset her. And I don't want Nan upset."

"Does Windsor know what she's doing?"

"She's probably said all the same things to him."

"He never really listens to Hazel when she gets off on these tangents."

"That's not a good way for a husband . . ."

"He's fond of Hazel, Shelton. And really she is a great girl—kind, clever—all that. But when she rants—Dewey's developed a tin ear. In self-protection."

"And we should too."

"Well, that's difficult. At least we should not repeat or

tell about what she's doing and saying. Spread the word."

"Oh, no. I certainly hope she doesn't say them to Nan! That's what I thought Dewey might be able to prevent."

"You could try speaking to him."

"I wish the other wives, Gene and Ginny, would silence her. They'd be the ones." His head lifted. A nurse's cap had tucked around the door. "I'll be right there," he said loudly. He glanced at Bob, and the two tall men went swiftly out of the room. Their night's work was beginning.

Chapter Four

It was a cold day for so early in October, and Ginny vetoed her cub den's decision that *that* day they would ride the horses. She had, in a moment of weakness, said that sometime they might go down to the pasture and perhaps learn the rudiments of riding. How to mount and dismount was as far as her plans went.

But today—with the wind swirling the first leaves from the trees, she said they would stay indoors and begin their work on first aid. "Elementary first aid," she pointed out. "I'm not training anyone to be a doctor."

They expected to work with gauze and mercurochrome. Ginny had old magazines to roll for splints. Newspapers to use for pads. Leaves to soak for poultices . . .

And chocolate cupcakes to reward their efforts. In planning her year as den mother, she had chosen Tuesday afternoon as a meeting time. She had said they would meet at the church parish house.

"We can meet at your house if we go swimming or ride the horses."

Yes, but for most meetings the boys were to assemble at the parish house. And in uniform, unless told different.

It was a chore to carry supplies—but an easier one than cleaning up her family room if they met at her house.

She had secured the use of a certain basement room in the parish house, the claim on a tall cupboard in which to keep supplies. Sometimes Mr. Linders would be available—he was good at sawing things and hammering, the boys decided.

Ginny told him of this talent recognition, and he had laughed. "Just better and stronger than they are," he agreed. "How is the Gaines boy doing?"

Ginny started to say "All right," then she stopped. "I don't know," she said. "He bothers me."

"He bothers other people, too, Ginny. Does he get along with the other boys?"

"Well, not really. Sometimes . . . He doesn't seem to know how to play, or to talk to the other boys. For one thing, he doesn't have a buddy. And generally the boys pair off to some degree. Danny sticks too close to me."

"You'll have to work on that, won't you?"

Yes, she would. Though she did not know just where to start. Maybe she could talk to Hazel. For a few years Hazel had taught school. Or—Gene Cornel seemed to know how to boss the kids around. Of course children adored Nan; she did wonders with the youth choir in the church. If all four women could put their heads together, the situation with Danny Gaines was precisely the sort of thing they could iron out. But just now, each one seemed preoccupied with her own affairs. Gene had Carol and the girl's convalescence. Nan of course had the new pregnancy on her mind. Hazel was trying to rehabilitate the boy who had found, or had stolen, Bitsy, and returned him. Bob said he wished her lots of luck in that project, but she was occupied.

Of course Ginny was busy, too. But she had taken on the cub den! And Danny Gaines. The others would probably feel that she was a nuisance if she would intrude him as a problem for their consideration.

Though he might not, really, be a problem. The child was shy and withdrawn. If Ginny had the time and patience— She should give some time—and patience— to him and whatever problems he had. In most cub packs there would be at least one boy who needed the scout work more than others did. So she should concentrate a bit on Danny.

He was a thin child, rather small for his age. He had dark hair. "Just one big cowlick," Ginny described his hair. Her records said that he was ten, and that he was an adopted child. He and his parents lived across the street from Hazel Windsor. Theirs was a red brick house, with foundation plantings of low evergreens and marigolds in the summertime. His parents were old enough to be the boy's grandparents, really. The father was sixty-five, the mother forty-eight. A strange household, to say the least. Ginny wondered if that strangeness would help her with the boy. And why should she decide that it was strange? The mother could have been only thirty-eight when Danny was adopted. Which would be acceptable, even quite normal. A childless woman of thirty-eight . . .

Ginny caught her thoughts up short. Here she was, imagining, not knowing, that she could have problems with Danny. She surely could handle shyness.

Only she was not handling it. She could settle him as part of a group in a certain project. And he never did become a part of the group. He would be started folding newspapers into pads, three other boys doing the same thing and chattering like squirrels. But those three boys would be tying on splints, while Danny still sat, slowly folding newspapers and watching Ginny. If she would urge him to join another group, he would go with her, and then become static the minute she left him.

She did wish she could help the kid. Didn't he ever play with other children? Of course he had no other children in the home, and with parents that old . . .

She gave herself a mental shaking. She would surely find a way to reach Danny, to get him involved in cub projects. That was her job, and it was not her province to take over his family relationships. Yet—she was surprised to find that Danny even was a cub scout. Though being one, being allowed to attend meetings, his family must have some interest in his project.

Ginny usually knew the other parents. Often she knew them before their little boys became cubs. And when they did become Scouts, in various ways she would get to know the parents. The kids, for one thing, gabbled a lot about their homes and families. "My dad says . . ." "My mom puts cherries on her sugar cookies." "We've got a new car but we can't afford it." Oh, yes, she got to know about the homes and families. She occasionally would talk to the mothers on the phone. There was to be a Blue and Gold banquet; it was hoped the parents would attend one hundred percent.

But she never—or not often—went to the parents and talked intimately to them about the boys' problems.

Though, for Danny—yes, she would go to see Mrs. Gaines. She would talk to her.

And she did go, the next day. The clouds had broken up without depositing rain, and Ginny needed only a sweater over her jumper and blouse. She glanced at Hazel's windows when she parked the station wagon at the curb in front of the Gaines home. Hazel would recognize it and expect to see Ginny. Well, this task accomplished, maybe Ginny would have time to run in and see Hazel.

For now, she wanted to get the call made before school would be out, and Danny at home. She went up the curving walk to the white front door, noting that a pane was missing from the stormdoor. She touched the bell and waited. And waited. Then, hearing noises from within, she touched the bell again. And eventually the white inner door opened.

Standing only half revealed was a large woman. A really fat woman. She wore a flowered blue dress, and her hair was what young Jan Ruble called curly-curled. Somewhat gray hair. Her face was puffy, and marred by several brown wens. Not too attractive.

Ginny stated who she was. "I am Virginia Ruble, Danny's . . ."

"You're the doctor's wife?"

"Yes. My husband is a doctor. Could I come in, Mrs. Gaines? I am Danny's cub den mother, and I thought it would be nice if we became acquainted."

"What's he done?"

"He hasn't *done* anything, Mrs. Gaines."

"He's a good boy."

"Yes, he is. Could I . . . ?"

Mrs. Gaines opened the inner door wide and unlatched the stormdoor. The missing pane had been broken by the newspaper, she explained. "And we just left it out. It's easier to open the front door now. Suction, you know. Come in, Mrs. Ruble."

Ginny stepped inside and gasped. The door opened directly into a large living room. That room, and the dining room beyond it, the sunroom to one side, were packed with furniture! Simply *packed!* Some of it was modern furniture, but mostly the things were antiques. Beautifully maintained, but crowded together. There were three *étagères* that she could see; the shelves were crowded with figurines, small porcelain and china bric-à-brac. There was a large glass-fronted and lighted cupboard or cabinet, packed with figurines—Dresden, Swedish, Copenhagen, Meissen, Cybis. There were two other "china closets." One contained handsome cut glass. In the sunroom she counted four couches—a day bed, a modern couch upholstered in gold velvet, a beautiful damask Victorian parlor sofa, and a tufted leather "fainting couch."

Did Hazel know about this horde? She was a bug on antiques.

Of course Ginny was staring, and Mrs. Gaines recognized that fact. "I suppose everybody stares," Ginny told herself.

"The basement is full of furniture, too," said Mrs. Gaines, who puffed and wheezed when she moved or talked. She led the way to the dining room. There were at least two full sets of conventional dining room furniture in the room. Two tables, with matching chairs, two large sideboards and other accessories. More cupboards and closets of matched china and glass ware, and silver.

"This was a Gaines set," her hostess explained. "This

was mine from my grandmother. That's Wedgwood china . . ."

Ginny nodded slowly, stunned by what she was seeing. How did a child live in such a house? She herself was terrified of brushing something from a shelf or table.

"Does Danny ever break anything?" she asked.

"No. He's a quiet sort of boy. And he knows not to touch things."

"He's quiet," Ginny agreed.

"There's bedroom furniture upstairs . . ." said Mrs. Gaines.

"The house doesn't seem too large . . ."

"No. There are just two bedrooms, but they are of pretty good size. Room for my big walnut headboard bed and a trundle bed for Danny in one room. Mr. Gaines uses the other room. There are two beds in there, too, but he sleeps in the brass one."

They went back to chairs in the living room, and Mrs. Gaines told of having to sell some things which they had inherited. Her husband, she said, was the last of his family. His parents had died, then an uncle, and an aunt . . .

With difficulty, Ginny brought herself back to the reason she'd had for coming to this house. "I felt like Alice in Wonderland," she afterward told. "*Queer* wouldn't begin to describe my feeling. It could háve been a bad dream, a nightmare. That woman even looked like the Duchess. She was, she is, unbelievable. She seemed to have trouble talking—she was short of breath, or something—but she talked an endless stream.

"But finally . . ." she continued the story of her adventure, talking to Bob later that afternoon. "Finally, I managed to say a few things to her."

"You don't like her," said Bob, who was painting the iron fence around the swimming pool.

"What difference does that make?"

"Some," he said. "Your sympathies were all with the boy."

Ginny gasped. "Well, of course they were. They are! I went there to get some idea of what could be done. In the scouting program, one wants . . ."

"To develop the boy. Yes. But should you start by being antagonistic to the mother?"

Ginny sat down in a chair and considered the charge. Her blue eyes were troubled. "I didn't go there in that mood . . ." she said.

"No. But once you saw the woman . . ."

"She's pretty awful, Bob."

"And that was evident at first sight."

"Well, she was fat. And rather untidy, though her house was clean."

"And . . . ?"

"I don't like fat women," Ginny agreed. "Not that kind. No bra, no girdle, puffy, fat feet."

Bob smiled. "Good thing you're not in my profession," he said mildly.

"It certainly is. I suppose you have to be nice to women like that."

"That type often needs help from a doctor."

"Yes, and maybe she does, too. But I believe I was fairly nice to her, Bob."

"I'm sure you were, Ginny. I was trying to get you to see several sides of your boy's problem."

"Yes. I did ask Mrs. Gaines if the boy should not have his own room. He'll be eleven in a few months."

"And she said . . . ?"

"That he would be frightened."

Bob nodded and asked Ginny to take the dog into the house. He was getting paint on his nose, and that could get transferred.

"There was a dog, too," she said when she came outside again. Willie was barking as if he'd been abandoned on a desert island. "There's a dog at the Gaines house. A poodle. A toy poodle, white, with very pink eyes and nose."

Bob chuckled. "And you didn't like him, either."

"Oh, Bob!"

"Did you?"

"I don't know. Usually I do like dogs. This one sat in Mrs. Gaines's lap all the time we talked. He'd look over her arm at me."

"Go on."

"Go on with what? I should be starting dinner."

"Have you told me the whole story? About Danny's home and his problems."

"Well— Oh, yes! As I was leaving, Mrs. Gaines told me she was expecting an organ to be delivered."

"This same afternoon?"

"I think so. I didn't think she needed one more thing in that house, but I asked her what kind of organ. Then I told her about the one you bought for Mary, and which I had learned to play. And she asked me—she said, 'Does your husband like it?' She meant when I played."

"Did you tell her I did?"

"Yes, and she said that she knew her husband wouldn't. But she'd saved the money to buy it . . ."

"How?"

"I don't know how. Maybe from housekeeping money. Maybe she has an income of her own. Anyway, she then said her husband didn't know she was getting it."

"Would she be able to hide an *organ?*"

"Maybe, in that crowded house. Who would notice another piece of furniture? But I asked her why she kept it a secret, and she said her husband would think she was silly."

Bob nodded. "A chronic infection among husbands."

Ginny laughed. It always made her feel better to talk to Bob.

"And then," she said, "I asked her how she could keep even a small organ secret."

"And . . . ?"

"She said she would play it when he was out of the home. And he never would know it was there, because she would put it in her bedroom and he never went into her room."

Bob whistled. "No wonder the kid's adopted."

"But the boy sleeps in that room . . . That worries me more than the organ, Bob."

"It should. He . . ."

The telephone bell rang loudly, and Bob went into the house to answer it. Ginny lay back in the long chair and looked up at the tall trees through which the sky showed a delicious glimpse of blue. The late sunlight washed the back of their old brick house, the enormous screened porch upstairs, the vine-covered, glassed-in one on the first floor, the paved patio, the flower beds . . .

Bob came out. He had some crackers in his hand and Willie at his heels. He had not washed, so she knew he was not going to the hospital.

"Fire drills at the schools," he mumbled through a cracker. "Cornel was setting up a schedule. I'll try to take my turn early tomorrow in one of the grade schools. Are we going to have those veal steaks for dinner?"

"Yes, if they defrost."

"They're doing it. I poked them with my painty finger."

"I'll take it off with turpentine," she promised.

"You just about would, too."

"Bob," she asked, "do you think I am crazy to be so— so astonished—with everything that happened to me this afternoon?"

"Well, I'm astonished, too. In fact, I think you made it all up."

"I did not."

"Then I think it was all part of a farce, and that you should join me in laughing about it."

She stared at him. "You certainly are no help!" she said accusingly.

"If you'll just sit there, pretty, and think about what you've told me, you'll laugh, too."

She leaned back and crossed her ankles. "I think I'll go to sleep," she said. "I could not *tell* you how much I wanted to go over and ask Hazel if she knew the Gaineses and their house."

"Why didn't you ask her? If they live across the street, she probably does know, and maybe more than you do."

"There couldn't be more!" cried Ginny, sitting erect.

Bob shrugged. "Ask Hazel."

She got up and started for the house. "Are you going to call?" he asked. "If Dewey's at home . . ."

"I'm going to core some apples . . . to bake." The screen door banged behind her.

"These women," Bob told Willie, "can you understand 'em, fella?"

* * *

Alison Cornel would have claimed that he made no attempt to understand women. Busy with his calls to the captains of the Volunteer Fire Department, of which he was chief, he was aware that his wife and his daughter were in a huddle about something. Beyond noticing that he had the phone tied up, they paid no attention to him, either.

They were sitting out on the porch, cutting and sewing carpet rags for a rug Gene thought she was going to crochet, and talking about the second letter Gene had, the week before, helped her daughter write.

"I told you this was to a different man, Mother," Carol was saying.

"Don't these fellows have names?"

"Well, sure they do. The first guy was named Derrick. Derrick Jordan. This one—" she waved a hand toward paper and envelopes on the table—"this one is Murray Shanahan."

Gene nodded and bit off a length of thread.

"Don't do that," Carol told her. "It makes grooves in your teeth."

"I thought bobby pins did that."

"They do."

"Tell me about this Shanahan. You called him a guy."

"Well, that's only a word. He's okay."

"Do you know him well? Do you like him?"

"Yes, I like him. Or I wouldn't be writing to him. I met him at a dance; he was with the same crowd I was. We danced some and talked. I haven't seen very much of him. Maybe I could have built things up. We are allowed to invite guests to Friday night supper. I did plan to ask him. Interns are always ready for a free meal."

Gene laughed. "I remember."

"But then I had to have this darned surgery . . ."

"You did have to have it, Carol."

"Yes, I know. But it sure put me out of touch with things at the hospital. Somebody else got my place at the nurses' home, and I don't know if Shanahan came back to University for his second year or went elsewhere."

"You could write to him, ask questions."

"I'd like to write to him, all right. If he'd answered my first note . . . Except, a girl can't write to a guy about chocolate cysts and . . ."

"She can if he's a doctor. They think such things are fascinating."

Carol laughed shortly. "Not any fellow I'd be interested in."

"You're wrong about that. If you made the letter amusing, and talked about yourself as a displaced person. Say something like feeling as if you'd been pushed off the escalator—"

"I couldn't make anything—there *wasn't* anything—funny about that surgery, Mom. All the tests and examinations—I hated every inch of it. And I don't think it's just hilarious that I have to be stuck here at home until Christmas. Sewing carpet rags!" She kicked the heap of bright strips at her feet.

Gene laughed. "Of course it's funny," she said. "Rapunzel of the carpet rags, or whoever the fair maiden was who had to spin gold. I'm not too strong on my fairy tales. You can write an amusing letter about almost anything if you try."

"If *you* try," said Carol.

So they spent that evening composing, changing, rewriting this second letter to a "guy" named Murray

Shanahan. "If he doesn't have red hair," said Gene, "he should dye it. But save that to say in your next letter."

"He'll have to do better than that stingy post card he sent after my note," said Carol gloomily. "And Jordan didn't even do that much."

But she mailed the letter to Shanahan, and by the first of the next week she had a reply from him.

Of course Gene knew that a letter had come. She took the mail when it came through the slot, and there it was, with a return address. A big envelope, the writing wide-swinging. "I'd think he would have learned to cut that down on reports and orders," said Gene, giving the letter to Carol, who only glanced at it and put it into her pocket.

Gene was disappointed; she felt Carol owed her at least an account of what Shanahan had had to say. But Carol said not a word. Gene stayed close, she fidgeted, she hinted . . . And she was, she knew, about to speak sharply about her rights in this matter.

But one thing stopped her. If she and Carol got into a row, Alison might hear it, and thus learn what Gene had been doing. He would hit the roof! And that weekend they didn't need, or want, a full-scale family blowup. Susan, the younger daughter, was taking advantage of one of the government-fostered three-day weekends. and was coming home from college.

"I don't know if we're celebrating Columbus or Armistice," said Gene. "Nothing actually ever happened on the eighth of October!"

But of course she was glad to see Susan, to have her vivid young face and her bright chatter in the home, her garments shed about, her laughter. Gene baked brownies for her, and fussed about the weight which the girl was acquiring.

Susan was much more outgoing than was Carol, but the two girls chattered at about an even pace up in their bedrooms on the second floor of the house. Gene heard them and made excuses to go upstairs several times during that first day.

Thus she came in on what seemed to be a quarrel between them. Susan had washed her hair, and she had come into Carol's room to use her hot comb. That surely had not bothered Carol, but evidently the paper in Susan's hand did. Carol was trying to take it from her, and screeching at her.

Gene pronounced the noise she made screeching. "What's wrong with you two?" she asked. "You act as if you were six years old!"

"I don't want her coming into my room . . ." said Carol, her nose red and her manner agitated.

"You said I could use your dryer!" countered Susan. "I asked you."

"Yes, but you—I didn't say you could be nosy and get into my mail and stuff."

Oh, oh! thought Gene.

"Susan knows better than to read anyone else's mail," she said aloud.

"She may know better but she does it just the same."

"Susan?"

"Well, jeepers, Mom! I never knew Carol to get letters like this before!" And she waved the sheet of paper at her mother. The envelope lay empty on the floor. Yes, it was Shanahan's letter.

But Gene must keep remembering her duties as a

mother. "I can imagine the girls in your house at college, how they would react if you came into their rooms and read their mail."

Susan smiled widely, put the letter down to change the comb to her other hand, and Carol snatched the sheet of paper. She was still half crying.

"At our house," said Susan, "we'd put a letter like that on the bulletin board! Mom, it's like *wow!*"

Gene laughed. "Is it, Carol?"

The girl made no reply. She was leaving the room, taking the letter with her.

"Susan . . ." said Gene, shaking her head. "You did know better."

"Aw, Mom. Who is this guy, anyway?"

Did all the girls call Shanahan a "guy"?

"Carol probably has met several men at the hospital where she is in training, Susan."

"But no fellow here in Bayard ever showed that much interest in her."

"She's probably learned to deal with the fellows, dear. Some girls learn that later than others." But what could be in that letter?

"I'm sorry I upset her. She's been sick and all . . ."

"I think she's getting well quite fast. Where are you going with all that hair primping?"

"Nowhere. I didn't get to wash my hair before I came home yesterday. Have you ever met this fellow named Mike?"

Mike?

"I'll bet he has red hair," said Susan.

Gene laughed, and with another word or two about not reading other people's mail, she too went downstairs.

*   *   *

That afternoon Alison took the girls to the pecan groves to pick up nuts, and told Gene not to fuss with dinner, they would go to the club, which they did, enjoying their friends. Carol and Susan danced with the men available, and even joined the square dancing organized by Ruth Kibbler. It was fun to do, and fun to watch.

Sunday was rainy, and except for church, the family stayed in. Gene cooked a standing rib and consulted with Susan about clothes. After their dinner she washed and ironed some things for the girl.

"Can't she do that for herself?" growled Alison.

"She can, and I'll be calling repairmen all week," said Gene. "She's death on gadgets and appliances."

"Remember when she put her fingers down the food disposal?" asked Carol, laughing. "Mom and I haven't told her that we have a compactor."

Her father grunted and went off to the den to read the Sunday paper. He was on call, and had been out a couple of times.

On Monday, the women did a little shopping, and then Gene drove Susan to the airport, Carol riding along.

During all that time, and in and out of all those activities, the girls' quarrel and the Shanahan letter was not mentioned. Gene didn't think Carol had spoken of it again to Susan. Their squabbles never lasted long.

But on the drive home, Carol said in a faint, stilted voice, "I brought Mike Shanahan's letter with me. If we stop for a Coke, I'll let you read it."

"If you want me to, Carol."

"Well, it's not so much *wanting*. But you helped me write to him, and I suspect I'll want your help in answering this one . . ." She was stiff with embarrassment.

"Whatever you like," said Gene. "I didn't know he was called Mike."

"Well, what else, saddled with a first name like Murray?"

Gene smiled, and nodded, and said they would stop for lunch, adding that Susan would be back in Colorado before they would get to Bayard.

"Yes. Because she can eat her lunch on the plane."

"I hope they have gooseberry pie," said Gene.

"Have to watch those gooseberries, Mom."

"Not to mention the pie crust. I was hoping to take a pie home for Father."

"Yeah. He loves it. But he'll mention the calories."

The highway north from the city ran pretty well along the river, sometimes edging inland, but always with the valley and the rippling water in view. The restaurant, of course called the Mark Twain, was built on a bluff, high above the river. It was a shining, clean place, not too large, and the owners had sense enough to keep the food simple and very good.

Yes, they had one gooseberry pie left. "If we cut it, Mrs. Cornel, we won't have one for the doctor."

"Then don't cut it. I want to take one home."

"We have strawberry and rhubarb."

"We'll get our sandwich, and see how hungry we are."

"Yes, ma'am. We just cooked a country ham."

"Oh, fine. I'll want coffee. Carol?"

"I want it, too."

So they had their sandwiches made with homemade bread, a crisp salad—and they watched a tow going upriver. Gene was debating whether to mention the letter, when Carol opened her purse and took it out. It was creased from being folded and folded again.

"I got really mad at Susan," she said.

"She should not have touched it," Gene agreed, putting on her glasses, She read the letter, knowing that Carol watched her. Then she read it again. As Susan had said, it was like *wow*. And surprisingly interesting.

As Gene read the letter for the second time, Carol turned her gaze to the view from the windows. Below them the river was slate blue, and the tree-crowded banks were showing all the colors of autumn. The red maples shone like torches among the trees that still were dark green and fully leaved. On the far shore a whole grove of hickory trees were tawny gold, washed with sunshine.

Gene read the letter through, and then through a third time. This Shanahan spread things out. He'd been pleased he said, in a half-dozen ways to hear from Carol. "I had hoped to get to know you better, but after that one evening you dropped from sight. Nevertheless, because I am not one to give up easily, I signed up here for a second year . . ."

The rascal! He had signed up nine months ago, and had known since last March that he would be at University for his second year.

". . . if I ever get a holiday, could I come upriver to see you? I am encouraged by your letter to think that we deserve more time together. So hold on, baby! Either you'll get well and come back to the world of bells and buzzers and bitch boxes, or the fates will smile on me, and I'll swim upstream to see you!"

Like wow.

Gene folded the letter. "He writes an interesting letter," she said, then laughed at herself. "A very interesting letter," she amended. "Tell me about him, Carol."

"Oh, he's a guy, Mother. I met him at this dance. I have already told you that. He's an intern."

"Red-headed."

Carol looked at her in surprise. Gene tapped the folded letter. "His name," she explained. "And he writes like a red-head."

Carol laughed a little then, and her cheeks were pink. "He has dark hair," she said. "He's tall and very thin."

"Do you like him?"

Carol shrugged. "I'm not very good with boys, Mom."

"Call them *men*, dear. This Mike must be at least twenty-five."

"Yes, I suppose he is."

"If you'd start thinking of him that way . . . You talk to Storm, and to Dr. Ruble, and Dr. Shelton."

"That's different."

"No, it isn't. They're men, and they are friendly to you."

Gene unfolded the letter again on the table top. "Interns in my day didn't have such—such—well, not *depth*, exactly. But certainly a way with words. Does he dance as well as he talks?"

"He's a good dancer. And you know, I dance pretty well."

"Yes, you do. There was a time when you studied ballet."

"I know. And we stenciled all those dancing girls around my room. Susan put horses on her walls. But she gets along fine with boys."

"She forgets herself in the good time she's having. Did you meet this Mike at other parties?"

"I would see him now and then in the hall, but, like he says, I got sick before there was another dance. The

106

nurses give them, you know. Several times a year. And the students and the residents, the interns, come."

"The parties must be fun."

"Well, sometimes they are. If, to start the evening, you get with a good crowd."

Gene could picture the dances. She had attended the same sort when she was in training.

"But you did get with a good crowd," she decided. "If this Murray Shanahan was with you."

"I suppose so," said Carol, lapsing again into despondency.

Gene paid their check, picked up the pie, and they went out to the car. Did Carol want to drive?

She did not.

Gene set her lips tightly and started the car on the homeward road. She was getting exasperated with her daughter, and she must not. The girl had problems. So—

"Do you know anything about Mike's background?" she asked. "Where he comes from, or anything about his family?"

"Oh, no," said Carol. "Not a thing."

"Why not? People often like to talk about their homes and their families. That's one way to start a conversation, especially when you're in training or at school."

"I guess."

"It shows interest, Carol."

"Yes, but . . ."

"Does Mike know anything about *your* background?"

"He knows I live in Bayard. As for the rest of my background, such as it is, who'd care?"

Gene sighed and drove the remaining miles in almost complete silence. Carol Cornel lived in a beautiful home, filled with interesting things, books, music, pictures. Her father was a successful surgeon, part owner of a well-known hospital and clinic. He was important in the civic projects of their town . . . Gene was a good cook, and welcomed the girls' friends.

Oh, dear! She would so *like* to talk over this particular problem with the other wives. She feared that Carol was about to go underground like a seventeen-year locust. And that would be tragic. Every girl needed to attract men, to be with them. What should her mother do? The other wives would probably have all sorts of suggestions. Ginny and Nan especially. When young women, they must have been popular. They'd love to help! And they would help. They might be shocked at what Gene had already done . . . but . . .

As they reached the outskirts of Bayard, she asked, "Are you going to write to Mike again?"

"If I thought I could find something to say."

Gene sighed. Again.

They passed the church, they passed the familiar shops and homes. "Will you help me if I do write?" Carol asked timidly.

"Yes. Of course. Though you shouldn't need help."

"But I do."

"Okay then. When a good time comes up. Tonight we have to feed Father gooseberry pie."

Chapter Five

That same week Ginny Ruble took her cubs on a field trip. She had wanted Jan to go with her, but Jan was not able to make the time. Girls, the minute they got into high school, became too busy for family matters. This sometimes lasted until they went away to college, but Ginny didn't think it would with Jan. She was, basically, a great girl. Of course senior high school did make a difference. She paid more attention to clothes, which was good. She picked up a lot of speech mannerisms, which both Ginny and Bob deplored.

"Don't make a thing of it," Bob cautioned. "It's like when Bobby was four and began to stutter."

"We ignored him and he stopped. But he *was* four . . ."

"So is Jan, in a sense. All this high school routine is new to her."

"Yes. So she curls her hair, and says 'I'm sure' to whatever is told her."

Bob laughed. "We were never much on smacking the kids."

"I feel sure I could learn."

"Will she take care of Sarah? While you are hiking?"

Ginny's pretty face set into firm lines. "Yes, she will! It's only after school."

"Where will you take the boys?"

"Oh, along the river. For cattails and other weeds. Next meeting we'll make a lot of stuff out of them."

"And they'll get to know cattails when they see them."

Ginny nodded. "And at least two will get their feet soaked. One mother will call me and protest. She'll expect me to do field trips on Missouri Street."

But Ginny took her boys—nine of them—upriver to a stretch of sand and gravel and marshy reeds which she knew about. The cubs had been instructed not to wear uniforms, just their yellow and blue scarves for identification. She herself wore jeans and a leather jacket which, years ago, had belonged to Bobby Ruble, now a giant pre-med student. Ginny tied a scarf over her hair, and looked like a young girl.

The boys had a fine time, and two of them did get their sneakers soaking wet; one boy fell on the shale and cut his knee, which gave the den a chance to practice first aid. He was the first boy Ginny took home, and the last was Danny Gaines, one of those who had got his feet wet.

"They're almost dry now," he told Mrs. Ruble. He had already said he was glad to be the last one with her in the big station wagon. She smiled down at him. "I'll tell your mother you just made a misstep into a puddle," she said.

"Don't tell her anything. I'll change my shoes, and these will get dry. She'd worry . . ."

Ginny nodded. "All right, if you say so." She wanted to think Danny was showing self-reliance. He was a strange little boy. Small for his age, his color was pasty. He had wispy brown hair, and large eyes. He didn't play well, nor know how to engage in the semi-abusive chatter which the other boys enjoyed. Mischief was entirely unknown to him. If one of the other boys should grab his neckerchief and run, Danny just stood where he was, feeling his neck, but not offering protest or pursuit. He liked to stay close to Ginny, and she debated whether to ask one of the other boys to buddy with him, and try to get him into things. If Jan had come along on this trip, Ginny could have asked her for advice. Jan claimed to have been in Scouting more and longer than any boy in town.

Ginny let the boy out, as he asked, at the end of the Gaines's driveway, and she went on, planning to drive up into the Windsor drive across the street, back, and turn toward home and dinner and her family . . .

"And a hot bath, first of all," she said. She had done as much hiking and weed pulling as any of the boys.

The lamps were lighted in the Windsor living room, and on impulse Ginny got out of the wagon and went through the open garage to the kitchen door. She touched the bell and called to Hazel, whom she heard moving about in the kitchen.

Bitsy barked, and Ginny called again. "It's just Ginny," she said.

Hazel threw the door open wide. "Ginny!" she cried. "What on earth . . .?"

Ginny stepped up into the kitchen. "You won't want me beyond the first chair," she said. "I've been den mothering." She rubbed Bitsy's ears. "I brought the Gaines boy home. Have you any use for a cattail or some chestnut hulls, or . . ."

"Oh, yes!" cried Hazel. "I make wreaths and things."

They went back to the station wagon, and Hazel selected a newspaper full of the things which the boys had gathered. "I haven't had a chance to go out myself this year," she said.

With a neat husband, a modern house, and one small dog, Hazel was always the busiest of the four wives.

"You look a mess," she now rewarded Ginny, who laughed and said that she knew she did.

"But I wanted to ask you, since you live just across the street, do you know the Gaines family?"

Hazel had found a flat box and was carefully putting her "weeds" into it. She was wearing a slim pants suit, bright red, which was pretty with her white hair. "They aren't very friendly," she said absent-mindedly. "And I keep busy." She turned to face Ginny, her eyes sparkling. "You would not believe how taken up I've been, lately, with Bitsy's return. If you could have seen him, Ginny! His coat, his ears, his feathers . . . I think he slept in tar! I had to give him baths, and then I took him to the vet's to be clipped and combed. I couldn't leave him there because he was so nervous. But the Vet wouldn't give me anything for his nerves, and he actually suggested that I ask Dewey to give me something for *mine!*"

"Did he?" asked Ginny, laughing.

"No, he laughed, too. But I was a nervous wreck. I'll agree to that. And then I've had to work to get Bitsy back on a proper diet. He must have eaten just anything while he was in that dreadful shack. Fishbones, and everything! I'm sure he has worms . . ."

"Wouldn't he have to get them from other dogs? Does he play with the poodle across the street?"

Hazel heard her, but it took a little time for her to realize what Ginny had said. "What poodle?" she asked.

"The Gaineses have one. A miniature. White."

Hazel stared at Ginny. "I've never seen one," she said.

"Well, they have one. I've seen it."

"Then they must keep it in the house."

Ginny had gone to the sink to wash her hands and splash water on her face. She now wielded a length of paper towel. "They couldn't keep a dog in the house all the time!" she cried.

"Oh, yes, they could. People do. Cats, too."

"And, I'd guess, that boy!" Ginny sounded angry. She went along the hall and into Hazel's bathroom. She wished she had not stopped in. But, no, she didn't. She wanted to know about Danny and his home. When she came back, Hazel was tying a red scarf around her head, and Bitsy's leash lay on the counter.

"I didn't get your bathroom dirty," Ginny said. "I even used this paper towel."

"That's all right," said Hazel indifferently, picking up the leash. She wanted Ginny to get going.

"Have you ever been in the Gaines home?" Ginny asked, perversely not ready to hurry. "All those antiques . . ."

"She does have a lot," Hazel agreed. "Family stuff, mostly."

"The place is packed!"

"She had a sale on the lawn one time. I went over then. She had a lovely cranberry glass muffineer, but she asked thirty-five dollars for it, and Dewey would have had a stroke . . ." She moved toward the garage door. Bitsy was wagging the whole rear end of his body; he, too, was anxious to go. "I walk him around the block four times a day," Hazel explained.

"What's wrong with his yard?"

"Oh, I let him out there when I can watch him. I don't trust him out alone."

"Do you think he got out, Hazel?"

"I don't *know*, Ginny. That's what is so bad. That boy, or some other boy . . ."

"Danny Gaines is in my cub scout group."

"Is he?" Hazel snapped the leash to Bitsy's collar. "I see him sometimes. As I told you, it isn't a friendly family."

"Maybe the parents were too old to adopt a child."

Hazel whirled. Her face was pink. "Don't say a thing like that!" she cried.

"Hazel . . ."

"I am planning to persuade Dewey—I want us to adopt that Fishtown boy. Jay."

"The one who . . ."

"Yes! The one who brought Bitsy back to us."

"Have you talked to Mac about this?"

Hazel was angry. She fairly stalked through the garage. "Why should I talk to *him?*"

"Because he knows Fishtown, and he probably knows the boy."

"Maybe so. But I'll take care of Jay, Ginny. I really will." She was almost in tears.

Ginny went to her car. She hoped she need not argue with Hazel.

"I know a great deal about children," Hazel was saying.

Yes, she had always been ready to tell Ginny, and

Gene, and Nan, how to raise theirs. "Would you take care of him the way the Gaineses take care of Danny?" she asked as quietly as she could.

"I am sure that woman loves her boy," said Hazel.

"I expect she does. But I do think she is mistaken in the way they live over in that house. It would not be good for a dog to be so protected and sheltered. And I know it probably isn't good for Danny. As for the Fishtown boy— It just wouldn't work, Hazel. He's no longer a small child whom you could mold . . . Good gracious, he might murder you in your beds!"

Hazel loudly protested this.

"He stole your dog," Ginny countered. "Oh, Hazel, do stop thinking about this! Adoption, maybe. That might be fine for you and Dewey. But not a boy of Jay's age, used to independence . . ."

Of course there was no arguing with her. There hardly ever was. She went, half running, down the street, led by Bitsy, who was deploying into every yard, under every bush. Ginny got into the station wagon. She should be getting home.

But she *wanted* to talk to the others about this absolutely crazy idea of Hazel's. She backed into the street and hesitated. Well, why not? She turned the wheels away from home and down the hill toward Nan's.

From a window of the tall Victorian house, Butch saw Ginny park her car, and he ran with the word to his mother. Nan met Ginny at the front door and welcomed her warmly. As she entered the house, Ginny had a good look at herself in the walnut-framed mirror in the hall.

"I think I had better not sit in your parlor," she said.

"You've been out with the scouts?"

"Yes. How are you, Butch?"

The little boy answered her nicely, and offered to fetch his sister, who would be happy to see Mrs. Ruble.

Nan said she thought Fiddle would be busy.

"Yes, she is," Butch told Ginny. "She's learning to be a stewardess on an airplane. Then she's going to Washington to see Abraham Lincoln. He's dead and in a tundra."

Ginny managed not to laugh, but her smiling eyes met Nan's. "We hardly dare read aloud to him," Nan told when she said that the boy could be excused, and he departed cheerfully, his shoulders straight.

"He's enchanting," said Ginny.

Nan led the way to the library and picked up a notebook. She explained to Ginny about the poetry reading she was doing.

"For the new baby," said Ginny.

"You understand, don't you?"

"Oh, yes. What little improvement my mind ever got was made before my kids were born." She leafed through the notebook and laughed aloud. "This one too, Nan?" she asked.

"Which one is that?"

Ginny read the bit of doggerel happily:

I passed by his garden, and marked with one eye,
That the Owl and the Panther were sharing a pie;
The Panther took piecrust and gravy and meat,
While the Owl had the dish as his share of the treat.
When the pie was all finished, the Owl, as a boon,
Was kindly permitted to pocket the spoon;
While the Panther received knife and fork with a growl,
And concluded the banquet by eating the Owl.

Nan flushed. "I'd enjoy a child with a sense of humor," she defended herself.

Ginny smiled widely.

"Hazel doesn't think the poetry will help," Nan said.

"How does she know it won't?"

"Well, she thinks I should not be having a baby at all."

"But . . ."

"No, she really doesn't, Ginny. She made a point of telling me that I should have an abortion, and she explained why."

Ginny stared at the pretty young woman in her blue jumper and white blouse. "But that's terrible, Nan!" she cried.

"Yes," Nan agreed. "I thought it was."

"You know?" said Ginny. "I came here because I felt sure something should be done about Hazel." And, swiftly, she told about their friend's idea of adopting the Fishtown boy.

"Dewey would not allow that," said Nan firmly.

"He tries to please Hazel . . ."

"Oh, yes, he does," Nan agreed. "But he is also a sensible man. And he's sure to consider the boy. Can you see him, or any lively boy, in Hazel's home?"

"She would have to make adjustments," Ginny asserted. "But, Nan—"

"We'd better leave it to Dewey," said Nan sweetly but firmly.

Ginny agreed, but she still thought she could tell the news to Gene.

At Nan's, even Butch had not expressed any wonder at the way Ginny was dressed—and probably smelled, she added to herself. "The Sheltons are real gentry!"

But Gene did exclaim, and Carol, in the background,

grinned. "As if you look any worse than Mother does five times a week," she told Ginny.

Ginny said she'd sit out on the front doorstep if Gene would get a jacket and come out there, too.

"What have you been doing?" Gene asked, obeying her suggestion, Carol with her. "Just to see what goes on," she explained. "I love the huddles you girls get into."

"This won't be a huddle," Gene assured her.

"Don't be too sure," said Ginny. "I've already been to Nan's, and I should be at home right now scrubbing sweet potatoes for dinner. But this thing—" She mentioned the cub hike, she told of stopping at Hazel's—

"Did you get any yucca pods?" asked Gene, tucking her hair behind her ears. A stiff breeze had come up. Leaves were drifting down thickly.

"Where would I get yucca pods down at the river?" Ginny demanded. "I could let you have some milkweed . . ."

Gene waved her hand. "I probably have a lot of stuff down my own hill. So what else happened?"

And Ginny told about Hazel and the idea of adopting . . . Carol yelped with joy. "I *knew* it was worth staying for," she said.

Gene told her to hush. "You're not serious, Ginny."

"I am serious in telling you that is what Hazel said."

"Dewey will put her in a cage."

"He—some of us—should take steps."

"We can't, Ginny."

"Well, we can't let Hazel adopt that boy. He sounds like an independent little fellow."

"An independent criminal in the making."

"Well, he may be that, too. In any case, Hazel cannot

be allowed to adopt him. She'd put him on a leash like she does Bitsy. You know? She's not allowing that dog to get out of her sight? She'd do the same with that boy. Scrub him, feed him what she thinks he should have to eat . . ." She was excited. Her cheeks were red, and she made gestures . . .

Gene watched her and listened. Finally she put her hand on Ginny's arm. "You're forgetting one thing, sweetheart," she said.

"What's that? You *know*—"

"Yes. I know what I know. But I still must ask you. Is all this any of our business? Whether Hazel does or does not adopt that Fishtown boy?"

Ginny stared at her. "Dewey would appreciate our help," she reminded Gene.

"If he wants it, he'll ask for it and get it. But until he does, Ginny—"

Ginny stood up. She felt rebuffed, and she was angry. "I came here, with the best intentions, to get help from our friends," she started. "And I would like to know just why that isn't our business. Yours, as well as mine."

"But we agreed . . ." Gene reminded her.

"It wasn't the right thing to do. I miss having advice, and I'll bet you do, too. Aren't there some problems you'd like help in solving? Just what has your business been lately, that you haven't had any advice on, and probably needed some?"

She expected Gene to flash out at her, but she had not expected the look of real guilt which swept into Gene's eyes and face. *Good Lord!* Gene was trying to hide something! What could be going on with her? When Gene was secretive, the earth could shake and cracks show in the walls of at least four homes, and sometimes the hospital.

Something important had evaded Ginny. She looked to Carol for enlightenment, but the girl only shrugged, got up and went into the house.

Ginny rose, too. "I might as well go home to my sweet potatoes," she said. Gene politely asked her what she was serving with them, but Ginny did not bother to answer. She got into her car and drove down the hill. Hazel, she thought, might be able to give her some clues. And even Nan . . . Or Nan . . .

But having been put down hard once that day, Ginny decided that she would go home and feed her family. Instead of warmed-over meatloaf, she would ask Bob to slice some of the country ham they had. "And apple salad," she planned aloud. With fresh, warm cookies for dessert.

The next morning, while Dewey was shaving and getting dressed for the day, Hazel came through the hall, wrapped in a plastic raincoat and hood, the skirts of her housecoat and her pajamas "flapping," Dewey said, "around her legs." She had plastic rainboots on her feet.

"Where are you going in that get-up?" he asked.

"To walk Bitsy."

"Let him out in the yard," said Dewey. "No self-respecting dognapper would be out this early."

"I won't be gone ten minutes."

"What about my toast and soft-boileds?"

"Everything is ready. And I don't plan to give you eggs. Anyway, I'll be back by the time you're dressed. If you don't keep me talking, I shall be."

Dewey turned back to the mirror. "You look like the devil," he said bluntly.

"I know. But who will see me?"

"*I* see you. People in cars will see you. The other houses on this street have windows . . . And you'll scare the birds out of the trees!" He washed his razor and dried it.

"That's nonsense," said Hazel. "The neighbors are used to seeing me . . ." She went on down the hall. Dewey was muttering something to himself.

She fastened Bitsy's leash, but at the door of the garage, she stopped, frowning. She was remembering Ginny's visit of the afternoon before.

"Dewey!" she said sharply.

"What is it?" He came out of the bathroom, his hairbrushes in his hands.

"I meant to tell you this last night," said Hazel. "But —I didn't."

"Something I should have known last night?"

"Well, we could have talked about it then. You never want to talk in the morning."

"No, I don't. I want my breakfast, and then I want to get to the hospital. Could you pour me a cup of coffee now? And tell me tonight whatever it is . . .?"

He went on to the bedroom, thinking that she had decided to wait. But while he was unbuttoning his shirt, there she came with a cup of coffee. She was still in her "get-up," and he frowned.

She put the coffee cup on his chest of drawers and sat on the end of the bed. "You can think about this during the day," she said.

Dewey put a shirt on and took the coffee cup into his hands. "Oh, sure," he said, "between the runny noses and the arthritic knees. I believe I have a surgical abdomen for Cornel . . . I'll have time for a lot of personal thinking. What do you have in mind?" He sipped the coffee.

"Well, I've decided that you and I should see about adopting Jay."

Dewey sputtered. His blue eyes flared wide above the cup's rim. "You—decided—*what?*" he gasped.

"You heard what I said."

"I don't believe I did, Hazel." He turned to set the cup down, his back to her. He was struggling to attain some self-control. Calmness worked better with Hazel than fevered argument. He knew that.

"I'm quite serious," said his wife, standing up. "That boy has no home. We have no child—"

"And you are serious."

"Yes. Yes, I am. It would give us a purpose in life."

Dewey buttoned his shirt. He already had a purpose in life, he told himself. To keep up with Hazel. He reached for a tie.

"Shouldn't we think a little about Jay?" he said aloud. "Like, ask him if he wants a home."

"He doesn't know what a home could mean."

"That probably is true." He turned up the shirt collar and measured the tie ends, then adjusted their lengths. "We should give some consideration to our ages, too. A chiild needs young parents, resilient ones. You and I are pretty set in our ways." He knotted the tie, which was blue and white striped. "I think you should take a good look at the little boy who lives across the street. Ginny Ruble says he is being raised like a flower in a terrarium. There seems to be a problem with an older mother. Mrs. Gaines is forty-eight."

"How do you know that?"

Dewey crossed the room to pick up his suit jacket.

"Is she a patient of yours?" Hazel persisted. "And you're remembering not to let me in on any privileged communications?" Her tone was sharp and her eyes shot sparks.

He turned. "Damn it, Hazel!" he cried. "Why in hell do you start out my day—and your day—in this fashion?" He reached for the coffee cup. "Is this all the breakfast I'm going to get?"

She took off the raincoat. "I'm sorry," she said coldly, and went around him to the hall and the kitchen. Bitsy looked at her hopefully. "Later," she told the dog, pushing the toaster lever down. She filled the coffee cup beside Dewey's plate and pushed the glass of orange juice forward an eighth of an inch.

"I'm sorry," she said again.

"About what?" asked Dewey. "That Mrs. Gaines is forty-eight?"

"Danny is eleven. He needs a home, just as Jay does. He's twelve, but . . ."

"And you're about to bog down in your complicated arithmetic. Couldn't I have something besides toast?"

"Eggs and bacon are not good for you."

"And you're the doctor around here."

But she went to the refrigerator and brought out a package of bacon.

"That's right," Dewey approved. "If you want me to go along with your ideas, you should treat me kindly, not starve me."

Hazel turned the bacon in the pan. "I am very serious about this thing," she told Dewey.

"If you mean adopting that red-headed kid, I am too. Damn serious."

"Don't swear, Dewey."

"Why not? I always swear about serious things. Isn't the Gaines kid—the one with the forty-eight-year-old mother—isn't he a cub scout, and Ginny worries about him?"

"Yes. I know him. He is a scout, though his mother says the boy is anemic. Is he?" She put the crisp strips of bacon between two sheets of paper towels, then transferred them to a plate.

"I don't know," said Dewey. "Thank you, Hazel."

She sat down across from him. "He has a bad color," she said. "Pasty. But his mother says he won't eat."

Dewey touched his napkin to his lips. "Then he is sick," he said firmly. He stood up, bent over to kiss her cheek, picked up his medical bag and started for the door. "That's as far as I will go," he said firmly. "Bye, Bitsy. Mamma will take you for your walk now."

Dr. Windsor put in a crowded morning. The abdomen was indeed surgical, and he had promised the patient to stand by during the operation. This always fouled up his schedule, but he would not do as some physicians did—walk out on the anaesthetized victim. In the remaining time, he made rounds on the run and concentrated heavily on his morning appointments, coming into the staff dining room late for his lunch. His colleagues commented on this.

"Hazel gave me a good breakfast," he reassured them, then grinned. "With a gun at her head," he added. "She's gone off on the cholesterol thing again."

"It probably has merits," said Rufus McGilfray.

"It does, within reason. But I do a better job of work

with a good breakfast. Dry toast, orange juice, and plain coffee don't give me much fuel."

He ate his bean soup, put cheese between his crackers, and asked McGilfray if Hazel had talked to him about the crazy idea she had . . .

"Which crazy idea?" asked Mac, and the other men chuckled. They were all very close friends.

Dewey nodded. "This one is down your alley," he told the public health man.

"Oh, oh!"

Dewey smiled and filled a small wooden bowl with salad. "She is doing good to us this time," he explained. "Or so she claims. But I'd hope she would talk to you before she goes very far in this idea she has that we should adopt the packing box kid."

"Oh, no!" said Mac fervently. "Not Jay!"

"That's the one," said Dewey.

"But—" Then Dr. McGilfray changed his tone. "I'm sorry, Windsor," he said. "I shouldn't . . ."

"Yes, you should," said Alison Cornel. "It's an impossible idea."

"I'm afraid," said Dr. McGilfray, "that I was thinking only of the boy. He's a bright kid, resourceful. He may do a great deal for himself. And with your help . . . Even so, I still can't see him in your wife's home, Windsor. They'd both be miserable."

"Hazel would adjust . . ." said Dewey unhappily. "I guess she'd have to."

"There would need to be a lot of adjustment, in various fields and directions," said Rufus. "A boy of that age . . . I don't know a thing about his health background, his inheritance." He laughed shortly. "I don't know if Jay would take kindly to the idea. Of course, adoption in itself is a viable thing for you, Windsor. But Jay . . ." He shook his head.

"Your veto would squash it," said Dr. Shelton.

McGilfray glanced at him. "I'd go no farther than advice," he said.

"I know you wouldn't. But—"

"I don't think it would work, either," said Dewey. "I pointed out to Hazel that the Gaines boy, adopted by older parents, was not a shining example. He's over-protected, probably anemic, his mother says he won't eat . . ."

"Ginny," said Bob Ruble, "had him out to our house for lunch one Saturday. The cub scouts had been riding our horses in the morning. She invited this kid on impulse. And he ate everything in sight. I think, like our friend Dewey, he is being starved of the food he really craves."

"Don't worry about me," said Dewey, filling his bowl again. "He may be a case of bad adoption, but I am not."

"You don't know he's such a case," said Dr. Shelton.

"No, I don't. But I'm sure as hell the Jay-Windsor combination would be a bad one." He was so fervent that the men laughed.

"How long has Hazel had this idea?" asked Dr. Cornel.

"God knows," said Dewey. "She broke it to me only this morning."

"I was wondering what the women would have to say about Hazel's adopting anybody. That boy, in particular."

"I don't know," said Dewey. Dr. Cornel looked inquiringly at Bob and Garde. Bob shrugged, Garde shook his head.

"They don't have a clearing house these days," Dewey reminded the chief of staff. He smiled a welcome to the maid who brought dessert. Hot gingerbread with lemon sauce.

"Do they like things that way?" asked Dr. Cornel. "I always thought their spice of life . . ."

"Nan doesn't like it," said Garde. "She loves her friends, and likes talking things over with them, if it's only the state of the gutters downtown."

Bob nodded. "Ginny likes to talk, too," he said. "I wonder whose idea this clampdown was."

"Probably Hazel's," said Dewey, not unkindly. "The others didn't have to go along with it, but she is always reforming or reorganizing something. If it isn't her kitchen cabinets, it's the small pleasures of her friends."

"Or your diet," said McGilfray slyly.

Dewey nodded. "You are so right!" he agreed. "Do you suppose I could take a piece of this gingerbread home in a doggy bag for a midnight snack?"

"Better come back here to eat it," said Alison Cornel.

"I better had. But, to be fair, I think this four-way consultation business did sometimes run away with itself. And even now, maybe they are talking too much."

Bob laid down his fork and wiped his small mustache. "How's that?" he asked. Their wives' huddles and the results had always been a diverting topic for the men's lighter moments.

"Well," said Dewey, "I understand my wife—Hazel, as ever was!—I *know* she told Nan to have an abortion."

For a second, maybe five, there was a deep, shocked silence. Then Garde Shelton knocked his spoon to the floor. Alison Cornel swore loudly, and Bob Ruble moaned a sick "Oh, no!"

"Why should she interfere?" he asked. "Why should she think . . . ?"

Dewey sat watching them, listening and nodding his head. "Spoken, or not," he said, "I agree with your every thought and word. I am just glad that you know her— and I think my loyalty extends to the belief that there was nothing personal in the advice she gave Nan."

"What did you *say* to her," Bob asked, "when she told you?"

"Oh, I swore. I always do. And that puts her off on my reformation. She reminds me that I am a church officer, and should be as pure as the driven snow."

The men smiled; Dewey shifted his shoulders and straightened the front of his white coat. "She reads a lot of stuff," he reminded his friends. "All about the population explosion, and its being immoral and selfish to have kids like Fiddle and Butch Shelton—and, well, when she reads things of that sort, she immediately applies the guff to people and circumstances around her."

"A lot of good guff gets watered down," said Garde, "by such application."

"I suppose it does. And I'm sorry, but I have to put up with Hazel. It helps if our friends would try to. I told her she was quite out of line with such advice. And I feel sure, if the wives had been in conference, they would have set her back on the track better than I can."

"They could," Dr. Cornel agreed. "I've known them to be brutally frank." He stood up. So did the others.

"What does Gene think about their nontalking decision?" Bob asked, walking toward the door beside him.

"I don't know," said Alison. "She probably doesn't

want anybody in on what she herself is up to these days."

"Oh, oh!" said Bob, grinning. The other men laughed, and they disbanded in the hall.

Gene Cornel definitely was up to something "those days." She had become so absorbed in the letters she was helping Carol to write that she thought about the project a great part of the time. She might have known that her husband, a clever man with people, would note her preoccupation, and, since he was a husband of experience, he would be somewhat concerned. She thought, those days, constantly about the letters—she planned things concerning them, she made notes of details to mention, of clever twists of a phrase, of a description. She eagerly awaited the replies to what she thought of as her letters, and resented the fact that she could not open the envelopes which contained those replies such times as Carol was not at home when they arrived.

She recognized her absorption and her impatience. "You'd think I was the girl involved," she told herself. "You'd think I was out to snag a man's interest in *me.*" And then she thought, "You'd think I was twenty, or twenty-two, back to being young and hopeful, shy and trembly."

Her youth renewed.

She recognized that fact, and faced it.

This time was better, she soberly told herself. Because now she was wiser, more experienced. Wisdom and experience, added to youthful and eager interest, changed what a person did. Or would have done.

Gene liked seeing what those changes were. If she could give Carol the benefit of her wisdom and experience—and interest—so long as Carol let her share in this flurry into excitement . . .

Carol did let her. She called her mother a genius, and asked her to help in writing another letter to Murray— no, *Mike*—Shanahan, and then another.

Chapter Six

Hazel Windsor was not one to give up easily on an idea once it had come into her head. Her friends could talk, Dewey could swear, but she usually persisted until she herself became weary or excited about some new project.

In the matter of adopting the Fishtown boy, Dewey refused to discuss any such plan. This might be one of those rare times when he would have to put his foot down, and when he actually would do it, but he was hoping things would not come to that. Meanwhile, he refused to talk about it.

He knew that Hazel felt thwarted, he knew that she had not given up the idea, but he was not completely prepared for the line her frustration led her to pursue. At first, he did not connect the two projects. Hazel had a bonnet particularly susceptible to bee-ideas. Her husband endured them, watched them burgeon and fade. He hoped this new one would do just that. He hoped it would serve only to obscure the adoption bee.

But before it did, it probably would be applied to him or to their friends. So he braced himself to hear about it, to watch its application, and either accept it or put up an effective objection.

It began first to manifest itself quite soon after she had begun to talk about adopting Jay.

He came home one evening, somewhat late and tired. He wanted nothing so much as a hot dinner and a chance to put his feet up before a fire on the hearth.

When he came into the house, he asked, "Isn't the furnace working? The place seems chilly."

Hazel was wearing a sweater. She nodded. "I turned the thermostat down a bit farther. I knew you would light a fire, with the wind outside."

"One fireplace doesn't do much for the bedrooms."

"The British thrive on homes heated that way."

"Well, hurrah for the British." He turned up the thermostat.

Hazel said nothing.

A half hour later she called him to dinner. He came out, sat down, and looked at the table, at his plate, which had been served in the kitchen.

There was no bread on the table, no relishes. For a centerpiece there was a small bowl of apples and a covered cheese dish. This contained a small wedge of cheddar.

His plate . . .

He leaned forward. There was a single thin slice of roast lamb and a small mound of yellow corn. He tasted it. Lightly seasoned, but without butter. He laid his fork along his plate edge.

"What's going on?" he asked, swallowing the "now" he wanted to add. He was too tired, too old, too saddle-sore to go over another of Hazel's hurdles.

"Nothing is 'going on,'" Hazel told him. She poured tea into a cup.

Jolly old England again, he supposed. "What's happened to coffee?" he asked.

"You have coffee at breakfast. You guzzle it all day at the hospital . . ."

"I don't guzzle anything all day at the hospital. I work all day at the hospital! And today . . ." He gulped and accepted his cup of tea. At least it would be hot.

"Where's the sugar?"

"I don't believe you need sugar, Dewey." Her tone was lofty.

He pushed the teacup away and picked up his fork again.

"People use too much sugar," said Hazel.

"They do, eh?"

She did not blink an eyelash. "Yes, they do," she said. "People—especially our friends—go to excess in a lot of things. They live entirely too well for their own good and the welfare of everyone."

Dewey ate his lamb, he ate the corn. "What's for dessert?" he asked.

Hazel touched the edge of the apple bowl. "Eat one of those and a slice of cheese."

He leaned back in his chair. "Get it all said," he told her. "What's going on now?"

"Nothing is going on, Dewey. Well, of course there is. But I've just stated it. People live too well. Here is Gene planning on a Thanksgiving dinner again this year. She called and told me what I was supposed to contribute."

Dewey watched her. He was glad the women were planning the usual dinner.

"I told her I didn't think you and I could face that sort of dinner this year."

"You did that. Well, let me tell you; don't speak for me on that matter, Mrs. Windsor. Because I damn well can face it. I damn well will face it. And I could do with a slice of it right this minute!"

"Dewey . . ."

He reached for the cheese dish, uncovered it, and transferred the whole wedge to his plate. He stretched his arm and took two apples. Not looking at Hazel, he sliced cheese, and he sliced one of the apples, cored it neatly and made sandwiches of cheese and apple, which he began to eat, crunching.

Hazel watched him. "There are many arguments for less food consumed," she said uncertainly. "We don't need hot homes. We don't need rich gravies, three vegetables, and sweet desserts. For our own health, we don't need such things." She was picking up steam again. "Another argument is the vast number of hungry people in the world. The hungry ones right here in Bayard."

Fishtown, thought Dewey. Packing box homes and fish to eat. He said nothing aloud.

"You yourself," Hazel continued, "talk at length of the high incidence of heart attacks."

Yes, he did that. He had, that day, ridden one hundred miles in the ambulance which had taken a stricken friend and patient to the city hospital for expert care. That was why he was hungry. And tired.

He stood up, gesturing to the barren table. "Are you going to keep this up?" he asked.

"I think we well could eat less."

"And get pneumonia in a cold house."

"I've heard you say, often, that one does not catch any sort of cold from being cold."

"No, they don't. But if you run down my resistance with inadequate food, and I pick up a germ or a virus . . . Gee jumping whillikers, Hazel! I am tired of you applying your ideas and theories to me. Tonight—I'm hungry! And after you make me a pot of coffee and put some cookies on a plate, I want you to call Gene and tell her you'll bake that chocolate cake and make the brussels sprouts *au gratin* for Thanksgiving dinner . . ."

He went into the living room and lit the fire.

"Did you get your coffee and cookies?" Bob Ruble asked him the next morning when Dewey told of the dinner he'd had the night before.

"I didn't wait to get the Ry Krisp and the Postum she was going to serve me for breakfast," he answered. "I came straight over here and ate everything in the kitchen."

The men laughed.

"And, no, I didn't get the coffee last night. I had to hunt for and find the cookies for myself."

He was changing his clothes with short, angry thrusts of his hands and arms. "Look," he said, lifting his head. "Be good sports and invite me over for a meal or a hand-out, will you? Dear Lord! I can't even *snack* at home. I wish you could see the shelves of our frig. I cleaned out the cookie jar last night. And there isn't enough food in our refrigerator . . .

"Skim milk on the top shelf, unsweetened grapefruit juice. Dry curd cottage cheese. Lettuce. Gobs of lettuce

135

and celery and carrots. Whole-wheat bread. The dreariest sight you ever looked at. And I'm supposed to keep big and strong . . ."

"And sweet-tempered," said one of the men.

"Don't be late for lunch," Dewey warned him. "I'll eat your share as well as my own."

The men told each other that they would not put up with it. "And Windsor won't, either, for long."

"Do you suppose she really won't share in the Thanksgiving dinner?"

"That's a month away."

"But she must have told Gene . . ."

That afternoon, the men asked Dewey what the other wives had to say about Hazel's latest kick. They hoped their wives would not accept her ideas.

Dewey smiled weakly and reminded them that they probably had said nothing. "They're not talking together about their problems, and certainly not about mine."

"What do they talk about?" asked Alison Cornel. He was reading the case book for the preceding week, but giving more attention to the talk going on as the men changed before going home.

The men said they didn't know what their wives discussed. "Nan calls the others to remind them of altar duty," said Garde. "But they don't talk beyond a polite 'How's the family?' and, I presume, a reply."

"They see each other."

"Oh, yes, they do. Ginny was at our house only a day or two ago. Butch told me. He asked me if she was going to get white hair when she became a grandmother."

Bob Ruble laughed. "Not if Ginny can prevent it," he said. "But do you fellows realize that these women are standing ready to lose the fine friendship there has been between them for the past years? And years."

"We'd be in on that loss, too," said Alison Cornel, the chief of staff, deciding to take the book home with him. "Our family closeness has helped us build up this hospital. We've ironed out all sorts of difficulties over a slice of apple pie and a cup of coffee. Gene thinks if Hazel sticks to her decision not to spend Thanksgiving with the rest of us, that we might as well give up the annual Christmas bash too."

Dewey Windsor swore aloud. The men laughed at his threats, but each of them was troubled. Their close alliance was indeed an important part of their hospital operation.

And each one determined to see what he could do with his particular wife.

Dewey saw this determination in the faces of his friends, and he was certain they were blaming Hazel for a lot of the problem. But if she was to blame, he was, too. For allowing her to go off on as many tangents as she did. The others didn't realize how unpredictable she was, and how hard and fast she pursued her notions; how completely absorbed she became.

Still—perhaps there was something he could do. Perhaps he could explain to her how the partnership was threatened . . . He could not believe but that she would listen to reason on that subject. If it were carefully stated.

He made plans. He would go home that evening and kiss Hazel. Then he would ask her to please, old girl, get a nice, marbled steak out of the freezer and broil it for him. And then he would ask her if winter were not approaching fast and close enough for her to bake some beans for him. She knew how he loved a cold bean sandwich . . . Then he would talk about the more serious matters.

He had a couple of house calls to make, and when he reached home, only Bitsy was there. Hazel had left a note on the table beside his plate. There was tomato juice and head lettuce in the refrigerator, a casserole in the oven. She had gone to a meeting at the high school, and should be home by nine.

Dewey looked at the tomato juice, he looked at the casserole. And he put his coat on again and went to the club for his dinner. He ate barbecued ribs and lemon pie —and he played cards with Howard Copeland, Tom Sandoxie and Bill Marquart, not reaching home until midnight. Hazel was asleep.

This troubled him. He and Hazel did not *do* such things to each other. It would be much better to have a real fight, which he would do the next day. Only—he was called to the hospital at five A.M., and he left without saying much of anything to Hazel.

Hazel was having her own problems. She did not think she was mistreating Dewey. That idea did not occur to her. But she spent the morning being depressed. She took Bitsy for a run; the air was thick with fog from the river. Shivering, she thought almost constantly about the meeting which she had attended the evening before. She had left it upset; she was still upset. Hazel never liked being opposed, or, as she termed it, "put down." And she certainly had been put down at that meeting.

She was cross and she felt far from well. She had planned to get some things out for the church rummage sale, but the idea of digging into cupboards and clothes closets made her feel even worse. She needed fresh air; she would walk downtown and get some wool for the sweaters which she planned to knit for Jan and Sarah Ruble for Christmas. She could guess their sizes closely enough to get the wool and wind it. Another day she would measure the kids.

She determined to think about the sweaters, the color of the wool, the pattern and design—and forget herself. Mind over matter would help, she felt sure.

She was coming out of the wool shop, the bulky paper bag cradled in her arms, when she met Nan. She was glad to meet her, but shook her head at the suggestion of coffee.

"Or a glass of milk?" said Nan brightly. She was looking lovely, her cheeks pink, her brown hair and the end of her red scarf flipping in the crisp little wind.

"Don't mention food," said Hazel. "Can't we just walk along?"

"Of course. Don't you feel well, Hazel?"

"I think my disposition has gone sour," said Hazel.

"Oh, dear."

"Well, not permanently, maybe. But I did go through an experience last night that has left me all crosswise this morning."

Nan laughed. "Tell me about it."

"I will. You know, lately, I have been very food and nutrition conscious. I think it began with my awareness of Jay, the boy who lives in a packing box and catches fish for food." She glanced at Nan, who said nothing. Hazel shifted the package from one hand to the other. "I should be knitting sweaters for him rather than for the Ruble girls."

"Buy him a warm, weatherproof coat," said Nan.

"Yes, I could do that. Dewey thinks I'm over preoccupied with nutrition."

"Are you?"

Hazel slowed her step. They must wait on a crossing light, and the corner afforded an interesting store window. "I don't think so, Nan. I believe our food can mean our health. That's why, last night, I went to the Weight Watchers meeting."

Nan turned sharply. "You did *what?*" she asked, plainly astonished.

"I went to the Weight Watchers. Their food plans are so nutritious but avoid all the trouble-making things. And I thought— But do you know? They wouldn't take me as a member." Her cheeks were red, her eyes wide with indignation.

Nan put her hand upon a lightpost for support, and she laughed. Hard. "Please forgive me, Hazel . . ." she gasped.

Hazel sniffed. "I don't think I shall," she said. "Those women laughed at me, too. I thought their behavior, and their rejection, was shocking."

"Your coming in there must have shocked *them!*" said Nan.

"But why? If their purpose is to achieve ideal weight..."

"It is, but you—" Nan touched Hazel's shoulder. She turned her toward the shining shop window. "Just look at yourself, Hazel!"

Hazel was wearing the red pants suit. Her coat hung straight and slim from her shoulders.

"How much," Nan laughed, "can a pipe cleaner like you hope to lose?"

"I thought I could keep a watch on Dewey as well as on myself."

"But Dewey isn't overweight."

"I don't let him be."

"Do you let him enjoy his food?"

Hazel stared at her. "It isn't like you to be critical, Nan."

Nan shook her head. "I am only trying to reach you, Hazel, dear. Lately—well, I'd do almost anything to get through to you, to make you remember that your friends love you and would advise you from that position. For the past month I have felt that we were failing each other. You were the one who thought we should each stand alone. I think you used that term. Attend to our own business, you said. But, dear, the world doesn't work that way. Nobody can, really, be alone. Not even that independent little boy down on the levee. And not you, not me. Because I can see very plainly, judging from the ideas which you've come up with lately, and especially from this notion of yours about joining Weight Watchers, that we miss our helping one another. For instance, if you had mentioned Weight Watchers to me or to Ginny and Gene, we would have dissuaded you—"

"You would have laughed at me, as you did this morning."

"Yes, I did. But lovingly. You surely know that I do love you. Those women last night—"

"Some were my friends. Ruth Kibbler, Catherine Sims . . ."

"They are your friends, but not in the close interdependent way we four wives have always been friends." She spoke very earnestly. "I am sure that Gene and Ginny would agree with what I have said. We know, and you should—you probably *do* know—that too much weight watching can be as bad as not enough."

"I don't want Dewey to have a heart attack!" Hazel spoke defensively.

"I feel the same way about Garde. I strive for a balanced diet, but a nourishing one. This, combined with rest and exercise . . . But not excessive weight watching, Hazel, especially not where it isn't needed. That can make one just as sick as being overweight." She watched Hazel closely, expecting her to flare out with a dozen arguments, all in one breath.

But she did not. She just stood, thoughtful.

Nan touched her sleeve. "Have you already been doing some of that, Hazel?" she asked. Garde had told about Dewey's constant hunger. "And has it made you ill?"

Hazel nodded. "Let's walk along. I might— Something seems to be upsetting my stomach. Maybe I have been fretting over things—but it could be the food. I was queazy yesterday morning, and really nauseated today. I blamed that on my getting so mad at the Weight Watchers."

They crossed the street. "It probably isn't anything," Hazel said when they reached the curb.

Nan bit her lip. She was worried, but she did not want Hazel to be. When she spoke, it was lightly. "Maybe you've caught my trouble," she said, "and are having morning sickness. The best remedy for that . . ."

"You know it could not be *that!*" Hazel cried sharply. "And it isn't kind . . ."

Nan slowed her step. Her house was less than a block

away. "How do I know it could not be that?" she asked softly. "How do *you* know?"

Hazel sniffled, and Nan turned to look at her. Why, Hazel was weeping. She actually was! And then, without speaking again, without answering Nan, she walked away from her. Across the street, and down the far side of it, turning at the corner . . .

Nan stood where she was. Sorry. She had not meant . . .

But, yes, she had meant everything she had said!

And she was glad that she had Garde to talk to! She would talk to him. She certainly would! She would get out the car, and—

She actually did go to see her husband. And at the hospital. "A thing I never do," she told Garde solemnly. "If we could have talked this out among us—Ginny and Gene and I—and then we three could have talked to Hazel . . ."

Dr. Shelton asked his secretary to hold calls for fifteen minutes. He took Nan into his office and made her comfortable in the chair beside his desk. She was right. She never had done this sort of thing before.

"I only wanted to help her," said Nan, her face pale with her earnestness. "But one thing did come out, Garde. Hazel is not well. And I got the definite impression that she was not about to tell anyone else. Probably, even now, she is phoning the house to ask me not to say anything. That's why I came straight out here."

In the doctor's waiting room, a half-dozen children were squabbling, playing, or just being miserable, waiting for him to attend to them. Mothers were visiting, or becoming impatient . . .

"Tell me," said Garde quietly, his dark eyes concerned.

So Nan did tell him. Garde laughed at the Weight Watchers bit, he expressed concern over the way Hazel had "taken care" of Dewey—and finally he agreed that Hazel herself should be taken care of.

"Do you think . . .?" Nan asked, looking up at her tall, strong husband.

"I think she needs attention," said Garde gently, bending over to kiss her cheek. His hand cupped her shoulder. "Drive carefully," he said, watching her go along the corridor to the parking lot door. He returned to his desk, wrote HAZEL largely on his memo pad, and buzzed for the next patient.

At the lunch hour that day, Dr. Cornel led his colleagues into a discussion of autotransfusion, and Garde watched Dewey, who took some part in the conversation but was, for Dewey, rather quiet. Preoccupied.

As the men departed, Garde touched his arm. "Can you give me a few minutes, Windsor?" he asked.

Dewey looked at him questioningly. "Something . . . ?"

Garde nodded.

Well, Shelton usually knew what he was doing. "Give me five minutes," he said. "I want to check on the possible coronary that came in this morning."

Garde walked along with him. At the desk, Dewey checked the chart, then went on to Intensive. Garde watched him through the window. Windsor was a fine, conscientious doctor. Compassionate. He was being attentive to the frightened patient.

He came out, and Garde took his arm. "Let's do a couple of laps around the parking lot," he said. "The sun's out nicely . . ."

144

It was. And the two men in white were in earnest conversation as they walked brisky around the perimeter of the big lot. Dr. Shelton was doing the talking, the watching personnel noted.

"What's Garde lecturing Dewey about?" Dr. Cornel asked Bob Ruble.

Bob shrugged. "Could be professional, could be church business— We'll hear about it."

"It's serious," said Alison. "Dewey's getting red in the face."

He was. Because the story which Garde told him irritated him no end. "Damn dieting!" he exploded. "It would upset anybody's stomach. If I didn't eat double here at the hospital—"

"There could be something wrong with Hazel, you know," Dr. Shelton reminded him.

Dewey stopped walking. He picked a red and yellow leaf from the hood of a brown car. Held it in his fingers. "Yes, there could be," he agreed. "Doctors never are any good, Shelton, at diagnosing their own wives."

"Maybe not," said Garde. "That's why there is a convention against our treating our own families. So—don't you think you should ask Hazel to see Bob?"

Dewey's head snapped up. "What the hell . . . ?" he cried. "Why should you suggest . . . ?" He was shocked.

Garde laughed. "You're as bad as Hazel," he said. "Nan says that she was stunned at the suggestion. But, let me remind you, Doctor. I need not be suggesting that a child is imminent. Bob Ruble is a gynecologist, and treats women for all sorts of ailments and ideas."

Dewey took a deep breath. "I'm sorry, Shelton. Ideas, Hazel gets. And *how* she gets them! And—well, I said two minutes ago that doctors are no good treating or diagnosing their own wives."

"Let's leave it at that, then. My intentions, and Nan's, are of the best."

"Oh, there's no question of that! And—okay. I'll try to get Hazel to come here and see Bob. At her age . . . Yes, I'll make her come in."

"Will she do it?"

Dewey sighed and shook his head. "It will take doing," he said gloomily. "But, yes, she'll come."

They started back across the lot toward the hospital. "Do the other women," Dewey asked, "Gene and Ginny —do they know that Hazel is having difficulties? Nan does, of course."

"I don't believe the other two do know."

"They will!" said Hazel's husband fearfully.

"Oh, yes. I am sure they will find out. But, Windsor, we should now treat her case at our level. Whatever ails her . . ."

Dewey managed a smile. "It would be a sight easier," he said, "to let the girls do it."

It was only a day or two after that when Ginny came home late from a cub meeting. Her husband and children were already at home. Even the dog and the cat met her expectantly.

"Don't say it!" said Ginny. "I know I'm late, but I knew I always would be when I let myself be talked into being a den mother again."

"We're just hungry, Mom," Jan explained. "I couldn't really start dinner. You use shorthand on your menus."

"Well, I will feed you. Let me wash up a little first."

"How often does your den meet?" Bob asked her when she came downstairs again. She had put on a fresh blouse and brushed her hair.

"Too often," said Ginny darkly. She looked at her watch. "Will an hour be too long to wait?"

"That's awful long," said small Sarah.

"Yes, I suppose it is. All right. You girls get the table set. I'll find some quick food. I had thought I could bake one of the pies . . ."

"Quick food," said Jan. "What did your scouts do today?"

Ginny laughed. She had a pretty, bubbly laugh, like that of a child. "We went to the bottling plant."

"Oh, oh," said Jan. "I remember going there. We really did get samples."

"I wish you'd continue with your girl scout work, Jan."

"I'm sure," said Jan.

Ginny glanced at her sharply, but she said nothing. Jan appreciated her silence, and said that the pork chops smelled "simply marv."

Ginny nodded. "The boys will tax the city's water supply tonight," she said. "Drinking all that pop. They'll be up and down until morning." Deftly she cored and sliced a half-dozen red apples.

"Oh, goody," said Sarah, "fried apples!"

"Certainly fried apples, with pork. Will you get me the brown sugar, sweetie?"

"It's in the tea canister," Jan told her sister.

Bob, in the family room, laughed.

"Do you think four bottles of root beer could hurt a boy?" Ginny asked him.

"Maybe I should alert Shelton."

"Maybe."

Bob watched Ginny moving about. She could tie apron strings more prettily than other women; her skirts did pretty arabesques around her knees. Even in flat-heeled shoes, her slender feet twinkled. Heavenly smells were coming from the kitchen.

And hot, delicious food came to the table. After taking the dishes to the kitchen while Ginny and Bob lingered over coffee and spice cake, the girls returned to their homework. The telephone rang and Ginny answered it, shaking her head at Bob to show that he need not be disturbed. He filled his coffee cup and went back to the family room. "I think you might get the dishes into the machine," he said to Jan.

Ginny hung up the telephone and came into the kitchen, her face thoughtful. She and Jan made quick work of the dishes and straightening the kitchen. Jan said she would study upstairs, she had a theme.

"All right. Don't let Sarah bother you."

"I'll dump her in the bathtub."

"That should solve a lot of problems." Jan would let Sarah come into her room until she got sleepy, then she would give the little girl her bath and tuck her into bed.

Ginny went to sit before the fire with Bob. "The wind's coming up," she said.

"Mhmmmn. Dinner was good."

"Thank you. I'm sorry I was late."

"No harm." He noted that Ginny was not discussing the telephone call she had had. Which was all right, though unusual. Bob picked up a magazine; now and then his eyes would go to his wife. She was sewing something or other.

After fifteen minutes, their eyes met. "Bob," she said, "do you think Garde would help me with a problem I have?"

"I didn't know you had a problem."

Ginny laughed. "I always have dozens of them!" she assured her husband.

"Mhmmmnnn."

"Certainly I do. The house, the family, my cub scouts . . ."

"A husband."

Again she glanced at him. "Oh, my husband is very good at taking care of his own problems," she said.

Bob chuckled and tossed the magazine to the floor, reached for another. "Let's go back," he said.

"How far?" asked Ginny.

"Don't put pins in your mouth, Ginny!"

"I—"

"Yes, I know you know better! Let's go back to the problem you—or maybe I—might take to Garde Shelton."

"Oh, yes," said Ginny, stretching her circle of red stuff across her knee. He could not imagine what she was working on! She glanced up. "Do you think he would take the case of my boy?"

"A cub? Sure. The parents have only to take him to Garde's office. Preferably with an appointment. He'd be the right age."

"But *that*'s my problem!" said Ginny earnestly. "This boy—I decided right from the first that he had a parent problem. And he certainly has."

"Oh, Ginny."

"I'm not meddling. I'm not taking sides. But this boy does have a problem, Bob. For one thing, he's an adopted child."

"And that makes a difference?"

"Yes, it sometimes does. In this case, it definitely does. Because, while he's eleven, his father is sixty-five, and his mother is forty-eight."

"Hard on them, a lively kid."

She was used to Bob's taking the other side of an argument or discussion. "The trouble is . . ." she said.

"And don't bite your thread. Use your scissors. What's the boy's trouble?"

"That he isn't a lively kid. You see, his parents— maybe they feel unduly responsible for him. I've known adoptive parents to feel that way. These parents try to —they *do*—keep Danny in the house all the time."

"*That* boy," said Bob.

"Yes. I've talked about him before. Their house, Bob —it's not very large, and it is crowded with furniture. But summer and winter, they keep the child inside. Summer and winter, Bob! He's pale. He looks like—like—"

"A shark's belly."

Ginny smiled ruefully. "I'm not too familiar with sharks' bellies," she admitted. "But I am concerned about this kid. And he really is colorless. His mother says he won't eat, but he did the day I fed him lunch here. Remember? Even your eyes popped."

"I remember," said Bob. "The Gaines boy."

"Yes. And he always eats well when he's with the cubs. One time we baked cookies, and Danny ate every one he baked. Today he drank quarts of pop . . ."

Bob laughed. "Then I'd say he was due to see Shelton."

"Yes. If his mother would call him."

"Won't she?" Bob sounded concerned.

"I don't know that she would. And that is what troubles me."

The doctor made no immediate reply. After fifteen minutes, he called the hospital to check on things, and Ginny went upstairs to be sure that Sarah was in bed. Bob could hear her talking to the child, and then to Jan. He put some soft music on the hi-fi, and stretched out in his reclining chair. He enjoyed these quiet, fire-warmed evenings.

Ginny came quietly back to her low rocking chair and picked up her sewing. "I'm not asleep," said Bob.

"I rather hoped you would be. You look very handsome on your sarcophagus."

Bob chuckled and raised the chair back. "A fine way to get me to recline," he said. "Have you talked to Mary?"

"Not since Sunday when she called. She said she was in fine shape then."

"She said she was in *great* shape. That's a frequent pregnant joke, you know."

"How would I know? Sarah is seven years old."

"Yes, she is. Maybe you should refresh your memory."

"Please!" said Ginny. "Aren't cub scouts enough?"

"They do seem to be. Tell me, if this Gaines boy is kept in cotton, as you say he is, how does he happen to be a cub at all?"

"Because—" said Ginny. "I asked about that—I have frequent consultations with the mother, you know. And she told me that the school counciling service told her to have him join. She thought she had better let him, because he was adopted. She had things to say, too, about the snoopiness of various people concerning adoptions."

"Did she choose your pack?"

"No, she chose the one sponsored by the church. She felt we would behave better."

"Do you?"

Ginny did not answer.

"She must be fond of the kid," Bob mused.

"Oh, she is fond of him!" Ginny agreed. "Too fond. You wouldn't believe, Bob . . ."

"Try me."

"Well, he's practically eleven years old, and she makes him take a nap every afternoon."

"How could he?"

"He does. He comes home from school and takes a nap. That makes him late for cub meeting. The mother explained the reason when I mentioned his tardiness."

"Did you tell her that the other boys . . . ?"

"I've told her *many* things! But her general response is that she wants to do everything she can for Danny. I feel sorry for him. He doesn't know how to play baseball or basketball, and certainly not football. When the boys talk about using the pool next spring, it turns out that Danny can't swim. I said he could learn, but he doesn't have trunks, and he doesn't think his mother would let him, anyway."

"You're making this up. Aren't you?"

"I certainly am not. And don't ask me what he gets out of cubbing, because I don't know myself. Though he does open up sometimes. He did this afternoon at the bottling plant. He was running up and down the stairs and along the catwalks. But on the way home I found out that he owns a ten-speed bicycle—the ultimate wish of every boy just now—but he never rides it; his mother says he's too young."

"And the other boys were ready to take over."

"Yes, they were," said Ginny. "When I suggested that we have a pet show, and ask the vet to talk to us, Danny said he didn't have a pet, though I've seen that miniature poodle . . ."

"It probably belongs to the mother. Have you ever seen the father, talked to him?"

"Not talked. I saw him once when I went to the house. He was leaving as I came in. I got the general impression of a tall man with a shock of white hair."

"I see."

"I'm glad you do, because I don't. For instance, why give a boy an electric train, then not let him play with it?"

"For fear he'll electrocute himself."

Ginny leaned forward. "How did you know?"

"It's typical behavior for overprotective parents. They want their boys to *have* everything, but they fear injury, so they try to prevent it. You bet it's typical."

"I'd not give him dangerous toys to begin with."

"*You* wouldn't. But these people—Gaines, is it? These people seem to be different."

"They certainly *do!*" said Ginny fervently. "That woman even told me not to let Danny play in the snow."

"We haven't had any snow."

"Not yet. But she's being forehanded."

"What did you tell her? That you planned the cubs'

programs for a group, not to accommodate one boy?"

"I did, and she said I could let Danny watch the other boys."

"But you won't have to do that, because she won't let Danny out of the house on a snowy day."

Ginny laughed bitterly. "You're probably right. She won't."

"Was she—Mrs. Gaines—the one who called you this evening?"

"Yes. She called to ask if Danny had been sick at the meeting."

"Had he been?"

"No, indeed. I told her that I'd never seen him sick."

"But she said she would plan to keep him home from school tomorrow."

"You're psychic."

"No, I'm not. I've just been a doctor for a long, long time."

"Presumably in obstetrics."

"Well, yes, but I've had Garde's office right next door, and he weeps on my shoulder."

"That I've yet to see."

"He gets burned about mothers of this sort."

"I would think so. From what I hear, she keeps Danny home from school quite often, claiming that he's sick."

"Now, there is where you could get Garde, or some doctor, to see the boy, through that practice. The school could use his frequent absences to ask for a doctor's examination of the child."

"Are they apt to do that?"

"I really don't know what the practice is in the school system here. Our own kids are healthy, and we never had much occasion to get acquainted with the health department and the school."

"Could I ask his teacher? Or should I just talk to her about Danny?"

"You'd better be careful, Ginny."

"Oh, I shall. I want to help Danny, not hurt him."

"Of course." He sat upright and asked Willy if he wanted to go outside. "Want to come with us, Ginny?"

She shook her head. "I've had my exercise for today. Bring some wood in when you come back."

Bob was gone for nearly half an hour and forgot about the wood, so he had to go out again. Willy refused this second excursion; with a scornful sniff he crowded into the side of Ginny's chair.

"What's that you're sewing?" Bob asked her when he had mended the fire.

"Quilted place mats. Christmas gifts for Gene and Hazel. Ruby makes Nan use tablecloths."

"She would," Bob laughed. "And that reminds me." He sat down in his chair. "How is Hazel coming along with her idea of adopting that Fishtown boy?"

"I don't know. Dewey's been against it, hasn't he?"

"Profanely. But that isn't enough to stop her, is it?"

"Not usually. Really, that man's patience with her is phenomenal."

"Oh, we husbands all have to be patient."

"You bet," said Ginny cheerfully. "The times I've seen Hazel recently—at church, and in the supermarket yesterday—she was on a diet kick. Lectured me for buying white bread. I was glad she didn't see the pound of butter I had in the bottom of the cart."

"Dewey should use a little more than profanity there.

He comes to the hospital acting starved. Of the people I know who don't overeat, it's the Windsors, first."

"I know. Hazel was telling about a no-fat cheese dip she has made. She says she plans to take a little tub of it to the next party."

"Dewey should put his foot down! What a thing that would be! She—"

The phone rang sharply; he groaned and went to answer. He returned with a handful of crackers and some cheese on a small plate. He gave Ginny a couple of these sandwiches. She smiled up at him.

"What's wrong?" she asked then.

"Why should anything be wrong?"

"I don't know, but you're looking mighty strange."

He sat down with his plate and his crackers. "Handsome on my sarcophagus, but strange when I come bearing Swiss cheese and crackers."

"That can happen," said Ginny, eating a sandwich.

"Ginny," asked Bob, "are you sure you're not talking to the girls?"

She brushed crumbs from her sewing. "Well, of course we *talk*, Bob."

"But—"

"We just are not solving each other's problems. You should be glad. You used to scold like the dickens when I worried about their affairs and spent what you called hours telling the others what to do, how to feel, what to say . . ."

"I remember," he agreed. "Advice, criticism, you told 'em what to wear, too, and what to cook."

"And they told me."

"Yes, that's what went on. All right, then. So you're not doing that interchange now. And I can break the news to you, that was Windsor on the telephone just now. He wants me to see Hazel tomorrow."

Ginny dropped her scissors. "Professionally?" she asked, her voice squeaking.

"Yes, I think so. At any rate, in the office."

"What's wrong with her?"

"That's why I asked. I thought you could tell me that, or some of her symptoms."

Ginny shook her head. "Didn't Dewey . . . ? Don't you have any idea . . . ?"

"I'll have more by tomorrow night."

"Mhmmmn," said his wife. "And after you've seen her, you won't tell me a thing."

"That's right," said Bob, smiling at her.

The next day, Ginny, thinking much of the time about Hazel, resisted her impulse to go directly to her and ask why she should be seeing Bob in his office. For one thing, Bob would "kill" her for acting on such privileged information. Secondly, Hazel well might resent his talking to Ginny about *her*, and she would snap at Ginny . . .

She didn't think she should try to find out things from Gene or Nan, and when she met Gene on the street, she sternly told herself to be careful. "Keep your ears open, however," she thought it safe to advise.

She had seen Gene on the sidewalk, and she pulled her car up to the curb. As she often did when marketing or "just running to the post office," Gene looked like the trash hauler's daughter. She had good clothes, she could spruce up and look like a million dollars, but often she was guilty of these lapses. Alison fussed at her . . .

Ginny rolled down the window, then opened the car door.

"You can't park here," said Gene.

"I'm not parking. I just wanted to say hello to you."

Gene grinned. "Hello," she said. She drew her old coat close to her body. "It's chilly this morning."

"Well, October should be a little chilly."

"Where are you going?" asked Gene.

"To the school . . ." She pointed down the street.

"About one of your kids? It would have to be Sarah."

"It isn't Sarah. She never makes trouble for anyone."

"Lucky you."

"Yes, I am lucky. No, I want to talk to the principal, or maybe his teacher, about one of my cub scouts. I hope to hit recess time."

"Maybe you will."

"Can I give you a lift?"

Gene brushed her blowing red hair back from her face. "I'm going to the bakery. For buns. My car is parked back at the supermarket. I'm assembling food for the hayride."

"What hayride?"

"It's for the church's young people. EYP, or some such initials. They go out in a flat-bed truck. I don't even know if they have *hay*—and they cook hot dogs and stuff —build a fire, naturally."

"Sounds like fun."

"It's supposed to *be* fun. Carol is going, so—"

Ginny had thought of the group as being made up of younger folk. Jan might be going. "How is Carol feeling?" she asked.

"All right. She's fine, in fact. And bored to death having to stay at home with the old folks."

"Oh, Gene!"

"I was quoting her. Mr. Linders thought this party up,

and probably to help me, he asked Carol and me to be the adults, the chaperones. I offered to get the food. How many buns can fifteen tean-agers eat?"

Ginny laughed. "You'd better count your money," she advised.

"You're no help."

Ginny edged back under the wheel. "I didn't expect to be," she said, still laughing. "Good luck, Gene! And have fun."

"Oh, I shall, I shall," said Gene gloomily.

Ginny drove on to the school, seeing Gene turn into the bakery. Neither of them had mentioned Hazel or even Nan, as formerly they would have done.

"What's Hazel up to?" they would have asked.

And, "Have you checked on Nan this morning?"

But not these days.

And Ginny, for one, missed their old interchange of news, ideas and opinions. As time went on, she kept missing it, as one keeps feeling of a hole in a back tooth.

Their behavior was not good, and she wished she knew how to stop it. This thing of politely ignoring the little personal details in the others' lives felt like, seemed like, indifference, and the habit of it might grow . . .

"I am not going to lose my best friends," she said half aloud when she parked her car at the school. "I want to *know* what's wrong with Hazel. I want to *help* her if I can."

The night was cool, but not cold. The river scarcely rippled in the path of the huge hunter's moon, and the hayride seemed to sweep of its own power along the road. Where Ferrell Linders had found an actual hay wagon and two fat brown horses to pull it, was anybody's guess. Carol had said no one should ask him, miracles could always happen. He had provided round bales of hay, too. Gene was leaning against one now, hoping that her ears would not suffer permanent damage from the noise the young people were making. She wondered if she would know it should one of the kids be jounced off.

"They can catch up with us or walk back to town," said Mr. Linders comfortably. He stood to drive, his legs spread apart for balance. "This smooth road offers no problems," he assured Gene. "Remember, I grew up on a farm."

"He's a lot like Storm, isn't he?" Carol found a chance to say to her mother.

Carol was having a fine time. And Gene was glad. As for herself, she wished she were safely at home with her feet up. "I never was young enough for this stuff," she told herself.

And promptly chided herself for even thinking such a thing. "By the time I'm forty-five, I'll want a wheelchair."

She should be glad that Alison had made her come, that he had said she should wear her plaid blouse, blue tweed skirt and the matching cashmere sweater they had bought at M&S in London last summer.

"Where else would you wear it?" he asked her. "You look like your own daughter in it."

This had pleased her. She didn't want to *be* her own daughter, but it was pleasant that Alison did not consider her old. He was an attractive, virile man. She meant to hang onto him.

But she was a little stiff when the wagon reached the

place which Mr. Linders had selected for their cookout. It was a wide, flat stretch of chipped rock, sand and dried grass stretching down to the river. He directed the boys on how to clear a space for their fire. The girls were to find driftwood and a few bigger stones.

This they did, scattering out, tripping, falling, laughing, screaming—laughing again, bringing up the wood they found, "snitching" a pickle, snitching a marshmallow . . .

"Stomach aches coming up," said the Rector.

"At their age, it's a shot of sensible food that would upset them," said Gene.

The fire was built, roaring high, then reduced to glowing coals for the wieners to be roasted. Gene's pile of buns melted away, as did the beanpot's contents. Carol had taken care of that, and had fun pretending to count the beans when plates came back for seconds and thirds.

Gene and one of the girls invented kabobs of apple slices and marshmallows to toast over the coals. "Next time, we'll bring cheese," said Gene. "Who planned this bash, anyway?"

"I think Mrs. Cornel was in charge of the food," said Mr. Linders slyly.

"I never heard of her," said Gene.

There were two stumps of large trees, long ago cut down. Between these the sand had drifted soft and clean. The young people made a hollow of this place and gathered there, crowding close together, replete with food, warmed by the built-up fire. One of the girls had brought a guitar, and the group sang. As usual with young teenagers, at first the boys lined up together, the girls facing them. These lines edged closer, and soon they were merged.

The girl with the guitar asked the boy in the blue windbreaker what to sing next. A boy in a yellow jacket pretended to read news items from a newspaper he carried rolled in his hand. He sometimes whacked one of the girls with this, to loud screams of pretended pain and protest. Now and then the talk became earnest.

"Why do you think 'Candyman' is a drug-oriented song?"

They hummed the tune and analyzed the words. 'Bridge over Troubled Waters' they *knew* had double meaning.

Almost any song could be read so. Nursery rhymes, too. Mother Goose was politically subversive . . .

"Back in the dark ages," said a girl of fifteen. Stretch pants did everything for her.

"Couldn't they apply now?" suggested Mr. Linders. "Take Humpty Dumpty . . ."

This idea was being pursued with great enthusiasm when a car came down the road toward them, its headlights gleaming upon the coats of the tethered horses. Mr. Linders rose and went toward the car. Perhaps he was needed . . .

He talked to the young man who had got out of the car, and both men gestured to the group around the fire.

They moved down the slope to the beach. "This gentleman says he was told," said Mr. Linders, "that he could find a certain Carol Cornel here."

Gene jumped and looked again at their visitor. Moonlight and firelight showed a tall man, young—his hair was dark—and—was that a beard? Yes, it was. Neatly trimmed, a jaunty beard. The fellow moved well, gracefully, as he came down the slope.

". . . he was told," Gene's mind repeated. Alison must have told him. How had *he* known which road they would take? He had called Mrs. Linders, was how.

Gene sat on the large, flat tree stump and watched the whole thing. Carol was being surprised and flustered. Lordy, was she ever flustered! Gene wished she could quiet her down. Mothers should come equipped with candle snuffers for their silly daughters.

Carol was laughing and standing in every awkward position in the book! While the man—yes, he did have a beard. And he was good-looking. Who in the world would he *be?* He certainly was in control of himself. He stood holding Carol's hand, talking to her, to Ferrell Linders, to the kids between the tree stumps.

Who in the world could he be? There were those two fellows Carol had written to . . .

He was not flustered. But Carol— Oh, for heaven's sake! She was talking too loudly, her voice was actually shrill. She pulled the scarf from her head and flapped her hands and laughed, then showed that she was embarrassed. She tugged at the sides of her sweater.

Gene slid down from the stump. This fellow must be, he had to be, Murray Shanahan. Mike. Gene had pictured him as red-headed, with an impish grin. This chap's hair was as black as night, and his eyes were steady. Watchful. He was older—quite a bit older—than Gene had expected. But—

Moving slowly, she walked into the rim of firelight, up to the strange young man. She held out her hand. "I'm Gene Cornel," she said. "Welcome to our clambake. Of course we don't have any clams, but there should be a marshmallow or two left over . . ."

The man's eyes brightened, then softened. He held out his hand. "I'm Shanahan," he said, his voice deep. "Are you Carol's sister?"

It was an old line. But a good one. Carol was shrieking with laughter. "She's my *mother!*" she screamed.

Gene nodded. "Stick around. She'll tell you how old I am, Doctor," she said dryly. "I'll get you some coffee and food."

"Maybe he's had dinner," said Carol, laughing over nothing.

Gene walked away.

In the firelight, her light red hair shone like a helmet against her warm skin. She was slender and erect, trim and tailored in her blue tweed and cashmere. Jeans and stretch pants were one thing. A short, well-cut skirt above good legs was still the best. And poise against excitement and flutter did more to attract.

Chapter Seven

Saturday was about to be the biggest sort of workday in the Ruble household. Sarah earnestly explained this to her father as he ate his breakfast. "It's a *hike*, Daddy!" she said. "It's a very *special* hike! Because, do you know what? The Brownies are going with the cubs! And *I'm* going!"

Bob laughed at his excited, dark-haired little daughter and lifted her to his knee. "Girls and boys together," he marveled. "When do you go? Is your mother going?"

"Well, of course she's going! She's the den mother. And our leader is Mrs. Carter, and then there's Mrs. Noble, who is her assistant."

"Does Mommie have an assistant?"

"No. She's supposed to, but she doesn't."

"Then you Brownie girls will have to help her."

"We will, only we're supposed to be learning things about hiking and what trees are, and how to make a fire, and how to cook . . ." Sarah's eyes fairly blazed with excitement.

Ginny moved busily about the kitchen, gathering equipment.

"Sounds like your busy day," Bob said to her.

She brushed her hair back from her face. "Start from here at ten, hope to be back by two. I have to fetch Danny Gaines . . ."

"What about the other boys?"

"Their mothers will bring them, or they'll walk. If I don't get Danny, he won't go."

"It's only four blocks, Ginny."

"Four blocks and his mother," she reminded Bob. "This will be his first actual hike."

"And you start by picking him up in your car."

"I know it's wrong, but it's right, too, Bob. That kid needs to be with people other than his antique parents and their antique furniture."

"Send Jan over after him."

"Won't do. Mrs. Gaines would object."

"I'd help you if I could. Plan on dinner at the club tonight."

"That's lovely of you, Bob. But I shouldn't make you pay . . ."

"Why shouldn't you?"

He kissed her good-by, kissed Sarah, and went out to his car.

At nine o'clock, Ginny went off to fetch Danny. She hoped his mother would cooperate to the extent of dressing the boy properly and providing the simple food supplies Ginny had said the boy would need. Of course she would take extras for emergencies, but—

She slowed her car and then pulled it up into the Windsor driveway. Something was going on—Hazel and her yard man, a neighbor or two, were out in the front yard excitedly watching something up in the pecan tree.

Not too close to it, but forming a half-circle and gesturing.

"What's going on?" asked Ginny, getting out of the station wagon.

Hazel's head turned. "Don't come too close," she called. "There's a puff adder up in the tree."

Well, it was warm. The days had been warm for this past week.

"Nonsense!" said Ginny. "It's not a puff adder."

She came close enough to see the snake—a pretty good-sized one.

"It puffed!" declared Hazel.

"But we don't have puff adders in Missouri."

"But, Ginny . . ."

"Look it up in the book," said Ginny. "I'll do it. Is your front door open?"

"Go through the garage," said Hazel, her manner distracted.

Ginny came back with the heavy dictionary. Danny Gaines, evidently seeing her car, had come across the street. "It could be a puff adder," she conceded. "Adders themselves, the venomous kind, are found only in Asia. But hognosed or puff adders do live in North America."

"I told you!" said Hazel triumphantly. "It's after the wrens. They stay all winter in that house."

"You're not going to kill the snake?"

"Orville is."

"Then I'm leaving," said Ginny. "I'll put the book back. How are you feeling, Hazel?"

Hazel looked at her coldly. "I am feeling fine," she said icily.

Ginny nodded. "That's good. Come on, Danny. Are you ready?"

Of course he was not ready. They had to pick up his pack and for five minutes listen to Mrs. Gaines's directions, but eventually they were on their way. Hazel and her neighbors were still gathered about the pecan tree.

"Mrs. Windsor is a smart lady, isn't she?" said Danny at her side.

"Yes, she is," said Ginny.

"But maybe you know more than the book?"

Ginny laughed. "I doubt that very much, Danny. What did you bring for lunch?"

"A can of soup."

"A can of *soup?*"

"Well, my mother said it wouldn't make me sick."

"Oh, we don't get sick on hikes."

"I'm glad," said the little boy.

At the Ruble house, the cubs and the Brownies were assembling. Which meant complete bedlam. Twenty children, three adults . . . Ginny went inside to talk to Mag, and to Jan. The scouts were, she said, going to cut down through the pasture and into the woods for a short way. "If I'm really needed, you could find me."

"I could tell by the noise," Jan agreed.

"Don't you want to come, too?"

"I'll fix Daddy's lunch."

"Okay." Ginny told about the puff adder.

"Oh!" said Jan. "That's one of the McLain boy's snakes. I'd better call him. They're pets."

"I'll never understand this generation," Ginny told herself earnestly.

She said Willie could go on the hike, the cat could not.

"And you don't want to, do you, Mag?"

"No, *ma'am!*" said that worthy woman emphatically.

"Well, I don't really want to either," Ginny confided. "Look after things, Mag."

The hike started, the three adults valiantly trying to combine a little instruction and safety into the proceedings. The Ruble horses regarded the ragged file of children dubiously but patiently. Someone lifted his pack upside-down and everything fell out, then was retrieved. No, the wieners were not ruined. A little dry grass and sand never hurt anyone, said Ginny. The girls were excited to be on a hike with the boys; the boys were patient, but displeased with the idea.

"Don't expect chivalry," Ginny advised the Brownie leaders. "Boys this age aren't as advanced as girls in the same group."

"That one little kid, he's having a ball."

Ginny looked at Danny, who was indeed having a ball. He was eager, he was excited. He raced all over the place, came back, and raced again.

"Dear Lord," prayed Ginny, "don't let him be the one to get hurt."

Their destination was the top of the old road up from the quarry. Ginny gathered her troops and laid down a law or two. No one, absolutely *no one*, was to go down to the quarry pool. In fact, not beyond the fence. "Now! Who knows how to build a good fire?"

Everyone said he did. "You just pile up a lot of stuff and light it with a match," was the general idea.

The sticks were found and assembled, the fire properly laid. Who had matches? Well, Ginny did.

"But when you're older," she instructed, "never forget your matches—in a tin box."

"Why a tin box?"

"In case you fall in the water."

"But you're not supposed to go down to the water."

"That's right. I'm not."

A typical hike. Some kids goofed off, some didn't. The girls wanted to play games. The boys didn't. There were disasters. A boy cut his finger, a little girl wanted to go home for lunch, Danny Gaines burned his tongue on a toasted marshmallow.

"Didn't you know it would be hot?" Sarah asked him curiously.

The boy shook his head, his hand still cupped over his mouth. He was uncertainly holding the stick and the wiener which Ginny had given him. Sarah took it away from him and held it close to the coals. "That's the way to do it!" she instructed.

"She'll make a den mother herself," laughed Alice Carter.

"I'll warn her," said Ginny grimly.

Having warmed his wiener, Sarah had to give Danny a bun to put it in, and she then offered another marshmallow. He regarded it dubiously.

"Hold it close to the fire," Sarah instructed. "Goodness, haven't you ever roasted anything before?"

"No . . ." said Danny. Then his face brightened. "But I like it!" he declared.

After lunch there was more hiking, more instruction, even a swift fight between two of the boys. Nut trees were discovered and identified, deer tracks were found —and their identity disputed.

Danny continued to be a mixture of fears and adventuresomeness. He fell and slipped down a short incline, tearing his slacks. He himself was unhurt, but he was dirtier than any of the other children. The toilet provisions, or lack of them, bothered him.

Ginny lectured his den-mates for laughing at him. "It's his first hike," she pointed out. "And our purpose is to help people learn about the woods, not to make fun of their inexperience."

She personally escorted Danny to a thick growth of buckbush, and in plain words told him what he was expected to do. Yes, she would stay close.

She waited, thinking harsh thoughts about Mrs. Gaines and her failure to make the simple facts of life a matter of relaxed procedure for the child. What the future held for Danny, she could not guess!

Today she had hoped . . . The boy wanted to be adventuresome, but he clung too closely to Ginny to accomplish much.

Before starting home—they had in fact reached the edge of the Ruble pasture—the leaders asked the children to form a circle and tell what they had learned that day. Did they want to have another hike?

"But not with the girls!" declared one freckle-faced boy.

"What about a bus trip sometime?" asked Ginny. "For that we would need to take in other dens, or some girl troops."

"Could we go to the zoo?" asked one child. "In the city?"

"And see snakes?"

"We have snakes in Bayard," spoke up Danny, and to Ginny's amazement, the boy launched into a vivid, gesturing account of the snake in Mrs. Windsor's tree that morning.

He talked for five minutes, and Ginny got him stopped

only by asking him if he had ever been to the zoo in the city.

"No," he admitted.

That figures, she told herself, even as she was making a qualified promise to take her den there. "But not before spring," she said. "From now on we'll be working on Christmas projects, and the Indian ceremony after Thanksgiving."

"Right now," said Mrs. Noble, one of the Brownie leaders. "I think we should have our closing ceremony and go home."

"We could sing . . ." suggested Sarah.

"Oh, yes," said Ginny. "We could sing. Two songs. The girls choose first, the boys choose the closing song."

So they sang "Plant a Tree," and the boys wanted to do "Inky Pinky Pider."

Laughing, they started for home. Ginny said she would drive the boys home from her house.

"I don't want to go home," said Danny.

Oh, dear. "Aren't you tired?" Ginny asked him.

"Yes, but—Will you drop me last?"

They started to cross the big pasture, Willie streaking for home. Danny wanted to help carry Ginny's pack. No, each must carry his own. What was he to do with his can of soup? He'd filled up on hot dogs and marsh-mallows and apples and snickerdoodles—Oh, he had had *such* a good time! He said this over and over.

Distributing the tired children into three cars, Danny still insisted on riding with Ginny and being dropped last.

"Don't you have a problem there?" asked Bea Noble.

"Yes," said Ginny. "I'm afraid I do."

But she dropped Danny last, refusing to do more than slow the car to a stop at his door. And when she reached home, she was not surprised to find the can of tomato soup wedged into the seat of the station wagon.

She gathered her things—her pack, the first aid kit, her sweater—and went into the house.

In the family room. Jan and Bob lifted their heads expectantly, but Ginny was going upstairs. Sarah came in, however, disheveled but content. She'd had a super day, but, boy, were boys dumb! "And Mommy's so tired she doesn't know a Bobcat from a Webelo."

Jan laughed.

"That's tired, all right," agreed the doctor. "We're going to the club for dinner, girls."

"If you don't get called."

"You'll go anyway. It's the least we can do for scouting."

On Monday when the doctors gathered for lunch, coming into the dining room at various times because Monday was always such a wild day, they talked about cases in the hospital. They decided that turkey had been served for Sunday dinner, since they were being fed something the waitress said was hot turkey salad. Alison was ready to dispute the name. How could a salad be hot? And if it was a salad, why were they given apple salad as well?

"Oh, eat your dinner," Dewey Windsor told him crossly.

"Had a hard morning?"

"All my mornings are hard. Could I have the rolls down here where a man is hungry?"

"Still being starved at home?"

"No, I am being the victim of a wife more solicitous of her mate than are other wives."

"Heaven forbid!" said Bob Ruble.

"I thought Hazel looked peaked at church yesterday," said Garde Shelton. "And since I shouldn't have said that, let me tell you Butch's latest."

Heads lifted expectantly. Butch was always a welcome diversion.

"More 'Tinkle, Tinkle, Little Star'?" asked Rufus McGilfray.

"No," said Garde. "Anyway, that was Fiddle. She's coming up a poor second to Butch. No, yesterday—" he reached for one of Dewey's rolls—"yesterday the Sims baby was to be baptized . . ."

"Well, he *was* baptized!" said Dewey. "Cried bloody murder."

"Yes, he really did. Probably wanted to be a Baptist or something. But before we started for church, Fiddle declared that she didn't want to be left in the nursery. She wanted to go to church and see the baby. Butch took over. 'You can't go to church,' said he.

" 'I can, too,' said Fiddle, and of course she appealed to her mother.

" 'And Nan said, 'Well, if you really want to. Though you are pretty young.'"

"Then Butch assured his sister that she would not *like* church. 'They won't let you say one single word!' he said. 'Who won't?' asks Fiddle. 'The hushers," said Butch. '*They* won't!' "

The men laughed. All took their turns being "hushers."

"Did she go?" asked Alison Cornel.

"That's right, you weren't there," said Garde. *He* had been a husher. "None of your family was."

"Was the preacher?"

"Can you imagine Ferrell Linders . . .?"

"No," said Alison hastily. "No, I can't. But he'd been on the hayride, too. That pooped Gene and Carol out. Besides . . ." He accepted his dish of custard. "We have a house guest."

The men's interest quickened. They'd known of no expected houseguest.

"Yes, we do," Alison confirmed. "Came in Friday night. Joined the hayride. And through that somewhat unexpected event, I am afraid my dear wife has caught her foot in a crack."

The men waited. Finally Dewey Windsor said urgently that Cornel could not drop things there. "Or you'd better not!"

Alison laughed and scraped his custard cup clean. "I won't. This is too good. And since we men have taken over the job of serving as clearing house for staff gossip . . ."

"Get on with it!" said Dewey.

Alsion glanced at him. "Aren't you being a bit nervy?"

"Nothing to what I can be."

"All right, then," said Alison. "This is too good," he repeated. He leaned back in his chair, which creaked in protest. Dr. Cornel was a big man. "Well," he said, "It seems that my wife has been helping her daughter Carol to snare a young man."

The men showed their surprise. "How?" asked Rufus McGilfray.

"Lord help us!" cried Alison. "I don't know *how!* But she's been doing it. And Friday night he showed up. On our doorstep, asking for Carol. He's a second-year intern at the University Hospital complex. That's where he met Carol. Seems to be a bright young chap."

"We could use him if Carol does snare him," said Bob Ruble. The coffeepot was going around the table.

"Don't rush things," said Alison. "I sent him off to the hayride . . . Gene invited him to stay overnight in the den, and Saturday there was every sign that, while he came to see Carol, he now prefers Gene to Carol. He followed her from kitchen to living room, intently talking to her. He has a line you wouldn't believe."

"Ignoring Carol?"

"No, he didn't ignore her. His manners were fine. But even when he talked to Carol, he drew Gene into whatever they were discussing. I can see that he must be a fascinating man. Gene, to give her credit, tried to brush him off or divert him. For example, he asked questions about where she trained, where she had grown up. She refused to discuss her past, she said. So the rascal sat on that round green puff Gene bought and invented a background for her. Even to me it sounded fascinating. All this has Gene considerably shook up." Alison was enjoying himself.

"I should think Carol would be shook, too," drawled Bob.

"She is, I'm afraid. She finally retreated to her room after lunch Saturday, leaving the field to this charmer and her mother. And he is a charmer. He'll go far in medicine. I knew his sort in med school and internships. They all have done very well in the profession."

"Poor Carol," said Dewey Windsor.

"Don't worry about it. Gene will think of something to get things back on the track. But her initial shock at the man's capitulation to *her* charms was very funny to watch."

"Aren't you jealous?" asked Dr. McGilfray.

"No," said Alison. "I'm not. I married Gene because I liked her. I am never surprised when other men like her, too."

The men sat thoughtful, appraising the situation which he had described. "Wouldn't our wives have some advice for her!" breathed Bob Ruble.

The others laughed. The wives certainly would have! They declared.

"How long do you think this situation is going to last?" asked Bob, standing up.

"I don't know. Shanahan left for the city by four Saturday. We may never see him again. I am sure Carol thinks we won't."

"But you don't agree?"

"I'm strictly the interested onlooker, Bob."

"Well, don't let it make you stay home from church again. And be sure to tell us more when you know more. Just now, I have a pre-office-hour appointment, and I should be on hand when the patient arrives."

Dewey got up to follow him. "Bob's patient has special interest for me," he explained, hurrying through the door.

Dr. McGilfray and Dr. Cornel, as if rehearsed, asked if Hazel was sick.

"She's been on this diet thing," said Garde. "Reducing drastically . . ."

"But, good Lord. man, she's as thin as a whip to begin with!"

"Yes, she is. But you've been hearing Windsor's complaints."

"I didn't think it was serious. Or lasting."

"I believe she had symptoms that made her think their eating habits were wrong. I don't *know*, of course. But I do know that Nan coaxed her to see Bob."

"Then Dewey told her she had to?" asked Dr. Cornel.

"Something like that probably happened. She was supposed to come in last week. And she didn't."

"Well, it's a good idea. And will probably get Windsor off the hook, too. I hope Ruble tells her to put on weight."

"You might try advising him."

Laughing, the men departed.

The clinic building held the doctor's offices, examining rooms, waiting rooms. This glass-windowed building adjoined the hospital, but was a self-sufficient unit in itself. The offices were set up in pairs. Bob Ruble, obstetrician and gynecologist, shared a large waiting room with Dr. Cornel's surgical patients; they had the same receptionist. This noontime, Hazel Windsor came in, looking miserable, which was not uncommon in that place, but looking angry, too, which was rare.

She was wearing a white blouse, a rosy-red skirt, and a white sweater. She shivered and told the receptionist that she was freezing. The young woman doubted that, so she made no comment. She said the doctor would be coming over any minute. Would Mrs. Windsor like to wait in his consultation room?

"What I'd like," said Hazel, "would be to go home."

But she went back to Dr. Ruble's office and was standing unhappily at the window when he and Dewey came in. "You needn't have hurried," she said.

"We were watching the time," said Bob. "Sit down. I'll be with you in a minute." He went into the lavatory, which he also shared with Alison Cornel.

Dewey crossed the room and touched Hazel's shoulder. "Come sit down," he said kindly.

"Why?"

"Well, it makes things easier for the doctor, and for you, too, if you sit near each other and facing each other." Dewey looked more miserable than Hazel did.

But she did sit down. Dewey took a position on the couch. Bob glanced at him when he returned, having put on a fresh white coat.

"Now!" he said, sitting down and drawing a pad of paper forward. He picked up a pencil. "I suppose the clinic has the vital details on record . . ."

"I'm never sick," said Hazel. "There's nothing wrong with me now."

"Oh?" said Bob. "Well, since you're here, suppose you let me be the judge of that."

Hazel glanced at Dewey. "He doesn't have to stay," she declared.

"Yes, I do, too," said Dewey. "I'm the husband. All husbands come to the doctor's office with their wives. Don't they, Dr. Ruble? You see them tagging along, scared to death . . ."

"Windsor!" said Dr. Ruble. "Shut up!"

Dewey gaped at him and settled back on the couch.

"That's better," said Dr. Ruble.

"Now, Hazel," he said, turning to her. "Relax and tell me how old you are."

But Hazel was prepared to fight him all the way. Dewey watched Bob with awe and admiration as, in one way or another, he got the information he wanted and needed.

And finally he asked about symptoms. Yes, her stomach had been upset lately. But she knew why. She'd found a new low-fat diet, and any diet needed adjusting to. With time, she would be all right.

Bob nodded. "What about medication?"

"Vitamin C," she told him. "Nothing else. I tell you, I'm healthy."

"Good. What about your periods?"

She stared at him.

"Your menstrual periods," he nudged her.

"Oh. Well, as you know, I'm at the age to miss a time or two."

"And you have missed?"

"Yes. It will start up again."

"It may. Now, I want you to let the technician take some blood for some tests. It's all routine, Hazel. Every patient I get has to do this. Then you're to go with the nurse and I'll examine you."

She balked at this. "This whole rigamarole is nonsense," she said. "I'd think you and Dewey both would have other things to do. It's silly for me . . ."

Bob nodded to the nurse who had responded to his buzzer. "Maybe it is nonsense," he told Hazel. "But doctors do a lot of silly things."

She sighed deeply and went with the nurse. Bob shook his head at Dewey. "Just sit quiet," he said, "or go over to your own office and do some of your own paper work." He put on his glasses and picked up a pen. Dewey roamed around the office, and when Bob was about to go to the examination room, he would have followed him, but again Bob shook his head.

"We keep all husbands out of here," he said firmly.

"But, damn it all, I'm a doctor!"

"Not today, not in here. Fifteen minutes ago you were proclaiming that you were a husband."

Dewey declared that it took an hour. Actually, of course, it did not. Within fifteen or twenty minutes, Hazel came back to the office, looking subdued and still petulant. "I don't want to talk about it," she told her husband.

Dewey had only opened his mouth to protest when Bob popped in. "Well!" he said cheerily. He waved a pink lab sheet at them. "Preliminary, of course. Sit down, Hazel. Dewey! This all looks quite good."

"To you," said Dewey dourly. Hazel put on her sweater again, and then did sit down—in a temporary sort of way.

Bob sat down, too.

"You took long enough," said Dewey accusingly.

"I took no longer than was necessary to give your wife the attention you asked me to give her. Will you two relax? Hazel, stop being mad at Dewey. Dewey, stop resenting me in my own office."

"Well, I need . . ."

"I need to get to work, too. So if you'll shut up and listen, I'll tell you my findings to date. The results of the lab work are not complete, but I am sure they will bear out my opinion that Hazel is pregnant."

He leaned back and regarded the astonished, the completely stunned Windsors.

Hazel gulped. "Are you—sure?" she asked in a thin voice.

"Oh, yes. I'm sure. You're about ten weeks pregnant."

Dewey was entirely speechless. He got to his feet; he

pulled tissues from a box on the shelf behind Dr. Ruble, he used them to mop his face and dry his hands. He walked the length of the room and pulled the curtain aside so that he could look out at the lawn and the street beyond.

"Well!" he said at last, gasping the word. "At least I know what's wrong with her lately. After all that thing with Bitsy, I thought she'd gone crackers."

Bob chuckled.

Hazel paid no attention to what was being said. She sat, still shocked and stunned. She shook her head from side to side. Once she glanced at Dewey. "This can't be!" she said.

"Why can't it?" asked Dr. Ruble.

She looked at him as if surprised to find him in the room. "How long . . . ?" she asked.

"It takes two hundred and sixty-six days," he told her gently. "That means early next summer. May."

Hazel stiffened. "It won't happen!" she said firmly. "I'm too old . . ."

Bob glanced at the notes which he had made. "You're forty-two," he affirmed. "Now, I'll agree, that's not twenty-two. But it should not be too old, provided the mother is in good health, as you seem to be, and if she has had no major obstetrical problems. You haven't, have you?"

"No," said Hazel hesitantly. "I just never got pregnant. Before."

"As for her health . . ." said Dewey.

"She seems in fine shape, Windsor. Of course I want her to put on ten pounds . . ."

Dewey was recovering. "Me, too?" he asked eagerly.

Bob laughed, then he sobered again. Hazel was not

accepting the situation at all well. And even Dewey seemed unable to believe what Bob had told them.

"Look, you two!" he said sternly. "Don't you *want* a child?"

Dewey looked up, astonished again. "Of course we want one!" he said loudly. "We've been wanting one for more than twenty years!"

"But not now!" cried Hazel, anguished. "Not at my age. I'd be embarrassed to death!"

The men laughed at her. Dewey came to her side and put his hand on her shoulder. "We won't tell anybody," he teased.

"And I don't believe Bob when he says it isn't dangerous," she declared.

"I didn't say that it could not be dangerous," Bob corrected her. "I told you that you could go safely through a pregnancy at forty-two, with a good doctor in attendance, and if you would do what that doctor tells you to do."

Dewey laughed again. He was getting excited. "Which good doctor would that be?" he challenged.

"Oh, *hush*, Dewey," said Hazel. "Maybe I should remind you how old *you'll* be when this—this *kid* graduates from college."

Dewey bent over and kissed her cheek. "If it's his turn to be embarrassed then," he promised, "he can call us Grandpa and Grandma."

Hazel gulped, and tears began to run down her cheeks. Dewey gave her some tissues and comforted her as best he could. He smoothed her hair, and she pushed his hand away. He patted her shoulder and tried to look miserable himself, though he was prone to grin widely. He murmured things to her . . .

"Yes!" she cried. "Of course I've wanted a child. But not like this. Not this way!"

"You'll get used to the idea," Dewey told her. "I shall, too. And we'll both like it."

Bob sat back in his chair, listening to them, watching them. He himself had, really, been surprised to have these long-time friends finally come to him, and . . . He leaned forward. "Listen, Hazel," he said briskly. "Think of all you've learned, think of all the theories you've had about raising children. Now you're all set for this experience."

Hazel sniffled. "You're making fun of me."

"I certainly am not!"

Again, Dewey patted her shoulder. "You're not to worry," he said. "Everything is going to be fine. Bob's right here to give you all the attention you need; Gene and Nan and Ginny will help you . . ."

"No, they won't!" Hazel cried loudly. "They'll just—they'll just *flip!* Gene will laugh her head off."

"Oh, I don't think so."

"Yes, she will. Besides, we went and decided not to help each other."

"They'll do it anyway. Nan will, I'm sure. Remember, she's in the same boat."

Hazel drew a deep, deep breath. Yes. Nan . . . She sat looking down at her hands, thoughtful. When she looked up, she said diffidently—though Hazel was seldom diffident—"You fellows, don't tell anyone that I'm pregnant."

Bob and Dewey laughed. "I told you . . ." said Dewey.

"The word will get out, Hazel," said Bob gently. "I won't need to promise. You'll tell it yourself."

But she was intently serious. "I won't tell, and I don't

want you to. Something could happen, and then . . ."

"Something won't happen!" Bob assured her. "Just put that out of your mind. You're a fine, healthy woman —or you will be when you've put on that weight I told you about. And you do need that, Hazel; you really do. The baby needs it, too. His nourishment and growth are at stake. Not only now, but through the next seven months. Right up to term. The last three months are especially significant." Now he turned to talk to Dewey. "There is a growth spurt then, a growing time for the infant's brain, and those months are very important. I want Hazel to get her weight and strength up to normal, and in the sixth month begin to help the child's brain develop. There are to be no stringent diets. From the start, I'll give you a diet list which you must stick to."

"But I thought . . ." said Hazel.

Bob nodded. "That a smaller baby helped the mother have an easier delivery. Well, the time is right here and now, Hazel, when your *child* is to be considered above all else. I am in no way in favor of obese children, but I do want your child to grow as fast as possible in this first period." He looked sternly at Dr. Windsor. "I think we should start worrying about coronaries a bit later in life. Say eighteen months later. Now, of course, babies usually pull through. This thing of diet isn't a matter of life or death. It's just that if a baby's brain cannot grow during this vital period, he may not turn out to be the man he could have been."

Hazel and Dewey looked at him, white-faced. An eighteen-month-old child—a man—those were entirely new and startling concepts to them. Dewey coughed and turned away. The truth was sinking in. Hazel stood up and straightened her sweater. "You think then," she said, "that I should try to have this child."

Bob turned her to the door. "I think you are going to have that child!" he said firmly. "Come back in a week, but earlier if anything troubles you."

Initially, Dewey was delighted at the thought of a child of his own, but a passing week or two turned that delight into a gnawing, increasing fear. He could not talk to Hazel about it, not sensibly. But he knew her so well, and he could not sleep for the fears which crowded into his mind. He would wake at four in the morning and worry for fear his wakefulness would disturb her. So he would slip out of bed, put on a sweatshirt and corduroys, heavy shoes and a knit cap, and slip out of the house, Bitsy with him. The green-white yard light still was keeping its watch along the driveway. He walked toward the river, watching a thin band of rosy light spread upward along the curve of the eastern sky, glowing upon the still water of the river, gilding the limbs of the tallest trees. A bird called a crystal note in the darkness, and the stars began to fade. He turned toward home. Soon the sun would be up and the world of people would be ready for the day.

"I woke early and took Bitsy for his run," he told Hazel when he returned, having solved nothing. Fear, joy, and fear again, tormented him. He was caught between moments of joy and anticipation, and his fears. Hazel—what was she feeling? What was she fearing, and what might she do? He took those worries with him everywhere he went, and thought about them constantly.

Hazel had gone to Bob's office again, though protesting. She was obeying his diet list; whole milk appeared again in their refrigerator, chops and roasts on their dinner table, and she was beginning to lose that hollow-eyed, hollow-cheeked appearance of a skull thinly covered.

Dewey looked better, too, and should have felt better. "But he doesn't act better," murmured Garde Shelton, the day Dewey came into the staff dining room for lunch and found a clipping slipped between his ring and his napkin.

"Hunger is said to spur the sex drive," the headline read. "A scarcity of protein increases fertility in women."

With four pairs of eyes on him, Dewey crumpled the paper, thrust it into the pocket of his white jacket, and, white-faced, reached for crackers to break into his soup.

The men exchanged concerned glances and began to talk again of hospital matters. A newly purchased vaporizer was not working. A stroke victim, ninety years old, had, against his physician's advice, been taken to the city for carotid artery surgery, then had suffered heart arrest and had died.

These were matters in Dr. Windsor's field, and by the time he was ready for his sausage cakes and lima beans, Dewey was stating his position on what he called cruel and unusual measures for senile patients. "A stroke can be the hand of God extended to a lonely old man," he said firmly. Then he put his fork down and turned to Garde Shelton.

"Is it true?" he asked. "Did Hazel really tell Nan she should have an abortion?"

Garde was not an easily shaken man. "Yes," he said readily, "she did. She said exactly that. But you know Hazel and her ideas. She was buying, without reservation, the idea that a family should have no more than two children. She took that statement and rode off with it."

"I know she did. I know she would. She reads too much—and now she is being concerned about the age for childbearing. She thinks she is entirely too old to have a family."

"Not so much to *have* one," said Bob Ruble. "But to *raise* one."

"If she ever has a child," said Dewey grimly, "she'll raise it."

"Yes, she certainly will. Right now—she's forty-two." His eyes went around the group. "I would like to have her undergo amniocentesis."

Dewey groaned and covered his eyes with one hand.

Bob regarded him sympathetically. "I am trying to think how to approach her on the subject," he explained.

"The suggestion would drive her right up the wall," said Dewey.

"So would a mongoloid child," Bob pointed out grimly.

"Yes, it would. It certainly would."

"Could she face an abortion if indicated?" asked Garde.

"Oh, yes," said Hazel's husband. "Abortion is her solution for everything, for anything. She has no idea of its emotional impact, or any of the rest of it."

"Are you worried?" asked Alison Cornel, "about her resorting to abortion even without testing the amniotic fluids for abnormality?"

"Yes," said Dewey, "yes, I am. Her reasons haven't extended to mongoloidism yet, though she may get around to that. But she is confused and embarrassed by this late pregnancy . . ."

"We're still not supposed to know about it?"

"I made no promise."

"Have you talked to her?" asked Garde.

"A little," said Dewey. "And I've tried to put my foot down. I've said things like, 'It's my child, too. If you let me give it to you, you should be ready to give him to me.'"

"That's one hell of an argument," said the chief of staff.

"I know it is."

"And you're still afraid."

Dewey made no answer to that, but the men could see that he was.

Garde Shelton cleared his throat. "Maybe you should have Linders talk to her," he suggested. "He is a very wise man."

"We're lucky to have him," Dewey agreed. "And I could speak to him—for her sake, you understand, not only mine."

"Do you really think," Dr. Shelton asked, "that she may be moving . . . ?"

Bob sat up straight. "I certainly would not do it, as things stand now!"

Dewey glanced at him. "Hazel knows that."

"But you still fear . . . ?" Bob began to sound alarmed.

"Yes. I do fear just that, Ruble. I think she might go somewhere. To New York, even to Sweden . . ."

"Then you must not let her leave town."

Dewey laughed. Without humor of any sort. "Now, look," he said. "Hazel has always done things on her own, and not always things I have wanted her to do. Now I just can't tie her to the bedpost. There's a trip coming up next week. The Garden Club is going somewhere . . . Hazel helped organize the expedition. I'll *have* to let her go. There's to be a mum show, and advice on spring bulbs . . ." He threw out his hands in a gesture of helplessness. "Abortions are available in the city now."

"Are the other wives going?" asked Dr. McGilfray. His glance circled the table.

Each man looked doubtful. "I wouldn't let Nan . . ." said Garde. "She'd get too tired."

"They're all busy," said Dr. Windsor. "Ginny and her cub scouts . . ."

"And Gene has her new boy friend," laughed Alison. "Does he still . . . ?"

"He drives up every week. He comes to see Carol, and spends his time with Gene."

Dessert came in then, and almost immediately following it there was an emergency.

But Dewey had given his colleagues quite a lot to think about, and that evening when Bob and Ginny went up to their bedroom at ten o'clock, Bob asked Ginny if she was planning to go on the Garden Club trip with Hazel the next week.

Surprised, she turned to look at him. She had been laying out his fresh clothes—slacks and jacket, shirt and shoes, tie, underwear, socks . . . She checked off the items before she answered.

"How do you know there is a club trip?" she asked.

"I heard about it today. Windsor spoke of it. I'd like you to go, if you could, and stay with Hazel, watch her. Most especially not let her do anything foolish."

Ginny stared at him in amazement. "What's got into you?" she asked. She came toward him.

"I'm worried about Hazel," he told her.

Ginny sat down on the chest at the foot of their wide bed. "Hazel?" she asked. "What's she up to now?"

Bob laughed a little. "She's *up* to being pregnant," he said. "And she . . ."

Ginny knew he was talking, but she didn't listen, she couldn't. She was too surprised, too stunned.

Then she laughed. "*Whoooppee!*" she cried. She got up and made a dance of taking off the bedspread, of hanging it on the rack. Talking to herself, and still laughing, she backed up to Bob to have her red jumper unzipped.

"Are you serious?" she asked, her face still flushed, laughter dancing in her eyes.

"Very serious," said Bob. "A bit over two months. And Dewey is afraid she'll try to abort."

"That she'll . . . ?" Ginny was shocked. "But she couldn't do that, could she? Not without his permission. And she *wouldn't*, Bob!"

"Dewey thinks she might try."

"I don't believe any of this," said Ginny. "I don't believe she's pregnant, and if she is . . ."

"You'd better believe what I'm telling you. That's why I'm asking you to go with her on this trip. Whenever it is."

"It's Wednesday. But, no, Bob, I can't go. I decided that I wouldn't weeks ago. And I've filled my time. But even if I were free, I couldn't decide to go and watch Hazel, and my reason would be the same that I can't pick up the phone right this minute and tell Gene and Nan this news."

"Do you want to do that?"

"Well, of course I want to. All these years we've listened to Hazel tell us how to have and raise our kids we've been saying we wished she'd ever have one of her own so that we . . . But now that it's happening . . . It really is?"

"Oh, yes. I say so, and the frogs and the rabbits say so."

"Oh, dear," said Ginny. "And I can't tell Nan, or Gene . . . Do they know?"

"We usually wait for the family to make these announcements. The men know."

"Of course," said Ginny. "Hazel has been acting strange lately. Goodness, she isn't still planning to adopt that Fishtown boy, is she?"

"I imagine not. Have you heard anything recently about that?"

Ginny shook her head. "That's the trouble. We don't hear anything about anything. That's why I can't call the wives now, and it's why I can't go to the Botanical Gardens and watch Hazel. I'd like to, Bob. I really would. Oh, dear! I don't want things this way, Bob! Poor Hazel. She should have been sharing with us her first suspicion, her first queasiness—I'd have told her about crackers. Gene favors 7up. We could—we *should*—be telling and talking about everything, comforting her. But instead, you will remember, we are leading our own lives!"

"I do remember," cried Bob roughly. Ginny looked up at him in surprise. "I think that decision has gone on for long enough!" he said. "I think you four women, you good friends, are failing each other. Perhaps you will agree with that, Ginny."

"Yes," she said soberly. "Maybe we are failing each other, and we'll be sorry."

"Can't you cut it off?" he asked. "Starting right now?"

She sat down before her dressing table. "I don't know," she said. "I'm all mixed up. I am trying to remember how we ever started the whole thing, and why we did it."

Bob went toward the bathroom. "I'd say the important question, my dear, is how to *stop* the damned thing." He turned on the shower and stuck his head around the door. "You'd better not wait too long, either!" he shouted above the roar.

It did not seem possible, but there it was! November had crept up on Bayard and the people who lived there. Almost at once, it seemed, the leaves were all gone from the trees, except for the clusters of dry, rustling oak leaves which would hang on until a gusty day in March. The evergreens showed up rich and dark, and sometimes people would drive out just to look at the holly trees against the red brick walls of the Cornel home. Hazel was envious of that holly. She, too, had planted trees, three of them, without a berry to show for her trouble and loving care. Of course she had barberry which glowed rosily under her windows . . . and barberry was getting scarce.

This particular day was a crisply cold one, but the sun was shining, and she found herself enjoying her walk with Bitsy late in the morning. Just now Dewey was taking the dog for his early morning run. Poor man. He was branching out in all directions in an endeavor to help and reassure his wife. Hazel did feel sorry for him.

She swung along briskly, with Bitsy as usual tugging at the far end of the leash, wanting to strike off and investigate each more distant and fascinating smell and sound.

Hazel circled the four sides of a two-block area, noticing that a neighbor had a very attractive swag of dry corn and wheat and green velvet ribbon on her front door. She stooped to lift and set aside a tricycle abandoned on the sidewalk by a child. She regarded her own home from a two-block distance, and decided it was looking as she wanted it to look—clean, attractive and warm, not overplanted and yet not stark. The Gaines house, across the street from her, was stark. Just recently, that woman had cut down every juniper and yew, and a truly magnificent sugar maple. Now her foundations showed up like—like—

Hazel leaned forward. Someone was sitting on her red brick doorstep. She should have brought her glasses . . .

It was a boy—no hat or cap—red hair— Why, it was Jay! From Fishtown! Why wasn't he in school? What did he want? Well, she knew what he wanted. Of course. Food, and what he called a piece of money. He always wanted that. She and he had come to expect her to do for him, to help him.

Well, she had bought a sweater and some knit shirts at the church rummage sale . . . And a bowl of soup would not be too much trouble.

Though she knew that Dewey did not think she should, when alone, invite the boy to come into the house.

"Why aren't you in school?" she asked when she reached her front walk.

"I've gone every day this week."

Today was Wednesday.

Inside, Hazel fed Bitsy and took off her coat and scarf, laid her gloves on the small chest beside the garage door, and asked Jay if he was hungry.

"Yeah. Sure."

That was what she thought. Well, she could and would help the boy there. Though now, of course, there was no chance of adopting him. She was glad she had not spoken of that idea to Jay. She would not completely abandon the idea—but nothing could be done for the timebeing. Not now!

She thought about what she would feed Jay—she had learned from experience not to bring forth too much food or to give him a choice. What he didn't eat, he thought he was privileged to take away with him. There had been the day when she had brought out the end of a ham which she had baked. Jay had said, sure, he could carry what he didn't eat. He even knew where to find a plastic bag to put it in. Dewey did not think her story funny. He said she was a sap, and the boy was taking advantage of her. And again he had urged Hazel not to bring him into the house.

On this day she fed him generously. Two bowls of hot soup, toast. No, she said, she did not have peanut butter. Yes, there was jam, and a bowl of doughnuts which Ginny had brought the afternoon before. She produced the sweater and shirts, and firmed her will enough to tell him that a quarter and three pennies was all the change she had. "I don't keep cash in the house, Jay."

"Why not?"

"Because you'd come around begging for it."

He grinned engagingly and asked if he could watch TV.

"I don't think so, Jay. I'm not feeling very well. I think I'll lie down."

"Gee, don't get sick, Hazel."

"You are *not* to call me Hazel!"

"I know. I forgot."

"The doctor doesn't like it."

"I know he doesn't. But he's a nice guy. I like him."

Finally she got rid of him, and she actually did go to the bedroom, knowing that she would not lie down. Though she might as well. She didn't know what else she should do. This matter of—

She was a person who liked to plan things. Her days, her life. But beginning last September when Bitsy had been lost, nothing had gone according to her plans. Then she had just dropped everything until the dog was found. And after that there was Jay to be thought about and planned for. She and Dewey could have adopted the boy; they could have worked with him and taught him not to lie and steal—to keep himself clean and go to school. With Dewey's cooperation, they could have. The boy liked him. Much better than he liked Hazel. She had an idea that he despised all women. Well, at times she couldn't blame him.

Standing where she had stopped in the middle of the bedroom, she was faced by her own reflection in the wide mirror over the dresser. She leaned forward a little to study the woman she saw there. She put her hand to her white hair. She had had gray, then white, hair since she was twenty-six. It had never bothered her before, but now . . . If she were going to have a child . . . She wore it short, in loose, pushed-up waves, vigorously brushed and burnished. Now, should she color it? Let it grow and twist it into a knot or a French roll? And her clothes— slacks and pullover sweaters had become the rule with her. Today the slacks were dark blue . . . She did have some dresses, a suit with a skirt, one long dinner dress . . .

She folded her hands across her abdomen and turned

sideways to the mirror. If this thing were happening to her, this dismaying thing . . . Fifteen years ago, and certainly twenty, she would have been delighted, and by this time in the process, she would have rushed out and bought what Dewey called hatching jackets, or she would have made some for herself. She liked to sew. She would find out about maternity slacks, and shorts, and skirts, and . . .

But *now?* Now, *what* was she going to do?

Make plans, that was what. It was what Hazel did for any circumstance. If she and Dewey took a weekend trip to the Ozarks, or a three-week trip to Europe, she made plans. Lists, lists, and lists. Now there were other plans and lists to make. For herself, for her time, for the house —for the yard. A baby in May would upset her whole gardening schedule.

As for the house . . .

There were two guest rooms. One was a rather large room with twin beds, rattan, shellacked, with spreads and draperies of white sprigged with pale green vines and pale yellow flowers, a yellow carpet. A cool and lovely room. The other guest room was small, and next to the huge room which she and Dewey enjoyed, with their own bath and TV and bookshelves, and a picture window that overlooked the fenced yard and garden.

When Storm Linders had spent some time with them, the small guest room belonged to the visitor. If Jay had become a member of the household . . . It, too, had its tiny bath, with a green curtained shower. The bed was pushed against the wall, without headboard or foot-board, covered with a quilted spread of violet and pale green. There was a pale green carpet, and a deep purple armchair.

Not a nursery! Not a baby's room. Though she would have had to change it for Jay . . .

Now must she . . ? Yes, she must. If things were to go along as Bob Ruble thought they would . . .

She positively would not use teddy bears or kittens, or rabbits . . .

Oh, she didn't want to use, or think of, *anything!*

And certainly she didn't want to *do* anything! Because what, what, *what* was she going to do?

That evening, Dewey was late coming home. Hazel had things ready for their dinner—small steaks defrosted, potatoes and salad ready for the last half hour of preparation. The table set.

She was sitting in the living room, Bitsy at her feet—until the dog heard Dewey's car come into the garage. Hazel listened to the noisy greeting, but she did not lay aside her knitting. Dewey would hunt her up at once; he always did these days. And he did tonight.

"I'll take you out later," he told the ecstatic dog. "Let's go see Mamma first."

He had called her that from their first year of marriage. It had no special significance now. But now, instead of stopping in the kitchen for a can of beer, or for some cookies, or to peer into a pot on the stove, he strode right through the dining room into the living room, with a quick, concerned first look at Hazel.

She knew he was worried about her, from his eyes. He'd been looking at her that way ever since Bob Ruble had said she was pregnant.

Now he bent over and kissed her cheek, then went to his chair on the other side of the hearth; he picked up the evening paper, but he did not look at it.

"I'm late," he said. "Flu shots and bad throats and worse stomachs."

He laid his head back against the leather cushion. Dewey's hair was white too, cut into as much of a crew cut as he could get from his barber. When had his hair turned white? Not as long ago as had Hazel's.

Alison Cornel jokingly claimed that it was something they ate.

Dewey didn't look old. His skin was as pink as a baby's . . . Hazel shivered and looked down at her knitting.

Was something wrong with her that Dewey knew and Bob Ruble had not told her? In which case . . .

Did Dewey wish she were not pregnant? That first day he had seemed delighted, foolishly so. But afterward—he just looked troubled and anxious. If he, too, were dismayed at her pregnancy, why didn't he say so? He must know that she had every doubt in the book! She believed she would ask him . . .

"Hazel!" She jumped a little, having been so absorbed in her own thoughts that she had forgotten . . .

She looked up, then glanced at her watch. She should turn on the broiler . . . "Jay came to see me today," she said quickly.

"And you fed him."

"A bowl of soup and some doughnuts. An apple."

"What else did he want?"

"I don't give him money, Dewey."

"Well, that's good. I hope he doesn't help himself."

"He wasn't out of my sight. Besides . . ."

"He took my drill from the garage."

Yes, he had. And Dewey had put the fear of the police into the boy when he claimed it. "What does he need money for, Dewey?"

"Food. Winter shoes. He can't wear sneakers in the snow, though I'll bet he has. Hazel, how about our taking a trip?"

Was that what he had started to ask her? "Can you get away?" she asked, turning her knitting in her lap and fastening the needles. She must get dinner ready.

"I can get away for a few days. I had only a short trip in mind."

"Where . . .?"

"The city, if you'd like that. Or Florida, perhaps. Far enough, and for long enough, that we both might consider the decisions we have to make. Maybe we could go to New York, take in the theaters and a concert."

And the clinics where abortions were easily possible. He must have decided that abortion was their only sensible course. This trip was going to be his means, his chance to persuade her . . . He was unaware that she herself had reached such a conclusion days and days ago. From the first. Bob objected, but if Dewey stood ready to agree and help . . . Of course she wished this pregnancy had come early enough that they could go through with it, accept the child and happily raise it. But now—She shook her head from side to side, and her hand smoothed the red wool in her lap.

As he so often did, Dewey read her thoughts. She knew that he could, and had protested the ability. Now he dropped the newspaper to the floor, stood up, then came across to her. He bent over and laid his cheek against hers.

"The day is coming," he said, his voice so close that it vibrated, "when you—when we both—will be swept with a great, hurting love for that child you are carrying, Hazel. You will be fierce in your protection of it, you

200

won't want anything to hurt it. So, if that is in your mind, you'd better get rid of it quickly, or you'll find yourself protecting it and defending it. Either way will hurt, but the time is here, right now, for you to decide which hurt you want." He kissed her cheek, straightened, turned on his heel and walked out of the room.

She sat where she was. She heard him whistle to Bitsy, she heard the garage door open and close. On the hearth, the logs slipped; sparks and a flame shot up into the chimney. And she sat there, her head back against the chair cushion, her hands clasped across her stomach, a dreamy, faraway look in her eyes. *A great, hurting love.*

Dewey . . . Sometimes he did talk to her that way. Stating his position, but making her know that it must also be hers. The hurt he had spoken of was the hurt which was his, and would be.

Chapter Eight

It was, of course, a November evening, too, in the Cornel home. Dark was pressing against the windows, and the doctor was fussing with the fire in the den.

"Why don't you build one in the living room?" Gene called above the noise of the blender in the kitchen.

"You just cleaned the hearth in there."

"Oh, Plumy did that. She thinks I want the ashes out completely."

"Can't you explain to her . . .?"

"Not to Plumy," said Gene, and she heard Carol and Alison both laugh.

She stopped the blender and looked at the salad dressing she hoped she was making; Carol and her father were talking in the den. Carol had some foolish idea of doing Plumy's work until she went back to her nursing studies.

Gene had no intention of allowing that. She thought about the salad dressing; she thought about Plumy, and fireplaces, and largely against her will, she thought about Mike Shanahan.

Once encouraged, that young man was proving to be impossible to get rid of. The first time, he had stayed until the last possible minute, sleeping in the den which often served as their guest room; the couch made into a comfortable bed.

And Mike had returned. "To see Carol." Three times since. Every time he had a thirty-six-hour break in his hospital duties. He had a small foreign car, and it ate up the fifty miles between Bayard and the city in no time.

He came back, he was lovely to Carol. This past weekend he had brought her some Wyeth Christmas cards to use that year. They were wonderful, exactly the sort of card Gene hunted for and liked to use. When she said so, Mike beamed at her and said for her to come back with him; he'd introduce her to the shop; it was called Printer's Ink, and . . .

And before she really knew that it was happening, he had moved in.

From the first, Carol knew what was going on. Gene saw the way she would pick up a book and tuck into the living room couch to read. While Gene and Mike . . . The visit before, the weather had been as warm as summer, and they had sat out on the side of their hill, overlooking the river. The trees stretched down and down the slope; where they sat, the outcropping of bleached rock was warm in the sun. Gene wore a gold-colored pullover and white stretch pants. Mike took out his comb from his light jacket and combed her hair, parting it, drawing it down into a thick, uncurled bob . . .

"There! You look younger than Carol!"

She felt younger, too, enjoying the intimacy of his attentions. He had knelt beside her, close and warm.

Once he had threatened to slip and she caught at him—he caught at her—and held her there in his arms for a long, long minute.

She freed herself and looked up at him. "You could have had a nasty fall," she said.

"And you'd care."

"Well, of course I would care. Think of the fuss. Rescue squad, ambulance—with your face spread all over the side of the bluff . . ."

He leaned closer and kissed her swiftly. Now she could still feel the brush of his soft beard.

That afternoon she had panicked, and she panicked each time she thought of what had happened.

She was in a panic now. She liked Mike; she liked him a lot. She liked feeling young and attractive enough to interest a most attractive young man.

But of course she must get Mike straightened out. He had made ways of getting off alone with Gene—that hour on the hillside, or five minutes in the kitchen when he reached glasses down from a high shelf for Gene. He'd even gone to church, and had sat with her. Carol was in the choir, Alison was on call at the hospital. So the handsome, bearded young man sat beside Gene, his arm in his blue tweed suit jacket against the hound's-tooth arm of her suit; they'd sung from the same hymnal; Gene had left the church beside him and introduced him to her friends.

"Dr. Shanahan, a friend of Carol's, here for the weekend."

"Hey!" he had whispered. "I'm a friend of *yours!* I am here to visit *you!*"

If he should ever say or suggest such a thing to Carol, it would crush the girl. And Carol was not the one to take that sort of bruising experience. Gene didn't want to find out if she could bounce back.

So she must talk to young Shanahan, and tell him . . . He had a way of twisting her words, of overpowering her and taking over the conversation.

She could, she supposed, write him a letter.

She unwrapped the hamburgers and thought of what she would say. It must not sound like any letter she had helped Carol write. She must be brief and explicit—and in a letter, she would avoid a face-to-face discussion with him, avoid the feeling that this brash young man, this charming young man, was about to take charge of her life, and with it her home, her family . . .

But of course a letter would not do. It already was Wednesday and any letter she might write that night would not get into the mail before tomorrow. The post office, as it stood those days, could not be counted on to move a piece of mail fifty miles in less than two days . . .

And before he could pick up his mail on Saturday, Mike would be on his way to Bayard. If he had only twelve hours, he still would come, and she would have to handle him face to face.

She knew that he would come, and she alternated between the determination to have a showdown with him and a wish to run away. She even suggested to Alison that they drive to Kansas City over the weekend.

"Can't get away," he said gruffly. "I'm on call this month."

There were times when she thought he detected the panic Mike Shanahan had put her in.

"But you and Carol might go . . ." he added, his eyes sparkling.

Yes, he probably did guess.

Saturday came. Gene was right there at home. She had a roast for dinner, and Mike did not arrive.

This threw her into a panic of another sort. Was he taking the initiative and abandoning the Cornels? After the way she had done with him, taking him to church, letting him comb her hair, she must be the one to step aside. But if he didn't come around . . . Then of course she must write her letter to him. And she panicked again. She even asked Carol why she supposed he had not come.

Carol only shrugged. "Did he say he would?"

No, he had not *said* . . .

"Have you invited him for Thanksgiving?" asked Alison unexpectedly.

Gene stared at him. She went numb at the thought of his being there. She never could conceal from the other wives the way Shanahan was behaving . . . nor from Susan . . . or Jan Ruble. And certainly her own behavior would be under scrutiny . . .

"It's strictly a four-family affair," she said coldly.

"He probably would like to come," said Carol. "Maybe he expects to."

"Tell him how things are the next time you write," said Gene, her fingers cold to the tips.

"Oh, I don't write to him," said Carol. "Now that he comes up here so often."

So panic continued to hold Gene, and she hated it. She had not felt so since she was in high school and afraid she would not be invited to a dance, and even more afraid that she would be.

She was acting and feeling younger than Carol, and just about equally inept. The idea of a woman of her age, and supposed poise, not being able to handle a man!

All she would need to do was to tell him plainly that she would not hurt Carol. He was to pay full attention to the girl, and let Gene devote her time and attention to household and family affairs. Unassisted by any—any *intern!*

And if that did not work—it should at least keep him at the hospital!—she would tell him that she had composed the letters which Carol had sent him and which evidently had attracted his attention.

As it happened, on Sunday, when he did show up, she had to say most of these things. To do it, she chose another walk along the bluff. At the last minute she had the inspiration to ask Carol to go with them. "I think I know where there still might be persimmons." She would tell Mike, in front of Carol, about the letters, making a big joke of it, depicting Carol as a tease—with too much time on her hands. She would tell that, together, they had "whomped up" lots of letters to various men.

Carol agreed to go with them, but said she was pretty sure that, by now, the raccoons and squirrels would have eaten every persimmon.

They had a fine hour or two in the briskly cold sunshine, scrambling over rocks, cutting some bittersweet; finally Carol went down the hill to see about the persimmons, leaving Gene with Mike, who denied having any goat's blood.

And Gene made her little speech about not wanting to hurt Carol, but she didn't quite come out with the confession about the letters.

Mike said he quite understood Carol's being bored with her lengthy convalescence. He was glad if his visits had helped relieve that.

Then his hand fell on Gene's arm. "And fondly glad," he continued, "because I have come to know you. Look, Gene— Can't you get away during my next break? If you'd come to the city, we could have a real whirl. There are restaurants, Previn is conducting the symphony— and we could explore a shopping center. You wouldn't believe what they turn up in those places!"

Just minutes before he had to start back to the city, Gene came back into the house in a fine glow, followed by a panic that was worse than she had felt before. She had basked in the sunshine of this man's flattery, and her sunburn was going to show! It certainly was!

She knew the dither she was in. And she could not remember if she had invited Mike for Thanksgiving—or not.

Holy hailstones! She had better get hold of herself, or enter the funny house voluntarily.

Garde had talked to Nan enough about Hazel and Dewey that she knew Hazel was pregnant, and that Dewey was worried about her, and about what she might do to herself.

"Does he think, because she told me to have an abortion . . .?"

"No, I really don't think that is the argument with Hazel, nor that Dewey feels it is. But her age—he calls it embarrassment—perhaps she overexaggerates the danger possible—Dewey feels sure she has abortion in mind."

"Wouldn't she risk their marriage if she did anything of the sort without his consent?"

"I'd think so. There seems to be grave danger in the Windsor household, Nan."

She sat troubled. "I'd do anything I could," she declared. "But, Garde, dear, I don't see how I could offer help. I have to wait until she comes to me and tells me there is a problem."

"Couldn't you girls get together, decide that it would be better to do a little meddling in each other's lives?" Anxiously, his fine dark eyes searched Nan's pretty face.

She nodded. "I suppose we could do that," she agreed. "But—" Her face brightened. "I'll think of something! I promise you that I will."

"Quickly?"

"Right away. I'll find some way of getting Hazel here to help me do something. She is always in a good mood when we agree that she knows more than we do."

Garde laughed. "All right. If that's what it takes."

Garde had said Nan must not lose any time. And she would not. That evening and the next morning she went around in a fog of thinking. She could speak to Ginny and to Gene. And they would eagerly respond . . . Too eagerly. Hazel, jumped at by the three women, might declare her right to make such a decision on her own, and she would do, most probably, something foolish. She had done that way before. Of course not over anything so big as aborting a child she had desired for twenty years! But, advised by her friends not to change the color of her house, she had immediately had it painted light green, then had hated it. Dewey had firmly refused to let her change it at once back to white.

"You gotta wait until I earn the thousand bucks," he'd told Hazel. That four years had been funny—at times.

The results of this threatened reaction would not be

funny at all. So Nan redoubled her thinking about ways
. . . and means.

At eleven o'clock, she decided to call Hazel and invite
her to lunch. She planned to have Ruby fix her good
sauce over shrimp and cheese on a toasted English
muffin. Hazel would like that. And Nan would talk to
her.

She made the call, Hazel said yes, she guessed she
could come. Was there something important . . .?

Nan said she thought there was.

Hazel said, all right. Was twelve-thirty good?

"Fine. We'll get the kids fed at twelve—have our own
lunch in some peace and quiet."

She would set a small table before an open fire in the
back parlor of the Victorian house, she thought. She
pulled on her plaid lined coat and ran up the street for
a few fresh flowers. She found red and pale pink button
mums; she brought them back and filled a pewter syrup
pitcher . . .

Hazel was enchanted with the arrangement. She
shrugged out of her tweed coat, pulled the scarf from her
hair, and went to the fire. "It's really cold outside," she
said, warming her hands. "The sun is shining, but—"
She shrugged and did not finish the sentence. She was
wearing a red plaid skirt, a white blouse, and a red pullover sweater. She looked tired and pale.

"She's worrying," Nan told herself. "If we could just
talk—perhaps she could relax, we'd both get rid of our
worries, and break down some of the barriers that have
risen between us . . ."

Hazel was being polite. She again commented on the
fire, the table, the flowers. She asked Nan how she was

feeling. Was she still reading poetry?

"Oh, yes," said Nan. "And trying to memorize it. The current one is Santayana."

Hazel laughed. "That doesn't sound like you."

"How do I sound?"

Hazel shook her head. "I should wait until you recite today's poem. Let's have it."

Nan smiled. " 'It is not wisdom,' " she said, " 'to be only wise, And on the inward vision close the eyes. But it is wisdom to believe the heart. Columbus found the world and had no chart.' "

"How's that?"

Hazel's blue eyes were wide. "I like it," she cried. "And I withdraw my decision. Oh, hello, Ruby."

"Good morning, Mrs. Windsor. Are you ready to eat now, Miss Nan?"

They were ready, and the warm plates were brought in, with a salad of lettuce and avocado slices, fragrant coffee in a small silver pot.

Hazel began to eat with appetite. "I get so tired of planning my own meals," she confessed.

"I suppose you do. You must come here more often."

"I thought you had some other reason for asking me today."

"I do," said Nan, entirely composed. "I thought you could help me figure out some way—the best way—to tell Butch and Fiddle about the new baby."

"Don't they know?"

"Not yet. It's still so early . . ."

"Well, there's the bootee bit."

"They'd decide I was making doll clothes for Christmas."

"Mhmmmn. I suppose they would. Well, then there's—" She and Nan turned their heads at the small sound from the hall doorway.

There stood Butch, looking at them, uncertain that he would be welcome. Ruby had told him that his Mommy had company . . .

"Hello, Butch," said Hazel, and his face broke into a relieved smile.

"Hello, Mrs. Windsor," he said ecstatically. "Mommy, may I shake hands?"

"Of course. Come in."

He came quickly and held out his small paw, which was clean because he himself had just eaten lunch.

"We had soup," he volunteered, "and applecot juice, and what else?"

"Cookies?" Nan suggested.

"Oh, yes. Do you have cookies?"

"No, I'm afraid not."

"I could get some. Ruby keeps them in a heavy jar, but she'd put some on a plate if I'd ask her."

"Butch . . ." Nan attempted.

He glanced at her. He was a handsome lad, and would be tall like Garde. Nan was always thankful that her daughter, not her son, had her own physical characteristics—small bones, delicate features . . . Both children had her glossy, dark brown hair.

By now the little boy was ready to take over the conversation. "Mrs. Windsor," he said chattily, "I have been wanting to ask. How is Jay, the boy who lives down in Fishtown? By the river, you know. Did you know that the river, farther downstream, gets called the Big Muddy?"

"Yes," said Hazel, "after the Missouri joins it. That's

because the Missouri is muddy; it brings down all the silt from the mountains and the plains . . ."

Nan sat back in her chair and listened to Hazel instruct Butch, who always was ready to be instructed.

"But you didn't tell me how Jay was," the child said. Like Garde, he never lost the thread of a conversation. "And I've been wanting to ask you: how big a packing case does he live in?"

"Well, Butch . . ."

"Do you have one at your house?" Butch persisted. "Is he going to live in it when he comes to live at your house?"

Hazel look wild-eyed at Nan. What was she going to say to this child? How was she going to deal with a question which she had put to herself, and found no answer?

How did he know so much about Jay? Had she, to her friends, committed herself to care for Jay? Had she made promises to the boy?

"Do you know Jay?" she asked Butch.

"No, ma'am. But I know Bitsy, and when he got founded again . . ."

"*Found*," murmured Nan.

Her son glanced at her. "Yes. *Found*. And I liked it when people said a little boy *found* Bitsy, and . . ."

Nan sat helpless. She well understood the situation in which Hazel found herself. She seldom told Butch to stop talking, though there were times . . . She scrambled through her mind for ways to divert the child. Usually she could do this, guide the line of his talkativeness. She could see that this lengthy consideration of Jay was disturbing Hazel—and Nan had not brought her here to be disturbed!

Unable to find any other effective way to quiet Butch or, at least, to change the direction of his talk, she said, gently but firmly, that Mrs. Windsor was preoccupied just now . . . "Do you know what preoccupied means, dear?" she asked.

Butch's face brightened. He dearly loved big words. "Oh, yes!" he agreed. "It's a long word for busy!"

Nan laughed, and so did Hazel. With relief, no doubt.

"Well, Mrs. Windsor is *preoccupied*," said Nan, "because she has decided to have her own child, and of course she has to think about that first . . ."

Belatedly she glanced at Hazel, who was staring at her in amazement. "How did you know that?" she cried.

Nan filled their coffee cups. "Don't you remember?" she asked calmly. "I was the one to tell you first that you might be."

On his part, Butch was taking the whole thing casually. "That won't make any difference," he assured Hazel. "If Jay lives in that box, you'll have plenty of room in your house for a baby." He turned to throw out his small arm in an all-inclusive gesture. "I live here, and Fiddle does," he said, "and one of these bright days Mommy is going to have another baby. We have room for one, and so will you. They're little, you know."

Leaving his elders speechless, he said he guessed he'd go see if Fiddle was taking her nap. He would play with his truck, or maybe read . . .

Sturdy brown Oxfords, brown knee socks and shorts, and tan pullover all disappeared around the hall door, leaving Nan and Hazel to gaze at each other, and then, when they felt it was safe, to collapse into laughter.

"Why should we ever, *ever* worry about the kids?" Nan asked. "We should always let them handle things!"

"He's a remarkable child," said Hazel, wiping her eyes.

"Cuts things down to the essentials, doesn't he?" Nan agreed. "Do you want more coffee, Hazel?"

Hazel did not, and Ruby cleared the table. "Since Butch brought it up," said Nan, settling comfortably with some knitting in the corner of the velvet loveseat— Hazel sat in the wing chair close to the fire, "what about Jay?" she chuckled. "Somehow I can't see him and his packing box on your patio."

Hazel nodded, smiling faintly. "Dewey and Rufus McGilfray have promised to take care of that boy. I don't know what they plan to do, or even if they'll do anything —but just now, for the time at least, my hands seem to be tied." She sighed deeply.

"If they have promised, they will take care of him," Nan assured her. "I think you can trust those two."

"I hope so. He needs so many things. But Dewey thinks he stole Bitsy, and he caught Jay in a fib and made a big deal of it . . ."

"He's interested, Hazel, or he'd just tell the boy to clear out, and give him no more thought."

"I suppose."

"He'll keep his promise. Now! What about you? How do you feel? And what are your plans?"

Hazel did not answer at once. For several minutes, she sat gazing into the fire. She looked tired and sad.

"Hazel?" Nan jogged her.

Hazel looked around. "Oh, I'm all right," she said. "Bob Ruble does say I may be pregnant, but I probably am not. I'm at the age . . ."

"You are not."

"Forty-two."

"So what? That would be young . . ." Nan frowned over a kink in her yarn. "Don't you want a child, Hazel? I always thought you and Dewey . . ."

"It's not a matter of *not* wanting one, Nan! I do want one." Hazel leaned forward in her chair. "Oh, I *do!*" she cried earnestly. "But what I want—what I *really* want—is to be as young as you are, with years ahead of you to spend with your child, to raise him, and enjoy life together."

Nan put her knitting aside. "Hazel," she asked anxiously, "are you *afraid?*"

Hazel gulped. Nan heard her do it. Her hands were clasped tightly in her lap. "Yes," she said, almost in a whisper. "I am afraid. This is—it would be—too much to ask at my time of life."

Nan shook her head. "Bob will take very good care of you," she said.

"It's more than just having the baby," said Hazel. "That won't be easy, but I'd take that. It's more the thought— Oh, say he's a boy and wants to play football. But his mother would be so arthritic and old she couldn't go to the games, or have parties afterward . . ."

Nan stared at her. "*Gee whiz!*" she said, and Hazel looked at her in surprise.

"Well," Nan acknowledged the uncharacteristic exclamation. "But you're worrying about fifteen or twenty years from now! With kids, you take one day at a time!"

"Not me," said Hazel. "I see *ahead!*"

"And make yourself miserable! About a future that never happens," Nan rebuked her.

"I know . . ."

Nan picked up her knitting again. "What color was

216

your hair?" she asked. "And Dewey's? Were you blond or dark?"

"Dewey had a sort of reddish-blond hair. Mine was strained dishwater."

Nan smiled. "I'm trying to picture the fat, healthy baby you will have," she explained. "He will turn brown and delicious in the sun, like a plump cupcake. He'll play in the sand, and tumble about on your grass. Of course you want that baby, Hazel!"

"I know," said Hazel. "I used to think I knew what I wanted. Exactly. And would make plans. But now . . ."

She got up from her chair and moved about the room. She looked at the oval-framed portrait of Nan's grandmother, she picked up a small gold frame that held dried violets, she smoothed her hand across a curved chair back.

She was upset, worried, and Nan decided it was time to talk of other things.

The weather seemed changeable. Only normal winter weather, said Bob.

"But it isn't winter yet!" Ginny protested.

"Oh, you're a calendar watcher. When I get cold between my shoulders, it's winter."

And so it was, she decided that afternoon when she and her station wagon full of cub scouts met the Reverend Ferrell Linders on the street corner, with his church only a block away.

She pulled to the curb and rolled down the window. "I would ask if you'd like a lift," she said, "but we seem fresh out of space."

Laughing, he came to her. "You mean you have a boy

in there for each pair of hands and legs?" he asked.

Bright boy-faces, blue and gold neckerchiefs, the wagon was full! Ginny's face, too, was bright, and her dark-lashed eyes were merry. A thick blue tweed coat must be keeping her warm.

He spoke to the boys, asking what project they were up to now.

"We were going back to the church," Ginny explained. "This afternoon we collected magazines—well, mostly pages from magazines. The boys are gathering material for the boxes they are going to make for Christmas gifts. We want appropriate pictures to *découpage* the lids. They'll be handkerchief or jewel boxes, we'll line them with stick-on paper . . ."

"Contact paper," explained one of the boys.

"That's right," said Ginny. "Thank you, Franklin. And we'll put hinges and hasps on the lids . . . But just now the *découpage* is our interest. I'm afraid several mothers will get pictures of football heroes. One of these sprouts wanted to cut pictures from Bob's medical magazines; he was fascinated by those gory things. How would it grab you to open a package on Christmas morning and find a straight-on view of a gall bladder?"

Mr. Linders laughed and shook his head. "Holly would be better," he admitted.

"Say, Mr. Linders!" called a boy from the far end of the wagon. "Do you have some pictures of angels and stuff?"

"I might have," the clergyman agreed. "We can look."

"They want chromos," murmured Ginny.

"Of course. Primitive art, like cub scouting, is for eight-year-olds to eleven." His attention focused on the small boy who sat in the front seat—who sat there quietly, not saying a word, not squirming, not getting on his knees to throw jabs at the boy behind him. His eyebrow went up to the den mother.

"It's Danny Gaines," she reminded him. "I don't think he knows what picture he wants to put on his box."

"We could talk about it," he suggested.

Ginny nodded. "Yes, we could—sometime."

The Reverend Mr. Linders needed much less than that clue. He reached a long arm and opened the door of the wagon.

"Why don't you boys," he said, "stretch your legs a little before getting down to this *découpage* work? You could run down the hill to the river and back . . ." Boys already were spilling out of the station wagon. "Not stopping to throw a single rock!" he added, raising his voice.

And there they went, whooping off, a scamper of feet and bobbing heads in the winter sunlight. Even Danny Gaines went, though more slowly than the others, and he kept looking back at Ginny.

"Do you have a crush?" asked Ferrell Linders, getting into the seat which Danny had vacated. He rolled up the window.

Ginny was laughing. "I have more than a boy with a crush," she said. "Haven't I talked to you about this before?"

"Evidently not enough. Doesn't your problem get any better?"

"Sometimes I think so. Generally, I don't. He—I talked to his teacher at school. They, too, think the problem is in the home. He skips school. He doesn't engage in games or projects at school. I find that he seems to enjoy the hikes we take, and he eats any food offered him, but he shows no initiative, and doesn't talk freely. He clings to me . . ."

"Because you're a nice person to cling to."

"Because he must live, he has had to learn to live, in an atmosphere of shelter, perhaps repression."

"You're quite a psychiatrist."

"I'm not, really. But I have to find some explanation. I don't think Danny is getting anything from cubbing."

"Oh, he probably is. Do you know the parents? Have you talked to them?"

"I've been to the home. Do you know that house? It is simply crowded with antiques! I can't imagine their survival with a small boy around. I have not talked at all to Mr. Gaines. I've seen the mother a few times; she calls me on the phone—usually to caution me about letting Danny eat too many marshmallows, or to ask if he got sick on a hike. He never does, incidentally. But—no, I've never really *talked* to her."

"Perhaps you should make that effort, Ginny."

From where they sat they could see down along the steep street; the boys had reached the river's edge, and some were making brief side excursions along the stone-paved levee. They would soon turn and come back, taking longer on the uphill climb. "I suppose," said Ginny, "that I should try to get to know Mrs. Gaines. I am really interested in Danny, and I want all the boys to get something out of scouting. But it won't be easy . . . Hazel Windsor lives just across the street, and—"

"And Danny's grandparents live next door."

Ginny turned to face him. "Why, I didn't know that!" she said. "Do you know them?"

"No, I don't. Just that they live there; they are Mrs. Gaines's parents . . . I've had no reason to call. But, you know, Ginny, since I've come to Bayard and hope to continue here, I have been trying to learn the pattern of the town. Not just the people of my church, but others as well. So—I know about the Gaines family, though not much."

Ginny smiled at him. She liked Ferrell Linders; she liked him very much. Now he asked her what she heard from her daughter Mary, who was the wife of his son Storm. The young people were expecting their first baby early in the new year.

"I hoped they could come for Thanksgiving," said Ginny. "I know Christmas is out of the question."

"You could go there?"

"The whole family would want to, and that would be as disastrous as for her to drive here. Bob and I shall probably go down a time or two in the next weeks."

"Storm and my father will see that she has proper care."

"Oh, we know that. They talk of her going to the Maternity Hospital in the city a week before she is due."

"Yes, and Gertrude is available in the home if she is needed."

"Me too," said Ginny. "I'll probably go down whether I'm needed or not." She sat back in the car seat, smiling gently.

"Everyone seems to be having a baby," said Ferrell Linders. "How is Hazel doing?"

"That seems to be the worst-kept secret in town," Ginny said, laughing. "But she . . ." Her eyes widened. "I have to confess, Mr. Linders, that I know very little about her and how she is. I ask Bob nearly every day, and he says she's all right. But he doesn't *talk*, and I am realizing, forcibly if not for the first time, the twit

221

we wives—the wives of the four clinic doctors, I mean
—and we would *be* in a twit over Hazel's having a baby
after twenty years of marriage. Normally, we would
be."

"Normally?" asked Mr. Linders.

"Yes. You see, until just a few months ago, we four
wives—Bob said we lived in each other's apron pockets.
And we did! We came here to Bayard together. Well,
Nan didn't, but she and Garde were married only a year
after the clinic was enlarged to take the four men in. And
being strangers and doctors, we families clung to each
other. We selected our homes and remodeled them. That
is, the Rubles remodeled. The Cornels built their home,
and that really did take the concerted effort of the four
families."

"I can imagine."

"It did. My Sarah was born, and both of Nan's babies.
We did *everything* together! We gave advice, whether it
was asked for or not, or welcome or not."

As she talked, Mr. Linders was watching her vivid
face.

"We'd telephone each other, see each other, every day.
And then—last September—I think it was over whether
Hazel should buy a brown coat—suddenly we women
decided not to interfere so much in each other's lives, to
be friends, but independent, to let each other alone. And
this just about completely changed things for us. That's
why we learned slowly about Hazel's baby, it's why we
don't know exactly how she is, why we aren't trying to
do things for her . . ."

"As you normally would have been doing."

"Yes! Bob says we've lost something important."

"He could be right. Was this a vow you four took?"

"Oh, no. We just agreed—it was just a mistake we made. Bob is sure it was a mistake."

"Well, a person can always acknowledge one of those, Ginny, and retrace one's steps."

She smiled at him. "Thank you," she said.

The boys had come up the hill again; some elected to walk down to the church, Mr. Linders with them. Danny crawled into the seat beside Ginny.

"It was cold down there," he said when she asked if he had enjoyed the run down to the river.

The boys worked for an hour, and when she took them home, Ginny was still thinking of the "mistake" she had confessed to Mr. Linders. She drove from house to house; she answered the boys' questions, she made comments of her own—and she thought, depressed and sad, of the time which the women had lost, of the events not shared and so forever lost in the chronicle of their lives. This seemed a terrible sacrifice . . .

She took Danny home last, as had become her custom. The other boys didn't mind. In fact, some of them had brought their bikes to the church, and they took themselves home. But Danny . . .

"I didn't know your grandparents lived next door to your house, Danny," she said, by way of starting a conversation with him.

"Yes, they do. Only they aren't really *my* grandparents."

"Don't they feel that way about you? I mean, don't they love you?"

"I guess they do. But they're real old. And they call me 'Baby.' "

Ginny laughed. "Grandparents do things like that, Danny. Don't you like it?"

"Oh, I guess it's all right. They buy me anything I want."

That was enlightening. "Did they buy your bicycle? The ten-speed?"

"Yes, they bought it. For Christmas last year."

And he had never learned to ride it.

"Bicycles like that are very expensive," said Ginny admiringly.

Danny shrugged his thin shoulders.

They had reached his house. Ginny glanced at her watch, but she turned into the driveway instead of dropping the boy at the curb. Mrs. Gaines had the front door open before Danny could get out of the car. Ginny got out, too, to go speak to her. The large woman was wearing a housecoat.

"Good evening, Mrs. Gaines," she said, clutching at her hair in the brisk wind. She stepped up into the shelter of the small entrance.

Mrs. Gaines had kissed Danny, and now stood half in, half out of the stormdoor; she tightly held the folds of her blue robe. "I've been lying down," she said, sighing and puffing. "I live on medicine, you know, and sometimes I get dizzy spells. I expect it's the medicine as much as anything. You know? I am allergic to bee stings. I have to carry some medicine for that with me all the time." She fumbled in the robe's pockets, brought out Kleenex, a candy bar, and finally a small glass tube. She shook it at Ginny. "I swell up," she confessed, "and I could just die within minutes."

"But there aren't any bees about now," said Ginny.

Mrs. Gaines probably did not hear her. "My nerves are about to collapse," she said. "Poor Danny . . ." She looked around for the boy, who had ducked into the house. "It's no wonder he's a nervous wreck."

Danny's teacher had said the same thing. "It's no wonder . . ."

"Shouldn't you go in out of the wind?" said Ginny.

"Yes, maybe I should," said Mrs. Gaines, backing into the hall. Ginny followed her, again struck by the crowded furniture, the duplication of literally everything! Who needs three pink china lamps? she asked herself. "Is he?" Ginny asked aloud.

Mrs. Gaines looked at her in surprise; she had sunk into a green velvet platform rocker. Ginny did not sit down. "Is he what?" asked Mrs. Gaines.

"You said Danny was a nervous wreck, and I asked . . ."

"Yes. Oh, yes. Well, of course he is, and why shouldn't he be? I am a sick woman—and his father—he's three years past retirement age, but he keeps on working, goes to his desk every morning, comes home by five-thirty every evening. He eats supper and is in bed by eight-thirty. I don't think he says three words a day to the boy. Or me neither."

"Are you worried about Danny?" asked Ginny, wishing that she knew what to say to his mother. She had never had such a problem with her cubs. Some boys dropped out, some were half-hearted, some families didn't seem to care, but . . .

"Of course I'm worried about Danny," Mrs. Gaines was saying forcibly. "If anything—" She broke off to clutch her breast and to pant for air. "If anything should ever happen to that boy, I'd kill myself."

"Oh, now, Mrs. Gaines. Nothing is going to happen to Danny."

"Well, I sure hope not. You do take care of him on the trips and at the meetings, don't you?"

"I take care of all the boys, Mrs. Gaines," said Ginny with dignity. "But the idea is for the boys to learn to be independent, to learn to take care of themselves."

Mrs. Gaines sighed again. "But he's so little . . ." she said pitiably.

Ginny could think of no answer to make, so she left the house.

Danny, who must have gone out through the back door, shedding his cub neckerchief but not his uniform, was riding up and down the driveway behind her station wagon. He was seated on a tricycle much too small for him, his knees drawn up to his chin, his back hunched forward. Wedged before him was a battered stuffed dog.

Ginny laughed at him. "Who's your friend?" she asked.

He frowned.

"Is it a dog?"

Then he laughed. "Yes! He is my friend! I've had him since I was real young."

"Did you ever have a real dog?"

"Just Mamma's poodle. But he isn't mine. I can't really play with him."

"And he couldn't ride your ten-speed bike, either."

This also puzzled Danny. Ginny touched the handlebar of the tricycle. Then the boy laughed. "Oh!" he cried. "You know this isn't a ten-speed bike, Mrs. Ruble. Jan has one . . ."

"Yes, she does. She has lots of fun riding it, too."

"I know. But maybe I would fall off of mine. Anyway,

my trike is all Mamma wants me to play with. And my dog."

"Those are your toys."

"Yes. Mamma says I can't hurt myself with them."

"No," said Ginny. "I guess you couldn't. Would you go up on the walk, please, Danny? Where I can see you as I back out."

He obeyed cheerfully. Ginny gathered some of the magazines which they had collected that afternoon to search for pictures for the *découpages*. She held one out to Danny. "Would you like to have this?" she asked. "It's a sports magazine, full of pictures. There's an article on Johnny Bench . . ."

Danny shook his head. "No, thank you," he said. "I don't like to read."

"You don't?"

"No, ma'am. I guess it's because I don't read very well. I mean, it's hard for me."

"Oh, dear. Do you suppose that's because you don't go to school regularly, Danny?"

"I guess so. The teacher said I should 'tend 'mediable reading classes, but that made Mamma mad."

It would. Remedial reading would not ever be for Mrs. Gaines's precious "baby."

"I think you should at least go to school regularly, Danny. And learn to read. Someday you'll want to drive a car, and you can't get a license if you can't read. You know, don't you, that you have to have a license to drive?"

Danny nodded. "But that's all right," he said, his face brightening. "Mamma is a good driver."

And she wouldn't want him to drive a car, would she?

thought Ginny bitterly. "What sort of car does your mother drive, Danny?" she asked.

Again that shrug. He didn't know.

"Does your father drive a car, too?"

"Yes."

"What kind is it?"

He shrugged again. "His is just a little car. I think it's gray."

"Well . . ." said Ginny, turning the key in the ignition of her own car. "Stay on the walk now . . . I'll see you next week, Danny. Bye."

He waves his hand like a child of two, thought Ginny. Not at all retarded mentally, the boy still was not being allowed to grow, to develop. He was the first ten-year-old she had ever known who could not tell the makes of automobiles.

Ginny's head was still shaking from side to side as she drove under the carport at home. "I simply must *do* something about that boy!" she was telling herself.

She went into the house and was greeted joyously by cat, dog, her husband, and her children.

"Kitchen love," she told them, but she was equally glad to see them. "Let me go to the bathroom, and then guess who's going to help me unload the wagon."

"Can't we get dinner first, Mom?"

"We can, but I don't think we'll need to, Jan. With help, it won't take ten minutes."

She hung her tweed coat in the closet, and went on down the hall.

Of course when she returned, Jan and her father were unloading the wagon. Sarah was looking at the picture magazines. Ginny told about the boy who wanted to use a medical journal.

228

"D'you think he's a med school recruit?" asked Bob. Jan had made a face.

"I think he has a gory mind," said Ginny. "Bob, have you ever heard it said that scout work tends to form the young into a mold?"

"Oh, there are those who find ways to detract from anything that is well established, Ginny. Careful of that plywood, Jan, sugar baby."

Jan grinned at him. "I'll put it in a bag or something," she said. "This isn't the first year Mom's cubs have made boxes."

"I was thinking how different my boys are," Ginny told Bob. "They are when I first get them, and I've decided that I don't put my thumbprint on them to any great extent."

"Oh, I'm sure you do. Why? Are you having problems again?"

"Still," she corrected, going into the kitchen and putting on an apron. "Dinner by the time you get the table set," she told the girls.

Jan stared at her. "How can you . . . ?"

Ginny nodded to the corner of one of the green counters. "I've had an old biddy-hen cooking in my crockpot all day," she explained. "With potatoes and carrots and an onion. I'll bake biscuits for the gravy, make a fruit salad . . ."

"Then *voilà!*" cried Jan, going toward the dining room, calling to Sarah to come help. The younger daughter needed to learn how to set a table.

Ginny mixed and rolled out her biscuits, and told Bob about Danny Gaines. "Do I talk about him all the time?" she asked.

"Just some of the time."

"But, Bob . . ." She told about the tricycle and the reading.

"You've already talked to his schoolteacher."

"Oh, yes. But I believe they've given up on him, though maybe only on his mother. That woman really is incredible, Bob."

"What's inedible?" asked Sarah, who had come to the kitchen for napkins.

Laughing, Ginny explained to the child the difference in the two words. Sarah went off announcing that she wanted some funky jeans like Jan's. And a glitter t-shirt.

"Maybe you have a problem right here," said Bob.

"By Christmas, even Jan won't want funky jeans. But to go back to Danny. I really do mean to do something about that boy."

"As, for instance, what?" asked Bob, his tone dubious. "Won't you need advice and help? I mean, interfering can get sticky, sweetheart."

"Sure. I know that. Will you ladle the chicken into the bowl, Bob? Or put the crock down where I can see into it?"

"I'll fetch the ladder," said Bob, who already had the crock open and the ladle and fork in his hand.

"Lay the more prominent bones in the pie pan," Ginny instructed.

"I thought maybe a lesson in anatomy . . ." The kitchen was filled with the delicious perfume. The cat and the dog, the two children, all came to the door.

Ginny smiled at them. "Not bad for a den mother, is it?" she asked. "I thought," she said to her husband, "that I'd ask Mr. Linders to help me, Bob. For that advice and help. And perhaps Rufus McGilfray, too. Or would being a nervous wreck come under his jurisdiction?"

"You? Or is the boy . . . ?"

"Not really. He's insecure, dependent—"

"Go to Ferrell first. Then—" he spoke quietly. "I still think you should ask your friends, Ginny."

For a long second or two, she gazed at him, then she smiled. "You bet I will!" she cried. "It's exactly the sort of thing . . . It will be worth a get-together. Just this afternoon I was telling Mr. Linders how much I regretted our not getting into a tizzy over Hazel's baby."

"She's stirring up a full-sized tizzy on her own."

Ginny looked around from the oven. The biscuits were done. "Is she really?" she asked. "Poor thing."

"Why do you say that?" asked Bob. "Don't you think she's lucky, finally, to have the prospect of a child?"

"Oh, yes, I do! But, still . . ."

"You're dubious about how she will handle the whole affair."

"I guess I am. Maybe I'm going to have to think about that point—as well as about how we are going to handle Hazel's having a child."

"You can't do it alone, that's for sure," said Bob, picking up the tureen and starting for the dining room.

Chapter Nine

These thoughts of course stayed with Ginny for the rest of that evening. By the next day she had decided to start with the "mistake" made by the four doctors' wives. Someone had to make a move. She well might be that one, and with the matter of Hazel's pregnancy of prime concern to them all, she decided to act at once.

She could have called the women together—but Hazel would hear of the meeting, and perhaps be hurt by her exclusion, maybe suspicious of Ginny's motives. She could even be angry at what might seem to be disloyalty, a disrespect of their agreed-upon policy.

It would be better, though of course more time-consuming, to go to see the other wives, one at a time.

She would start with Gene, dropping in casually, and she could begin by asking about last-minute decisions concerning the Thanksgiving dinner. There certainly had been much less than the customary foofuraw about that, with no decisions made that she knew about.

It was a very gloomy day, not quite freezing or thawing, but with a mist in the air and a dusting of snow upon the ground, unexpected slick spots on what looked to be only wet streets.

She found Carol and Gene in the wide upstairs hall of the house, laboring over the making of a caftan. Now, when Gene sewed, her friends usually backed away ... It was not a talent with her, but a matter of labored trying and multiple frustrations.

"Do you know how to make these things?" she demanded of Ginny.

"Yes," said Ginny, laying her coat, scarf and gloves on a chair. "Hazel has made a couple of them that are lovely."

"Humph!" said Gene.

"You really should not have started with a border print, Gene."

"Now you tell me," said Gene grumpily. She had evidently washed and rolled up her hair; the edifice of curlers was covered, somehat, by a turban of pink toilet paper. This made her look topheavy and—

"If you stretch that material as you are doing," said Ginny, "your hem will curl." She found a chair and sat down.

"Oh," cried Gene, "I do wish you wouldn't know so much, and then tell me."

Ginny laughed. "I at least know you won't like a curly hem."

Gene nodded. "You're right, I won't," she said. She laid her scissors aside. "Come on down to the kitchen. I'll make some coffee."

Gene's kitchen was a beautiful area. Glass-fronted cabinets displayed her array of china, silver and glass. The breakfast space at one end had a wall mural of old French style paper—pale green, dusty blue, black and white—the scene one of carriages in the Bois, the time 1890 or thereabouts. The wide window looked out across the river valley, its colorings much like the essential ones of the wallpaper, though the sun was trying to break through the low clouds.

"How are your plans for Thanksgiving coming along?" Ginny asked politely.

"Is that why you came over?" Gene was frequently just that blunt.

"Not really," Ginny replied in kind. "I want to get your ideas on how we are going to manage Hazel if she is pregnant."

Gene did not turn from the counter where the percolator was beginning to bubble, and she was putting crisp cookies on a plate. "Is she pregnant?" she asked.

"Haven't you heard?"

"Only rumors. Hazel hasn't told me."

"And she won't, probably. But the frogs, rabbits, or computers—whatever they use—say she is pregnant. Bob says she is."

"That should be authority enough."

"We feel it is, but Hazel still hasn't accepted the fact. As a fact."

"Well, she will have to accept it, won't she?" Gene seemed cool, almost indifferent to what, normally, would have been an engrossing item for lengthy discussion among Hazel's close friends.

She brought her tray of coffee cups and cookies to the breakfast table. She talked to Ginny, she listened when Ginny talked. She made almost no comment when Ginny ventured to say that she missed their old way of conferring and talking over each other's affairs.

After a half hour of this, Ginny left, having decided that Gene had something on her mind other than the affairs of her friends. But what could be worrying her? She had said that Carol was doing quite well and hoping that her father would let her return to the nursing school in January.

But, yes, Gene was bothered about something, and Ginny had not found enough courage to question her. Which did seem too bad, under the circumstances.

Feeling this defeat in her purpose, she still decided that she would go on to Nan's and talk to her. She and Nan had been the ones not to want the regime of withdrawal into privacy. She would let Ginny talk about Hazel.

She entered the Shelton home by the side door, pausing to gaze at the river which lay like a sheet of steel just below their garden wall. Gene's house commanded a broad and distant view of the river; the Sheltons had it below their windows.

The children were in school—Fiddle in a private nursery school, Butch in the public school kindergarten; Nan was making stuffed dolls for their Christmas.

"Garde says this probably will be the last year that Butch will allow Santa to bring him a doll—" She laid the length of blue denim down and gazed at Ginny, her eyes troubled. "I don't like calling him Butch . . ." she said.

"You can't fight it," Ginny assured her. "Remember how Gene's mother always called her *Eugenia?*"

Nan laughed. "Yes, and even now one can get Gene's attention by using that name."

Ginny told that she had been at Gene's house, she

spoke of the caftan. "She had some beautiful material. Cotton as soft as silk, with a red and blue India print, some swirls of gold . . ."

"Border?"

"Yes, it was."

"She'll ruin it. She should ask Hazel to help her."

"I doubt if she will. I tried to talk to her about Hazel, and she didn't seem interested. I think she has something on her mind."

"What kind of something?"

"I don't know. I didn't ask her. I settled for stating my concern about Hazel."

Nan looked up in alarm. "Has something new happened?"

"If you mean, has Bob said anything— No, he hasn't. But it has occurred to me that we should all be rallying around Hazel just now, helping her, talking to her, and to each other about her."

"I agree with you," said Nan. "But if Gene won't talk to you, and Hazel won't . . . Dewey is worried about her. So I am, too, of course. It was one thing to have her talk to me about my obligation to have an abortion because I already have two children. It's quite something else, and more serious, for her to act, talk, or whatever it is she does, to make Dewey worry. He's afraid she'll go off somewhere and have one."

"That would be terrible, Nan."

"Yes, it would be. Garde says it might destroy their marriage."

"I would have thought . . ." mused Ginny. "I always did think she wanted children."

"Yes. Though, of course, at her age—"

"Is she afraid?"

"I believe she is. Not for herself, maybe, but because she thinks she can't carry the child to term, or she thinks something is sure to be wrong with it. As you know, she doesn't talk to us, but I invited her and Dewey for supper on Sunday—just clam chowder and hot bread before the fire . . ."

"Sounds great."

"It was, somewhat. But Butch came in all excited because Ruby's daughter's cat had kittens, and he wanted to know if he and Fiddle could have one of them . . ."

"And Hazel . . . ?"

"Yes. She got pretty excited. I'm afraid she frightened my little boy somewhat; she said, rather loudly, that it would be terrible for us to have a cat in the house when I was expecting a baby. She said it was dangerous! And —you know Butch—we let him speak up, because we think that is his right. Not to be rude, of course, but . . ."

"I understand," said Ginny, looking sorry.

"I know you do. We base our child-raising on the successful Ruble method."

Ginny's face pinked, her eyes shone. "What a nice thing to say!" she cried.

"It's true," said Nan firmly. "Your children are human beings."

"So Butch asked Hazel *why* a cat didn't belong in the house . . ."

"Yes, he did. And she said that cats sometimes carried a disease which could be harmful to the unborn baby."

"And Butch decided . . ."

"Yes. That we couldn't have the kitten."

"What did the men have to say?"

"After Butch left the room, you mean? Well, Hazel

explained for them. She said this disease could cause a miscarriage or a malformed child. Then Dewey changed the subject."

"But— We could ask Bob."

"*I* asked Garde, and it seems that Hazel has told Dewey enough that the men had had a discussion on the subject."

"I'm glad *they* are getting together!" Ginny spoke emphatically.

"Well, they are. Incidentally, I don't think any one of them approves of our recent standoff attitude."

"What did Dewey find out, what did Garde tell you about cats? Why, we've always had a cat!"

"I know. And Ruby says Miss Hazel is sure crazy!"

"She has a point, perhaps." Ginny folded her hands in the lap of her blue skirt and waited.

"Well," said Nan, now stuffing the blue denim leg of Butch's farmer-boy doll with shredded foam. "Garde said that cats *sometimes* do carry a small one-celled organism called toxoplasma-something-or-other which can invade the expectant mother's body and be transmitted to the fetus by way of the afterbirth. Just *sometimes*, Ginny!"

"I understand. Go on."

Nan laughed ruefully. "That's precisely what I said to Garde at that point, and very reluctantly he told me that in rare cases—he accented the *rare*—the invasion might cause a miscarriage or the enlargement of the fetal liver. It also may cause calcium deposits in the infant's brain."

"And of course all those things could happen to Hazel's baby."

"I'm afraid so."

Ginny sighed. "Well, I've always thought that we'd

have a time handling Hazel if she ever got pregnant."

"And we are. Though poor Dewey . . ."

"I don't see how he endures it. But one thing is certain —He, and all of us, must *do* something about Hazel's ideas."

Ginny stayed with Nan for another hour, and late that afternoon she told Bob about her visits. She said she was really worried about Hazel. Was he?

She had waited until he had got himself settled in his recliner chair before the family room fire, with their own cat on his knees, and Willy snoring on the hearthrug. She brought a bowl of apples, a pan, and a knife with her.

"Now what?" asked her husband.

"I'm going to make hot apple dumplings for dinner."

"I meant, now what about Hazel?"

"Oh, well, today Nan told me about the cat thing." She looked up questioningly.

Bob nodded. "Yes," he agreed. "That must have been pretty tough on Windsor. And I don't think it did much for Nan's serenity. We have a cat, and the Cornels do. If we all go there for Thanksgiving dinner . . ."

"Is there a chance, Bob?"

"There's a *chance* for all sorts of things to happen. There was for each of your babies."

"Nan seemed to think Dewey's main worry was that Hazel might have, or try to have, an abortion."

"He's worried just about sick over that," said Bob, getting up to mend the fire. "He knows that if an abortion were indicated, I'd speak up. But he doesn't want Hazel to dash off and have the thing done out of embarrassment."

Ginny's head lifted sharply. Bob's eyes were grave.

"But you can't mean that!" she cried.

"Yes, I do. It is her basic fear. She hides it—she thinks she hides it—behind all her arguments concerning cats, and mongolism, and their being too old to see a child through college, but really—"

"She thinks people will laugh at her."

"Yes. That's why she didn't want it told that she was pregnant."

"But there's no reason for her to be embarrassed, Bob!"

"People don't always need a reason for their behavior, Ginny."

"Oh, dear," said Ginny. "Don't they?"

"No, they don't. That's why I've been urging you girls to persist in an effort to talk to her."

"And go on the Garden Club trip."

"Yes, though that was called off. But I do wish she could be persuaded that her pregnancy is a normal thing, and should be, literally, a happy event, whenever it happens."

"I see what you mean," said Ginny, picking up the last apple. "And I have been trying, Bob. Nan and I are in full agreement, but Hazel . . . Can't *you* talk to her? Though I suppose you already have. You're her doctor."

"That sounds reasonable," said Bob. "Only—Hazel hasn't been to see me since those first two visits."

"Why not?"

Bob shrugged. "I told her what to do. And I told her to come back in a month."

Ginny stood up. "Let's go to see her. Them."

"Right now?"

"No. I'll make my dumplings."

"With caramel sauce," he specified. "Cream is fattening."

She rumpled his hair as she passed him. "And the kids will be coming in . . ."

He followed her to the kitchen. "Do I make a fair conclusion that you are ready to give up your no-meddling agreement?" he asked, nibbling on an apple peel.

"Gracious," said Ginny. "I gave that up before we started. I have been meddling for so long that I wouldn't know how to stop." She got out the rolling pin and a small bowl. "Anyway," she said, dipping flour, "we won't have to mention our agreement. Tonight, you're to do the meddling."

"Me?"

"You."

Shaking his head, Bob returned to the family room. But he knew that he and Ginny would be going to the Windsors'.

They did go, of course. The girls came in from their post-school activities, Sarah from her Brownie meeting, Jan from junior choir practice at the church. Both must be given time to tell about their day. Ginny listened and commented and went on with her preparations for dinner. The dumplings were greeted with cheers; there was a letter from Bobby to talk about. He said he thought he'd go respectable, and could he have a camel's-hair topcoat for Christmas?

"You're sure that's from *our* Bobby?" his father asked, reaching for the sheet of notebook paper.

"I've read that the college kids are more serious these days, dear," said Ginny.

"I'll wait and judge for myself."

The table was cleared. Jan said, sure, she'd stay with Sarah. The familiar reminders about phone calls, and keeping the doors locked, were gone through. Yes, Jan knew the Windsor number . . .

And finally Bob and Ginny were on their way in his small blue car. Ginny had wrapped a soft white shawl about her head, and Dewey called it a fascinator when he admitted them to his house. He bent and kissed her cold cheek. "Doesn't that tightwad have a heater in his car?" he asked. For some reason, the kiss brought tears to Ginny's eyes.

She helped Hazel finish their dinner dishes, while Bob and Dewey lit the fire in the living room, talking about the emergency which had made Dr. Windsor late coming home from the hospital.

When finally they all settled down, Bob and Dewey occupied the fireside chairs, Ginny sat beside Hazel on the couch. Hazel was knitting something from brown wool, and Bob told about Bobby going respectable.

"It won't last," Dewey predicted. "Pre-med students aren't the style setters of any campus."

"How would you remember?" Bob challenged him.

Ginny thought that was not the right thing to say on this particular evening.

Quickly she told Hazel about Gene's caftan, and the men must be told what a caftan was.

"She'll ruin her material and end up with a bare summer dress," predicted Hazel.

"Not for tonight, I hope," said Ginny, pretending to shiver. "It's damp and cold out."

She hunted for another subject for conversation. She decided she would ask what the brown wool was turning into when Hazel lifted her head, laid her knitting in her lap, and abruptly asked, "Will you do an abortion for me, Bob?"

For a long second there was not a sound in the room, not a movement of any kind. Pretty, curly-haired Ginny sat with her lips parted to say what she had been planning to say, before.

Beside her, Hazel, in her dark blue skirt, sweater and white blouse, sat rigid, her hands so tightly clasped that the knuckles were white. White-haired Dewey and handsome, graying Bob sat in their high-backed chairs like manikins in a shop window, their feet extended to the fire's warmth, Bob's fingers cupped around his pipe bowl.

Then, with a shower of sparks, the logs rolled on the grate. Dewey sprang to seize the poker and push them back . . .

"Let me," said Bob, quickly at his side.

"Watch your hands, surgeon," growled Dewey, kicking at a heavy log.

"Watch your own hands," Bob retorted, sounding angry. "Wait, Dewey! You're putting the big log in front —the fire will burn that way, but little heat will get into the room."

Talking so, the men, together, poked and jabbed at the fire, but they finally returned to their chairs. Dewey took out his handkerchief and mopped his face.

And again the room was silent.

"Are you going to answer my question, Bob?" Hazel asked, her voice brittle.

Bob glanced at her. "No," he said.

"It would be only simple good manners . . ."

"I meant, no, I will not perform an abortion for a healthy mother who should be having no problems." He was white-faced and stern. "Tell me," he cried. "Why *should* I do such a thing? Why *should* you ask me to do it?"

Hazel's fingers wove a basket against her skirt. Her eyes were wide, and intensely blue. "Because I—" she said. "Because Dewey and I are both too *old!* Too old to start a family, too rigid in our ways. We have made no place in our lives for a child, or in our home . . ." Her hand swept out in an all-inclusive gesture. "You know how we live. Look at this house. Every single thing in its own place, not to be moved, touched, or broken. Take Bitsy, for instance—" The toe of her shoe touched the fat old dog who slept on the rug before the couch. "Bitsy's too old, too, to be disturbed, displaced. As for Dewey and me, we'd be just like the Gaineses across the street. Any child of ours would be treated the way Danny is, the way that has been distressing Ginny all fall. We'd be so frightened of that small life that we'd wrap the child in cotton, and . . ."

"Oh, shut up, Hazel," said Ginny, too shocked to embroider her speech.

Bob made some sort of sound, not a chuckle, not a means of agreement, though certainly he was not protesting her bluntness. He pointed the stem of his pipe across the hearth at Dewey. "What do *you* think about all this, Windsor?" he demanded.

Dewey looked up at him, but he shook his head. Obviously too shocked to speak at all. Again he brought out his handkerchief.

"Okay," said Bob, rising to knock his pipe against the andiron. He sat down and took out his tobacco pouch. "You know, Ginny," he said, as if they both sat alone in the pretty room, or as if they were before their own fire. As if the Windsors were not present at all. "I am sorry for these people," he said thoughtfully. "Deeply sorry for them. I can only think that Hazel forgets she wanted to adopt the boy from Fishtown. Eleven years old, and you and I know what a boy going into his teens can do to a house. Heavy old boots, cookie crumbs, and tipped-over Coke bottles, doors slammed, or left standing open. But she thought she and Dewey had room and time and interest enough—not to mention youth and strength—to take on that wild kid with all his faults and bad habits firmly established. But she doesn't want a child of her own, a tiny baby to love and to cuddle, and teach to eat the things he should in the way he should, to speak and to be listened to, watched when he is sick, boasted about when he . . ."

"Stop it!" screamed Hazel, jumping to her feet. Bitsy yipped and slid under Dewey's chair. His hand dropped reassuringly to the dog's head. He was watching Hazel as if he looked at a stranger. Curiously. Waiting to see what this unknown woman would say or do next.

"You have to help me!" she cried in anguish. "You have to, Bob Ruble!"

"You don't think we should leave things to Mother Nature?" Bob asked mildly.

"No, I do not! Your Mother Nature is playing funny tricks on Dewey and me. Mother Nature should have given me a child twenty years ago!"

Ginny thought Hazel was close to hysteria, and she looked anxiously at Bob. He nodded reassuringly, got to his feet, went to Hazel, and took her two hands in his. Dewey did not look at them; he now seemed to be watching the wispy blue flame which licked along the backlog in the fireplace.

Bob was being firm with Hazel. He held her hands in

his and turned her. "I want you to look at Dewey," he said. "Do you see him, Hazel?"

Bob was a tall man, with an air of competent ease. He was strong, but always seemed relaxed, ready to wait out a crisis. Beside him, Hazel was like the shaft of a steel arrow, tense, quivering. And Dewey, that usually kind, humorous man, friendly, ready to laugh or make others laugh—Dewey sat sunken into the embrace of the tall-backed fireside chair. His fingertips dug into the velvet of the arms, his eyes still stayed on the fire, on the chiffonlike wavering of the flame.

And Ginny watched them all, her breath held in her wonder at what was happening, and what would happen next.

"Now tell me," Bob said, dropping Hazel's hands, putting an arm about her slender shoulders, "are you able, Hazel, to see Dewey the day that nice guy first holds his own child in his arms?"

Ginny's gaze moved to Hazel; she saw her friend's face grow still, she saw the eyes quiet and become thoughtful.

Her lips parted. "As a matter of fact," said Hazel, her tone one that she might have used to add some item to a grocery list, "it won't be the *day*, Bob, when that happens to Dewey. It will much more likely be at three in the morning." Now she was arguing. Gently, but still arguing. "He will have sworn mightily to have been wakened so early—he always does swear—and he would, he will, that midnight, even to take me to the hospital. Oh, yes, he'll be in a fine temper."

Now Dewey's head lifted, and he turned so that he could look at his wife. There were three deep lines between his eyes.

"And," Hazel continued, "when you take the baby to see him—you don't do that for all the fathers, but you will for Dewey. When you take the baby out to see him, you'll have to wake him again. And he'll swear again."

Dewey nodded. "Yes, I will," he said quietly. "I'll think we should have managed the whole business better!"

They laughed. They all laughed together, these good friends.

On the way home, an hour later, Ginny laid her head on her husband's shoulder. "Will it puff you up unduly," she asked, "if I tell you that you are wonderful?"

"There's a limit to how puffed up I can get," said Bob, smile crinkles at the corners of his eyes. "I only said what Hazel was keeping herself from saying to herself."

"You knew that?"

"I knew she had closed the door—a heavy, wooden-planked door—against what was going to happen next May."

Ginny nodded. "I do thank you."

"Remember, we have six or seven months still to get through."

"I'll remember. Is a case like Hazel's a challenge to you, Bob?"

He made a growling sound in his throat. "More like a persistent headache. She'll phone me at every twinge, Ginny, worry over every change in her body and its functions, panic about nothing . . ."

Ginny laughed. "And she'll be the source of complete information to poor Nan."

"Oh, yes," said Bob. "She will indeed. But Nan will

lean on the fact that she has accumulated experience which Hazel will ignore . . . But I think they will both survive."

"And their doctor, too, I trust." Ginny was laughing softly. Then she stiffened.

Bob glanced down at her. "Something?" he asked.

"Something. I just had a thought."

"Oh, my."

"But I did, Bob. And look! Do you know what is happening to *us*?"

"No," he said. "Is anything . . .?"

"There certainly *is* something. Here Hazel and Dewey are going to be getting ready for their first baby. And we—you and I—*we* are about to become *grandparents!*"

Chuckling, Bob swung the little car into their street. "And you don't like that?" he asked.

"It isn't that!" said Ginny. "Of course I *like* it! I'm happy and excited and worried—all the delicious things for Mary. But there's still Hazel. I *don't* want her going around feeling younger than me. She isn't."

"No, she isn't. As for her feeling—Do you want to do something about your status?"

Ginny slumped back into the seat. "Just get into the carport, Grandpa, without scratching my wagon. I had it washed today."

It was Jan who brought Ginny's attention back to her resolve to do something about Danny Gaines.

For the past months, Jan had been giving her mother some things to worry about. Ginny recognized the "phase" through which her daughter was going; it was natural for the tomboy little girl to attain adolescence, and to have the change noticeable in many ways, including her behavior. But she had not enjoyed seeing her little girl Jan, of the short black hair or the pigtails, turn into a long-legged, short-skirted junior miss, curling her hair religiously, worrying, thinking, talking about boys, chattering endlessly on the telephone—hardly ever going to the stable and pasture to care for and ride the horses. But this day—

Ginny was stopping in to see Hazel almost every day, so it was quite natural for her to drive home from a shopping expedition by a route that would take her past the Windsors', quite natural for her to stop, and thus to see Jan, who did seem to be . . .

Why, she actually was teaching Danny Gaines to ride his ten-speed bike!

The old, too small trike stood on the sidewalk before the Gaines's front door. But in their driveway and going down into the street—Mrs. Gaines would have a puffing, wall-eyed fit!—came the yellow and chrome ten-speed, Danny on the seat, Jan running along beside him, ready with a steadying hand should he falter.

They went up to the corner of the street, cautiously turned and came back. Ginny got out of the wagon and watched, fascinated. Jan spied her and smiled widely. They went on down the street, going faster and faster, and Ginny watched them, not believing what she saw.

Not only was Danny riding his bike—Jan now was only running along beside him—but this *was* Jan—she was wearing her old jeans tucked into her short, soft riding boots. She was wearing an old rat-catcher shirt under her leather jacket.

She smiled and waved at Ginny as she and Danny came back. "I'm ridin'," Danny proclaimed loudly. "I'm big enough, Mrs. Ruble. *I'm big enough!*"

"You certainly are!" said Ginny. "You certainly are."

The two swept past her, Jan yelling something about not changing gears "unless you're *riding*, Danny boy."

Ginny went into Hazel's house and told her about the miracle. That evening she told Bob—at the dinner table, with Jan present. "Do you think Mrs. Gaines will let him ride the bike now, Jan?"

"Oh, I hope so, Mom. What do you think? He was so proud . . ."

"Of course he was. And I'll do what I can." She glanced at Bob. "It may not be much, Jan, dear. And— I must say—you looked very nice, too, this afternoon in your old yellow shirt."

"I like it better than the funky stuff. That darn glitter scratches, do you know that?" Jan rose to get more milk from the kitchen.

"Do you think there is hope?" Ginny softly asked her husband.

"Maybe," he said.

"Maybe. Only that?"

"That's all hope is, Ginny. Only a maybe."

But Ginny was struck with the fact that Jan had really *done* something for Danny. The girl had heard her mother's worried wonderings about him, she had seen the child at their home—she knew about the ten-speed—and she had taken direct action. Surely Ginny could do the same.

But this time she would chart a course and follow it to the end. The hope for the boy must go beyond the maybe stage.

She made appointments, she selected her clothes.

When going to see men, she argued, it never hurt to look one's best. So she put on her red suit, slim and trim, the flat fur collar soft about her throat; she pulled the soft fur cap down on her head, letting a curl or two escape. She pulled fur-lined gloves on her hands and drove to the first appointment she had made for this day. Her family might not get dinner, but she was going to see all of these people.

She went first to Dr. McGilfray's office, and dimpled like a young girl to see the light in that handsome man's eyes. She let him hold her hand an instant longer than was necessary. She did like Rufus! And she had long wished that she were two women, one of whom would be Mrs. Robert Ruble, but the other she would be pleased to devote to Rufus McGilfray and his unrequited love for her.

Rufus—Mac—talked to her earnestly and honestly.

She next went to see Mr. Linders at the church. It was a satisfaction always to talk to Mary's father-in-law, happily now the rector of their church in Bayard.

She went to see Mr. Peredoe, attorney-at-law. Judge Peredoe, he was called, because of his prestige. In Ginny's memory, he had never been a judge . . . But he would tell her if the court could help her purpose.

And finally she kept an appointment with Garde Shelton. He was intrigued by the formality of the appointment. Ginny could see him at any time in his home or even here in the hospital and clinic . . .

But he respected her need and wish to make this a professional thing.

He greeted "Mrs. Ruble," seated her in the patient's chair at the corner of his broad desk, and then sat down in his own chair behind it. Ginny gazed at the man, her friend she was sure, and she told him quickly, compactly, about her concern for Danny. His adoption, his parents, his home—his lack of initiative. "He isn't growing up, Garde," she said earnestly. "I'd interfere if I saw a child in danger of being run over by a truck, and I think you would, too."

"Yes, I would," said Dr. Shelton. "So tell me about the truck, Ginny."

"I can't imagine why that awful . . ." She gulped and started again. "I can't imagine why Mrs. Gaines would adopt the boy and then— She treats him as she treats her shivering, pink-eyed poodle! She's smothering the boy, and something should be done before he actually does have the nervous breakdown his mother promises for him. Would you help me, Garde? Would you take Danny's case, and—"

The doctor shifted his weight in the big chair. "Wait a minute, Ginny. First, I'll assure you that I am as interested as you are in keeping that truck from running over any of your cub scouts."

"Danny's the only one . . ."

"All right. And I would take Danny's 'case,' but you know as well as I do that we have to move carefully."

"I do know that. I've already talked to Mac, and to Mr. Peredoe. They said . . ."

Garde listened, one thick eyebrow climbing his forehead at her thoroughness. When she had finished, he asked his secretary to bring them coffee, and he told Ginny that he had a story to tell her. "It's an allegory," he said. "By the way, Butch has decided that it is only confusing to talk about alligators and crocodiles. He thinks it would simplify the whole subject to call them all lizards."

Ginny laughed and waited.

"Er—yes!" said Dr. Shelton. "Well, my story is about something that happened to me when I was an intern-pediatrician. One day an attending physician telephoned to me and said that he was sending in a boy for a bronchoscopy. When the child and his mother appeared, she told me that he'd torn a button off his sweater and inhaled it. I couldn't see that the kid was in any great distress, and the size of the remaining buttons made me doubt that he'd swallowed one like them. So I inserted a mouth gag, put my index finger into his pharynx, and lifted out the button as easy as pie. Just about then the Attending arrived, and I showed him what I had done, as pleased as Punch with myself.

"But that doctor was not pleased. He turned bright red with anger, and he shouted at me. When he sent in a case for a bronchoscopy, he yelled at me, he wanted a bronchoscopy, and not interference from a blasted intern!"

Ginny laughed at his story and accepted the cup of coffee the secretary brought in. Garde drank some from his own cup. "I'll help you, Ginny," he said, "but maybe I won't do just exactly what you might expect."

"Goodness!" she cried. "If I had known *what* to do, I'd have done it myself, Garde."

"Fair enough."

Ginny buttoned her jacket. "How is Nan?" she asked.

"She's doing well. I don't like the poetry she is memorizing just now."

Ginny laughed. "Still Swinburne? She says he makes it hard to memorize."

"She could choose someone else. 'Hounds of Spring,' indeed!"

253

"The baby's due in the spring, isn't it?"

"Late winter. End of March. Of course, I suppose a woman in her condition does get tired of winter's rains and all the season of snows and sins."

"You seem to be memorizing yourself."

"Me, and Butch, too. He loves the brown bright nightingale bit, and fully expects to see one on our rose trellis."

Ginny rose, and Garde followed suit. He repeated his promise to help her with Danny. If she could get him under his jurisdiction. "I rather wish you had begun to work on the matter when he first came into your cub group."

Ginny turned quickly. "He already was in the den when I took over," she explained. "The former den mother decided to have a baby, and I took her place."

"I see. But you immediately detected—or did the boy's mother contact you?"

"I don't remember. Danny's problems are easily spotted. But Mrs. Gaines calls me frequently to tell me what not to let Danny do. He mustn't eat with dirty hands, for one thing. And with cub scouts, Garde . . ."

"You have a problem, all right," said the doctor, laughing. "Have you talked to Nan about this?"

"A little, perhaps. But remember, we have not been talking things over for the past few months. We wives, I mean."

"I know what you mean. It has been a matter of concern among your doctor-husbands. We are afraid you have been failing us."

"Nan and I have already decided that you felt so. We'd like to return to the old gossipy way we used to do. We think Hazel needs our interest . . ."

"It would take some of the load off Bob," said Garde, "if you women were to tell her when she's being foolish."

"I know," Ginny agreed.

"And I am sure both Hazel and Gene could tell you what to do about Danny Gaines. So perhaps you are failing the boy."

Ginny looked so shocked that he put his hand on her arm. "I'm being just a little facetious, Ginny. If you've talked to me, to Peredoe and McGilfray—what about Linders?"

"Oh, yes. Well, really, I've talked to him several times about Danny."

"Fine. Now, I think—at this point, I think—that you might get to the parents if you'd tell the court that you think the boy is perhaps neglected."

"I came to you hoping you might support that claim."

"I'd have to get to see him first."

"The court might so order."

"It might. But it would probably not designate me particularly. Any doctor would suffice."

Ginny's face fell.

"Don't be discouraged. I think your own opinion on the subject carries much weight. Your prestige as a veteran den mother is tremendous."

Ginny made a wry face. "Grandmother. Den mother…"

"You feel a lack of glamor?" asked Garde. "May I say that your appearance belies any such condition."

"Well, thank you very much, Dr. Shelton. But if I'm honest—"

"Which you must be."

"Of course. Well, the thing that really bothers me is that Danny is not a neglected child, actually. Over protected, smothered—we could claim that. But . . . About the worst I could claim is that she keeps him out of school because of his delicate health."

"And that complaint must come from the school?"

"Wouldn't it have to? Then, if a doctor would say he was not delicate, or a nervous problem . . ."

"I think something could be worked out."

"He can learn to do things, Garde! I know he can." And she told him about Jan and the ten-speed bike. "You never saw a little boy so delighted. To know that he could accomplish what other ten-year-olds do. Though by now I'd bet even money the bike has been taken away from him."

"That certainly is not a good condition," Garde agreed. "And I'll ask questions on my own. It well could be, Ginny, that the Gaines family will end up in a child-guidance clinic."

"Will that do any good?"

Garde smiled down at her earnestness. "Perhaps not as much good as his being a cub scout," he said warmly. "All such a clinic can do, really, is to advise the parents what *they* should do."

"And if that doesn't suit the mother— Oh, you should see her, Garde! I don't suppose she ever does anything she doesn't want to do. Because if, for instance, they'd tell her to get that boy out of her bedroom, she won't do it."

She moved toward the door. "I've probably worried more over Danny Gaines," she confessed, "than any boy I have ever had in my den. And I've had sixty-eight of the little monsters in my ten years of cubbing."

"Have you really?" asked Garde, impressed.

"I have all the bruises and scars to prove it. But there

are satisfactions, too. Thank you for listening to me."

"I plan to help you if I can. For one thing, Ginny, more people aware of the situation, and making the Gaineses know they are aware, should change things, shouldn't it?"

"Under normal circumstances, oh, yes. But with Danny . . ." She shook her head. "There doesn't seem to be any solution for him, and I do hate to see a boy—any boy—heading for trouble. I truly am afraid that is what lies ahead of him in the next ten years. He won't adjust to school, he won't adjust well to adolescence—he'll regress mentally, or rebel violently—probably run away from home and not be able to cope . . ."

"Hey, hey, *hey!*" cried Garde. "Let's not borrow too much trouble! You work on him through the cubs, and I'll see what I can set in motion. You know, this isn't the first troubled child I have had to handle."

"That's why I came to you," said Ginny frankly.

"Good!"

"He can have trouble ahead . . ."

"He'll grow, yes. He'll mature. And have all the problems any growing boy meets. But they must grow, Ginny. As much as we enjoy them when they are four or eight or twelve years, they will grow up. And we adults in contact with them must not give up on them. You won't for Danny, will you?"

Her blue eyes were wide. "Of course not!" she told him earnestly.

"I thought not. Here, I'll walk you to your car."

"It's cold out."

"My overcoat is right at the door. Tell me, has Hazel talked to you any more about the Fishtown boy that stole their dog? She, for a time, seemed ready to raise him."

"Yes, and we all said she was crazy. But now I think she has just about forgotten him."

"Nan says Butch told her there was room on their patio for Jay's packing box, and that a baby took up very little room."

Ginny laughed. "Good old Butch! But I don't think Dewey ever would have consented to their adopting the boy. Hazel will still think something should be done for him, once she recovers from the shock of being pregnant. She'll come to realize that life goes on, and when *her* life goes on . . ."

Garde laughed. "It really does, doesn't it? Dewey is prepared for that. Through him, Jay is going to try living with the Linders."

"Gertrude and Mr. Linders?" Ginny asked in complete surprise.

"Yes. Dewey asked for Ferrell's advice and suggestions, and Gertrude said the boy could try it with them. In fact, he's there now."

"Oh, my."

"Oh, my, indeed. You take a boy like that and try to hold him down to three legs-under-the-table meals a day —and then there's the matter of baths. Not just the first bath, which was an event, certainly. Ferrell tells about it very well. He says first the boy was just told to take a bath, and Jay mentioned how cold it was outside. But he was persuaded that the inside of the rectory was not arctic. And he went into the bathroom. He came out washed in streaks. So Linders, not without violent opposition, undertook the job, and he made it a thorough one, only to be rewarded by this classic statement. That 'Dr. Whitey did a better one on his dog!' "

"Dr. Whi . . . ? *Dewey?*" asked Ginny in delight.

"Dewey, indeed. When told the story, he predicted that Linders has a job cut out for him."

"He does. Hazel never in the world could have handled it."

"She never could."

"And it is very good of the Linders. Because they already have that invalid aunt."

"They do. But they claim that they are not being good. Gertrude says she misses their own boys."

"Well, I expect she does. But I see a couple of halos above the rectory, don't you?"

"Bright and shining. Though they—the Linders—have an idea about Jay, that he might be better off down at their Ozark farm."

"Mary . . ." protested Ginny in alarm.

"Oh, no, not Mary. Of course not. But there seems to be a grandfather, and one of the sons is a farmer with boys of his own."

"Harold, yes," said Ginny, accepting his solution. "Storm's brother—"

"Well!" said Garde. "That could work out. And—thank you for coming, Ginny. Nan was wondering last night if you were beginning to worry about Mary?"

"Of course I worry about her. I'm trying to get Bob to go down there to see her."

"Isn't she another item you girls have been neglecting lately?"

Ginny smiled at him. "Maybe Nan and I should be doing something about that neglect. Since our resident o.b. and pediatrician can't seem to get along without us."

Garde stepped back from the car. "If I help you with

your problems, you should stand ready to help us with ours," he said, watching her drive away.

"Your hair is coming into shape nicely, Mrs. Cornel," the beauty operator told Gene as she conducted her to the dryer. "You used only to come in to have your hair cut. But now you come regularly—"

"For special occasions," Gene told her somewhat bluntly.

"You must be having *them* regularly!" said the girl, laughing and adjusting the dryer over Gene's head.

Gene watched her heels depart. She picked up her book and laid it down again. "Special occasions—*regularly*—" The terms echoed in her mind, Well, yes, such things were happening. Ever since—

She made a wry face, and again picked up her book, determinedly holding her gaze to its pages.

"... Ever since Mike Shanahan," the words inexorably said themselves under the persistent whir of the hair dryer.

Mike Shanahan!

Mike Shanahan!

Mike Shanahan!

That dark-haired, bearded young doctor. Well, not as young, really, as the average second-year intern. Five years older, in fact. He'd explained about that to Gene, and to the whole family. Something to do with the Vietnam thing—and a decision to study medicine when he'd returned from service. He'd thought he would use his paramedic training— Yes, it did help. He could have found hospital work—

"But I'm one to want to be up there on top," he said. "Lab workers, emergency room aids, ambulance jockeys, are okay. But the doctors are the top boys. I did consider staying in the army, going to O.C. school, but this will give me both."

Oh, yes, Gene knew how Mike Shanahan talked, what he said, what he planned . . .

She'd seen him often enough, she'd heard him often enough—he'd been around, dear Lord! often enough—

Ever since that blasted hayride. Just last week she'd heard herself say to Ferrell Linders that she would not be in favor of a bobsled hayride, even if they did have enough snow! Sure, they were fun, but—

But too many things could happen on a hayride, and after one.

Like the results of that one in October. That had been the first she'd seen of Mike, and though she desperately wanted to see the last of him, he had kept coming around. He hung on, and he *hung* on!

She shook her head at the girl's offer of coffee.

She was thinking. And how!

Of the way Shanahan hung on, and on. Even when she told him, or tried to . . . Ostensibly he came to Bayard to see Carol. He made the date with Carol when he left their home, he called Carol when he wanted to come for an extra visit. When he came, he talked to Alison about medicine. He was spoken of as Carol's date, and he did come often. Nearly every weekend, he'd bob up.

"Carol's date." He came to the house. He talked to Carol, he took her places in his little car. He was nice to her, maybe with an air of tolerance, Gene suspected.

Because with Gene, he was not tolerant. He was—well —eager. His eyes shone, his voice quickened. He kissed Gene when he arrived. And when he left. While he was there, he found times when he could touch her hand, reasons to smile at her, places and occasions when he could steal another kiss—doing it in a way that would be absurd to protest. "My favorite doughnut maker!" he would declare, taking a hot, sugary circle from the grease-absorbent towel, and bending swiftly to kiss the cook's cheek.

He found ways of being with Gene. Should she start to market . . . "Let me drive you," would say Shanahan. "I was planning to go downtown for a paper . . ."

His car stood at the front door. Why should Gene insist on backing her car out of the garage and bringing it around . . .? There was not room for Carol in the small car . . . Gene and Mike went to market.

He went to church with her, and sat beside her, close. Because he shared prayer book and hymnal with her.

He never—well, seldom—did anything to which she could object in so many words. He was being courteously attentive to his hostess, to his "girl's" mother. Though once he was alone with that mother—in brief snatches as she held the door open for him to bring in an armful of fireplace wood—"Thanks, sweetheart," he would say softly. Or when he "hitched a ride" to go with Gene for the eggs, the sorghum, the fresh churned butter she bought from the Mennonites who lived in a colony five miles from Bayard—he would talk earnestly to Gene, turning in the car seat to look intently at her. Carol had not gone with them; she had become involved in making Swedish coffee cake for Sunday breakfast. She couldn't leave just when Gene was ready to go. "Bring me back some peanut brittle!" she'd called after Mike and her mother.

They got the peanut brittle, and Gene tried to keep their talk on the Mennonites.

But Mike had ways of turning a phrase about, of becoming too earnest, too—

Oh, the whole thing was ridiculous! Gene was almost fifteen years older than Mike. Perhaps he did like older women better. They didn't "twitter," he claimed. But not women old enough to be the mother of the girl he was dating.

She said this once to him.

"What girl?" he had asked gravely.

And Gene knew that she shivered.

It *was* ridiculous! She should tell him not to come to Bayard again. And what would Carol say to that? What would she do? Was she too naive not to see what Mike was doing? She treated him as she treated any young man who came to their house. Storm Linders, Bobby Ruble—any of them! As a friend, whom she was glad to see and talk to. Or not, as the case might be. Carol was just not ready to be serious with a man.

And Gene—well, of course she liked to have Mike admire her, to want to be with her—but she hated the whole thing, too. If her friends knew, if Alison guessed, they would howl with laughter. She, too, should laugh. In fact, she had tried that line, only to have Mike wait her out and say something, touch her, in a way to silence her, and to send that shiver again along her nerves.

Certainly there was the excitement, the filip Mike added to her life. Would he come this weekend? On Friday night? Not until Sunday morning? What would he say? What would he do? What would *they* do?

She knew that, once Alison discovered that the young man was somewhat serious in his attentions to Gene, he would, literally, blow his stack. He would be mad at everyone. Mike, Gene—maybe even at Carol.

And of course there was Carol. A difficult person to deal with under any circumstance. She always had been. Gene had gone through every childhood phase, when the plainer, more quiet, more introvertive Carol had languished in the shadow of her sister, who was prettier, more lively, more fun to be with. Adolescence had been very difficult indeed. Then had come the girl's decision to study nursing rather than go to college as Susan was doing. Carol had liked the school, had liked the friends she made. But now if it should occur to her that her mother was snatching one of those friends . . .

Oh, indeed, Gene was playing with fire! And she should stop before making the biggest error of all—that of making herself look ridiculous to Mike Shanahan. There was no sort of workable future to this episode.

Of course, day to day, it could be fun. Like the day Gene and Mike met Catherine Sims at the feed mill where they had gone for bird seed. Mike was to "tote" the bags of sunflower and milo. Gene went there several times during a winter. "Our birds eat better than we do," Alison liked to assert.

Though, as much as anyone, he enjoyed the wild birds that came to the feeder. He even would cook a pudding of suet and peanut butter, raisins and sunflower seed, and fill little molds with the mess—Jello molds he used —letting the contents harden. Then he would remove them from the molds, drop the little fluted cakes into mesh bags which he hung from tree branches. This was especially for the chickadees. Gene was gaily explaining all this to Mike on the morning they waited for their seed bags to be filled and brought out to the dock, on the morning when Catherine barged up, full sail, talking a mile a minute, as she always did.

"Oh, hello, Gene!" she cried. "I know I look a fright..."

Her eyes went to Mike. Gene introduced him. "Dr. Shanahan."

"Oh, yes! But I thought he was Carol's friend . . ."

"Given a choice," Gene told him when they were driving home, "she always says the wrong thing."

"She told me that I really would not like baked soybeans."

Gene laughed. "I don't think you would, either. But look, boy, I'm not going to bake some so you can find out."

The encounter had been slightly embarrassing. But fun, too.

When Carol went back to school, the whole incident would end, would be over. Nothing would ever come of it, of course. So Gene decided just to let the matter ride. She had already decided that she would not invite Mike for the Thanksgiving dinner. If invited, he would come! No duty roster would keep him from doing that!

And she simply could not face the four families with Mike behaving as he did. Not one of them but would guess and condemn what was going on. And if they didn't condemn, they would laugh, which would be worse.

She could just see and hear Jan Ruble, or Hazel—or even Dewey. He'd make a big laugh of the situation. Even Ginny would ask her why she was allowing that young man... And if Gene attempted to say that she was helping Carol, even Ginny would laugh at her.

So—the coming weekend, if the matter of Thanksgiving were mentioned, she would tell Mike . . .

The operator who came to take her from under the

dryer decided that Mrs. Cornel had gone to sleep. "You didn't move a muscle, dear."

Gene swathed her freshly cut and set hair in a scarf. She stopped at the bank and at the ice cream shop, and then went home, hurrying to put the ice cream into the freezer. "They had their spumoni in," she said. "And I got cranberry sherbet, too."

Carol helped put things away. She said, yes, she liked Gene's haircut. "Did Helen tint your hair?" she asked. "It looks nice."

"I've been using a rinse for some time," said Gene. "Red-blond hair is apt to look faded if you don't help it out a little."

"I have lunch ready."

"Oh, good. Was there any mail?"

"Not yet."

Carol waited for her mother's flurry to blow itself out, then she served their soup and uncovered the thin sandwiches she had made. There was a pot of fresh coffee.

"This is very nice," Gene told her daughter as she sat down.

"I thought we should have a little talk," said Carol.

"Is this that new brand of clam chowder? Your father will like it. Talk about what, dear?" She glanced across the table at Carol. "My, you look serious," she commented.

"I am serious," said Carol. "Mother . . ."

"Yes, dear?"

"And I want you to listen to me."

"Well, of course I am listening. Right here across from you? Did you put salt in the cream cheese?"

"Mother!"

Gene leaned toward Carol. "What is bothering you, dear?" she asked.

"Well," said Carol, "that's what I'd like to tell you. And of course I put salt in the cream cheese. But listen, Mother."

Gene watched Carol, who was not at all a pretty girl, though, as she matured, some people said that she was developing an "interesting" face. She had learned to wear her hair simply—a soft wave was the most adornment she ever risked. But it was clean, smooth, and its bright color was Gene's own. Red-blond. Susan's was really blond, and she curled her hair.

". . . think you should be seeing more of your friends than you have been doing all fall, Mother. Hazel and Nan, and Ginny Ruble. These days you don't call them or go to see them. They don't come here . . ."

"I've been busy, Carol."

"Mhmmmn, I know you have. And that's the trouble. But if you were seeing more of the wives, I wouldn't have to tell you the things I feel I must tell you this morning. They would have done it for me, weeks ago."

Gene sat back in her chair. "What things?" she asked, her face blank of understanding.

"Oh, things like pointing out how incredibly silly you have been acting lately."

Gene picked up her half round of brown bread and cream cheese, and laid it down again. "Have I been silly?" she asked. "In what way?" Would, she wondered — Would Carol mention the times she and Mike had sat on the hilltop, the times they had walked along the riverbank—the Saturday night at the club when he had dutifully asked Mrs. Cornel to dance, and then had led her outside, down to the pier . . . not returning her until one waltz, two shags and a rumba later . . . his own way of telling the time that had lapsed.

But Carol did not mention any of these things. "You know when you've been silly, and how," she told Gene. "And I take my full share of blame for your behavior. I suppose your age would account for the rest. Because, ordinarily, you are not a silly woman."

Gene's jaw dropped. She could not have spoken to save herself!

"I suppose," said Carol, "that it all began when I let you write my letters for me."

Hadn't she *asked* Gene for help?

"I myself knew it was a silly thing to do. I really did know that I couldn't fool anyone that way. And you should have pointed that out to me. You're older; you must have known how such things go. You should have realized what I had to learn the hard way. That anyone attracted by a letter settles for the paper and pencil used, not what should be behind the words written. You probably do know—you did know—that letters, and letter writing, are only the picture of the person involved. I could copy your ideas, just as I could copy a letter from George Bernard Shaw, or one from Elizabeth Barrett Browning, and send it off. It might please the reader, but it would give no idea of what I was like . . ."

Gene now sat back in her chair and gazed, unbelieving, at her daughter. That she could hold in her feelings, gather them, assemble them, and then bring them out . . .

Now she was talking about *découpage*. "Letters are more a *découpage* than anything else. Like the stuff Ginny Ruble's scouts do. You cut a picture out of a magazine

—ducks on a pond, or a bunch of daffodils—and you paste the picture on—and that's the way a picture should be. Nice to look at, to read, but not able, ever, to take the place of the real thing.

"And that's what I'm trying to tell you, and what I'd tell him if ever I tell him anything again. I'm talking about Mike. That you wrote the letters he liked. Not me. That it was *your* picture he liked. Not me. When he came to see me, he knew right away that it wasn't my picture . . .

"Though I shouldn't think any man would really want a *picture* of a girl. I should think he would want, that he should want, the girl's warmth, her person—yes, her body. By that I mean the way she looks and walks and talks, her hair and eyes and her voice. He should want that girl's goodness— Oh, I don't mean *goodness!* Worth, maybe, is more like it."

Now Gene hugged her arms across her breast. She was shivering. Not the shiver which Mike induced. This was hurt, and pain—for Carol. Fifty words back, she had stopped caring about her own hurt.

She had not meant . . .

She spoke the words, her voice harsh and dry. "I never meant to hurt you, Carol," she said.

"I don't say you did mean to hurt me."

"I was sorry for you. You seemed to want to reach people. We worked this up . . ."

"*You* worked it up," said the girl coldly.

"Yes, I did. Of course I did. But . . ."

Carol stood up and began to clear the table. "Well!" she said. "I hope the whole thing is over. And I for one will be very glad. Mike isn't coming back to Bayard, you know. Last Sunday I told him not to."

Gene stared at her. "You're not going to be dumb enough to lose him now."

"Oh, no. I've learned an awful lot. And I guess you've taught me all I know. I'll know how . . . Oh, not Mike! He never was anybody very special with me, you know, Mom. But there are other men. One man—he called a day or so ago, and Doc said, yes, I could go down to the city to see this special play—"

"Who is he? This other man?"

"Do you remember Dietrich Jordan? I wrote the very first letter to him, and he never answered. But now . . . he called me . . ."

"And you're going down!" said Gene, pleased. "Would you like to invite him here for Thanksgiving . . .?"

Carol looked over her shoulder at her mother. "No, thank you," she said coolly. "I think I'll play this alone. For a while, at least."

Chapter Ten

That year, the four-family Thanksgiving was a failure. "A complete flop," said Jan Ruble when the gathering broke up. "I don't think we should bother."

Nothing really had happened, though of course a great deal did. Without consulting the others, Gene, "at the last minute," decided to have Plumy and Mag cook and serve dinner. No one need bring food as they usually did. "And all the dishes match," commented Carol.

Everyone was dressed up and said polite things, but Plumy was not much of a cook, and, Friday morning, Mag told Mrs. Ruble that she hadn't really wanted to help with the Thanksgiving dinner at Cornel's.

"I don't blame you," said Ginny. "It won't happen again. I—*we* will see to that!"

And then it was Sunday again. There was snow on the ground, but the church steps and the sidewalks were clean. The men told each other that they were afraid the pigeons might be coming back to their tower and steeple. Hazel Windsor said sharply that Dewey was not to *con-*

sider climbing up there to put sticky stuff on the steeple louvers.

"I'll do it, Dr. Windsor," offered Jay, who was pulling his cotta over his head. Mr. Linders had found the boy interested in learning to be an acolyte.

"He only *looks* like an angel," Ginny whispered to Gene. "Watch him." She and Gene were attending to the altar. For the next months, they had agreed to double their duty to spare Hazel and Nan.

"Did Hazel ever buy a new winter coat?" Gene asked, helping Ginny get the protector on evenly.

"Did she plan to?"

"Oh, yes. A brown one, she said."

"A brown would be dead wrong for her."

Gene laughed. "That's what we told her at the time. And started all this business about tending to our own affairs."

"Oh, me," said Ginny, shaking her head, hurrying with their work. For the first time since September, the families were to take their Sunday dinners to Gene's, and they had asked the Linders to come.

"Will Jay . . .?"

"Jan will take care of him," Ginny predicted.

"I plan to get rid of the last of the Thanksgiving stuff. I've made turkey salad."

"That's all right. I have a pot roast cooking. The men will have their sliced meat to eat."

The whole group was gathering on the front steps and in the narthex. Dewey and the church treasurer were still in the vestry. They would see that the lights were out, the furnace turned back, everything tidy.

The families moved toward their cars, the women—all four of them—planning a day-long meeting together during the coming week. They would go to Nan's, they thought, but Ginny suggested that her house would be less tiring for Nan.

"But with Ruby . . ."

"She'll take care of the kids when they come home from school."

"Butch wants to be an acolyte. He thinks if Jay can—"

They all fell silent to watch Danny Gaines and his parents take their leave of Mr. Linders. And they heard Ferrell suggest that Danny, like Jay, might want to train to be an acolyte.

"That'll rub off some rough spots," Garde murmured to Ginny.

"But they're Baptists, I think."

"Let Linders handle the theology bit. He seems to have got action of some sort from the family."

"Don't be too optimistic. Look at the overshoes and gloves on that boy!"

Hazel was still talking about the women's get-together day. Would it be a quilting bee? asked Gertrude Linders.

"It could turn out to be. We have lots of things to do. You know, there are three babies to make things for, and Christmas coming up. That will be at the Sheltons' this year."

"You're invited," called Nan.

Rather quickly, then, the four families funneled into their cars and drove away, to reassemble within the hour at the Cornel home, bringing in their savory roasting pans, their bowls of salad, the spice cake and sauce . . .

Jan took charge of the children; their table was out on the heated porch. Food was spread buffet style on the breakfast table, taken to the dining room to be eaten. The men's voices rose and fell. A fire snapped and popped in the living room. The men laughed and talked, and watched the women move about, in the old familiar ritual of feeding their families.

Without exception, the men were beaming with delight to have the "girls" huddling together, so delighted that they decided to taste the salad of leftover turkey, decided that they liked it, and had eaten most of it before the women finished serving and could sit down. But there was food in abundance. Each family brought what had been planned for their own Sunday dinners, Hazel's two Cornish hens, her green beans and mushrooms, her bowl of custard tapioca. Ginny brought the pot roast, the potatoes and carrots, the hot rolls and jam. Nan brought sliced ham and sweet potatoes—the spice cake. Oh, indeed there was food in plenty.

The women moved about, chattering, laughing. Aprons had been brought from home and tied into place. Nan's ruffled white pinafore with a strawberry for a pocket, Ginny's perky pink apron, starched and flaring, Hazel's coverall, printed all over with lady bugs, and Gene's practical blue denim butcher's apron. Garde tweaked the bow of an apron's strings. "Four are better than one," he said contentedly. Hazel reached for a bowl on a high shelf; Gene gently prevented her, and they looked at each other, smiling.

Before the grownups were ready for their dessert, the children departed to slide down the hill on the snow. Fiddle cuddled into her father's arm and declared that boys were too rough. Within fifteen minutes she was asleep and carried in to Gene's bed, with a warm afghan spread over her.

The women talked again about the day which they

planned to spend at Ginny's. She was not to plan too much food, Hazel stipulated.

"I'll attend to that," said Ginny. "You can eat as much or as little of it as you like. Come early. Beds are made in our house by nine o'clock. And the kids don't get home from school until three-thirty at the earliest."

"A really all-day meeting," commented Mrs. Linders.

"Would you like to come?" Ginny asked politely.

"Oh, no, dear. There's Aunt Sophy. I was lucky to get someone to stay with her today."

"We'll need a long day to catch up with each other," said Ginny. "Lately we've been too busy to pay much attention to what our friends are doing."

"But on Wednesday," drawled Bob, "the floodgates will open."

"I think," said Hazel, "that we'll have to divide the day into four equal parts, and catch up on each family in turn."

"You'd better put four days to that job," said Dewey. "May we come, too? Cornel can sew real good."

"Oh, we have missed your corny jokes, Dewey!" Ginny told him.

"We've missed you girls, haven't we, guys?"

There was a hearty rumble of assent.

"We missed us, too," said Ginny. "I don't think one of us really liked the experience we've been through. We didn't do things for each other, we didn't quarrel, or laugh together . . ."

"Nobody told me how silly I've been behaving," said Gene ruefully. "And that I let my hair get too pink."

"But we knew," said the other wives in unison.

The men rocked with laughter.

Gene stood shaking her head. "You couldn't have

known," she insisted. "You'd have said something or done something."

"I will say this," said Alison. "I personally knew that you girls could not live for long without each other. It was just a matter of how long you were going to try the silly idea."

"Why didn't you tell us?" asked Nan.

"You wouldn't have believed me. Oh, maybe you would, Nan—"

She smiled at him. "I knew it wasn't working," she agreed.

"How long did you try it?" asked Dewey.

"Two or three months," said Ginny.

"It was much longer than that!" cried Bob.

"No, not much longer. But you're right; it was too long."

"Don't say things like that, Ginny," Hazel protested. "These fellows are unbearable when they're right."

They all laughed at that. "We'll stick together now," Nan promised the men. "We have to see Hazel through the next six or seven months."

"And me through the next twenty years," declared Dewey.

"Though maybe she had been right all along, you know," said Bob. "Maybe all of us are too old for her to have her first baby."

"We'll make it together," said Hazel, confident at last.